Murder at the Museum
& Other Fruithills Suspense Stories

Vol. One

Each story visits one of the many spirit-inhabited places in and around a small Town in the midst of the beautiful hilly landscape in the American midwest. The European settlers found the climate ideal and grew and shipped the plentiful apples, melons, strawberries and many grains, early on by riverboat and later by train to Chicago and beyond. Even today, in the valley of the Fruithills, the past still lingers to inspire dreams and haunt the imagination. From murders to mysteries to haunting spirits, each story presents a look into the past from the view of the present day.

Murder at the Museum

& Other Fruithills Suspense Stories

by
RoseMary McDaniel

Dedicated to my husband and my son for their love and
support over the years.

Special thanks to my fellow writers at the Soul, Ink.
Writers' Group at the Bristol, Indiana Library for their support and
friendship, and to the wonderful staff at the Elkhart County
Historical Museum who really have that hearse in their collection,
(although it doesn't have a coffin or a body in it) and who oversee
a fascinating collection of Michiana history.

To order additional copies, or find new series releases, go
to this website and order online:
http://www.thebookpatch.com

ABOUT THE AUTHOR:

Fascinated by the fairy tales told by her father, RoseMary
Sherwin McDaniel (a.k.a. Amy Hayle, pen name) felt an instinctive tie to
her Irish heritage.

From the age of five, she penned her own stories, but her serious adult
writing efforts were concentrated in Indiana and Michigan historical
writing that led to a weekly genealogical column in an area newspaper.

Sharing a September 15 birthday with mystery author Agatha Christie,
she yearned to be published. Some years ago, after joining a out-of-town
writer's group, she achieved her goal of getting a romance story
published in a national magazine.

However it was not until she retired after a 50+ year corporate career
and joined a new writer's group in the small northern Indiana town near
"the Fruithills," that she was able to devote more time to her writing.

Watch for future volumes, or contact her at:
mcdaniel.rosemary@gmail.com

Author's note: Although the stories have been inspired by some actual
places and events in history, they are all a product of the author's
imagination and not intended to represent any persons, living or dead.

Contents

Now, pour a soothing cup of cocoa, tea or coffee and settle back to read about life in the Fruithills, a place that has never lost its ties to a spirit-filled past.

Murder at the Museum

RoseMary McDaniel a.k.a. Amy Hayle

"There's a body in there!" was the last thing that long-time volunteer Flo expected to hear when Lily, staff member of the history museum, peered into a coffin left in the old horse-drawn hearse that was being donated to the collection by a local funeral home.

Flo loved exploring the past, but hadn't expected this tragic event to link to her own youthful indiscretions. But she soon discovered that not all in the past is dead and buried, especially in this small town in the Fruithills, a place that has never lost its ties to a spirit-filled past.

Special thanks to my fellow writers at the Soul, Ink. Writers' Group at the Bristol, Indiana Library for their support and friendship, and to the wonderful staff at the Elkhart County Historical Museum who really have that hearse in their collection, (although it doesn't have a coffin or a body in it) and who oversee a fascinating collection of Michiana history.

Murder at the Museum

Not all history is dead & buried

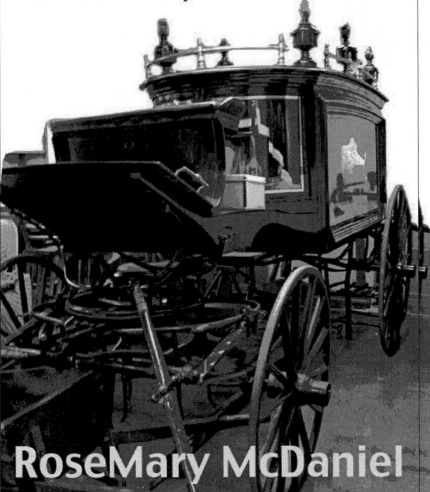

RoseMary McDaniel

Murder at the Museum

RoseMary McDaniel a.k.a. Amy Hayle

I heard a door slam and then I heard Lily scream. "There's a body in there!"

O.K., rewind - let's step back a bit. I'm a history nut. I'd be the first to admit it. I guess I'm just more comfortable with things that are over and done with. It's easier to deal with people and events that don't keep changing, that are set in place. You can leave them for a while and come back to find they are still the same as you left them, waiting for you to carry on and perhaps discover things you didn't know.

Rain was threatened that day, when I got up early, had my usual breakfast of peanut butter toast and a diet Pepsi and got ready to go for my stint at the local history museum as a volunteer. I carefully pinned my badge on my tweed jacket. It stated my entire name: Florinda Fletcher Waycross, and it took up two whole lines. I had cajoled a little to get it, because it had to be specially made, but the dashing young museum manager generally acquiesces to my more reasonable requests, since after all I am from a highly regarded local family which is a polite way of saying I have old money.

It is generally known in the community that I can often be counted on to chip in whenever a worthy group's fundraising efforts need a final boost to meet their goal. That's why most people will tolerate an old doll like me, and I'm not vain enough to assume it's for my good looks, talents or skills.

However, it suits a purpose in my life. Never married, since I always knew darn well anyone who gave me a second look had an ulterior motive: marrying money. So I've lived alone with my cat in the old family residence since my parents died. It's really too big for one person, but I refuse to give it up.

Now that I've reached what they call the "sunset years," I'm determined to poke around in the treasure troves of history, satisfying my curiosity among other things, about what I presume are my less-than-illustrious forebears, who managed to acquire and squirrel away more money than they or my parents could manage to spend. I've always been frugal and have just kept salting away

3

the proceeds from well-managed investments.

Now part of my pleasure is doling out carefully calculated chunks of it to what I consider qualified recipients.

I took my time, since I was early. The museum didn't officially open until nine, and I liked to give the the staff time for whatever morning pickup energy drinks or cups of fruited yogurt the young ones of today consume.

The entire staff, except for old Henry the janitor who had the job because he lives next door, and can still climb on the riding lawn mower, are young enough to be my grandchildren, which is fine by me. They have brought a breath of fresh air to the old place turning a collection of static display rooms into a more interesting, periodically updated and visitor-friendly history museum.

They have a knack for fundraising and have managed to plan and execute the building of an annex to properly store the vast amount of items that once sat moldering away in boxes and bags and added a library that attracts researchers of both local and family history from miles away.

In the transition, some of the old-time volunteers, generally relics like me, had run for the hills, fleeing the importation of the dreaded young ones who had actually been educated in the proper running and care of a place worthy of being called a museum. The new staff was polite and very considerate with them, but the aura of change penetrated the fading eyesight and diminished hearing capacity of some who had to decide to quietly withdraw or be resigned to change.

Even my cat Luke, the dedicated indoor/outdoor type, has the good sense to know that when it's raining, it's time to come out of the woods into a safe and comfortable environment. Although that's the name I use for him at the vet's, at home, I usually dub him Switch, which relates back to when I first adopted him from the shelter and took him, then as Lucy, to the vet to be, as they say, altered. That dang cat had so much fur all over, that I hadn't bothered to check the equipment, and the vet informed me in an amused voice that I might want to call him Luke, instead, which I did. He is my devoted companion and hangs on my every word, at least as long as I keep his food dish full.

But today was going to be a big day. I hoped the rain would fail to appear, since there was to be an outside event. An out-of-town funeral parlor was donating their old horse-drawn funeral hearse. There was to be a public ceremony at the museum, complete with refreshment table to thank them for the artifact and the $50,000 donation to the building fund that came with it.

I had even been asked to say a few words about the history of the old vehicle, which I'd researched over the past few weeks. I was planning to keep it short, since folks today have a limited attention span, especially when they know there's a cake furnished by a very popular local bakery and some non-Kool-Aid punch waiting at the end of the formalities.

When I got to the museum, the building energy spike had been elevated, and the three young staff members were in full readiness for the hoped-for crowds. Lily, the pretty curator of collections, was as usual, casually elegant in a flowery summer dress and matching sweater. The clothes weren't designer, but so carefully well chosen that you immediately knew she certainly had a knack for style and a particular eye and a talent for the work.

Mason, the museum manager was tall, thin and just the sort of polite young man with a ready smile who could charm the donors and be respectful to the visitors. You could tell that he, too, knew his stuff, so obviously the board of governors of the museum had made the right choice.

Liam, the education coordinator of programs, was the youngest staff member. Irish to his bones, a bit shy, but stepping up to his responsibilities, especially in designing events to attract visitors of all ages. He was a fast-developing asset.

They greeted me and offered some green tea, which I politely refused, since a diet Pepsi and water were my preferred solutions to hydration. I offered to let one of them review the notes for my speech, but Mason said with a smile that he trusted that whatever I chose to say would be appropriate. Dear boy.

So when we heard the beep beep of a horn, we knew that our exhibit for this afternoon's presentation had finally arrived. Lily and Liam hurried outside, while I helped Mason collect the brochures and holders that would be placed on refreshment tables for the public to take for information on joining the Historical Society or learning about upcoming events.

I found out afterward that the horse-drawn hearse had been delivered on a large flatbed. The vehicle had been lowered to the ground and landed with a slight thud, as something inside bumped against the door.

"There's a empty coffin inside that we kept there to make it look more authentic," the funeral home representative, a rather scruffy individual in a chauffeur's cap, told the staff, proudly.

Curious Lily opened the door to the carriage and with Liam's help lifted the lid. It was a tight fit, so they tugged and tugged, and finally, it came loose. The funeral home guy's chatter was cut short, as Lily pulled away and the door slammed shut behind her.

"There's a body in there," she screamed.

The sound of Lily in distress could be heard inside the museum, and Mason and I hurried out to see what was wrong, expecting to find that someone's foot had been run over or that the wheels of the carriage had sunk too deeply into the grass.

Lily had retreated in horror to the steps and was stabbing her finger in the air in the direction of the carriage. The funeral home guy and Liam had reopened the door and were staring in the open coffin.

Curious to a fault, I stopped to give Lily a hug, and then made my way to peek over Liam's shoulder to see what had caused all the fuss.

"My gosh," I exclaimed. "Louie Lamorata."

"Who?" echoed a chorus of voices.

"Louie Lamorata, a former godfather of the area," I replied. Then remembering that at least three of my audience were from out of town and would have no idea what that meant, I hurried on. "The three most prominent early settlers around here were the Irish, the Germans, and the Italians. The Italians generally settled a little further west of here, and many of them worked in the railroad yards. They had a godfather or head of a group of families who served as arbitrator of any disputes that arose. Locally, that was Louie, and he was the final word on family matters, but he disappeared about ten years ago. His son Little Tony took over the job."

Tony must be in his later 60s by now, I thought, a bit older than me.

"Like the Sopranos," Liam commented, nodding his head.

"But what's he doing in the coffin?" Lily asked.

"Someone put him there," I said stating the obvious.

"Oh dear, oh dear," moaned the funeral home guy. "Why do things like this always happen to me?"

Not having an answer to his question, but presuming that he believed he would be blamed, I turned to Mason.

"Do you want me to call 911?" I asked, but he was already dialing on his cell. After he had alerted the police, he called the funeral home director, and after a few words put the phone back in his pocket.

"Your boss will be here as soon as possible," he told the by-now-pacing man who had made the ill-fated delivery.

We could already hear the siren in the distance since the police station was only a few blocks away. The officer pulled into the parking lot and came over to us with a puzzled look.

"You called about a body?"

Mason took charge and led him over to the still open door of the hearse and the coffin.

"Is this some kind of joke?" the officer asked, as he looked inside. "This guy's been dead quite a while."

Admittedly the corpse must have been processed, and although there was an odor, it wasn't as unpleasant as one imagined. He was in remarkable condition, although his face, still recognizable to me, had the appearance of dried up fruit. He still wore a suit and tie, and a desiccated brown carnation was tucked in his label.

Mason explained to the officer how the funerary vehicle had been donated by the funeral home to the museum for its exhibit space, and delivered for a presentation this afternoon. He told him that I had identified whom I thought the body was, or rather, had been.

The officer who likely had been about fifteen years old when the old Don had disappeared came over to confirm my story. "Did you know this gentlemen?" he asked.

"Yes, everybody of a certain era knows of Mr. Lamorata," I told him. "I'm better acquainted with his son." No need to go into details, like I was once engaged to Tony. That was a story better left to the winds of history.

By now, the funeral director had arrived, and the officer moved off to speak with him. Mason joined them, while Lily, Liam, and I went over and sat on the steps.

"What happens now?" Lily asked, and I shook my head.

What happened next was that both the police officer and the funeral director made calls on their cells, and in a half hour or so, the front lawn was swimming with what we assumed were the local version of C.S.I., and a grim looking individual who undoubtedly must have been the coroner.

Mason had joined us, and finally both the officer and the funeral director approached and said that since the death did not occur here, that the vehicle and its contents were being removed to police custody. They furnished no other information.

I could see the faces of the three staff members drop for a moment, but Mason was the first to recover. He stood up. "Does that mean that we'll be able to take possession eventually?" he asked.

I knew that he must be experiencing the sinking feeling of realizing that the donation of $50,000 was evaporating before his very eyes.

Fortunately the funeral director reached into his pocket and pulled out an envelope. "Here's the check for your building fund," he said handing it to Mason. "You shouldn't have to be inconvenienced by a mixup on our end. We'll do everything possible to make sure that the hearse is returned here as soon as we are able to do so."

Mason just stood looking at the envelope and swallowing and politely thanked him.

"Of course we'll be canceling the presentation today," Mason said to all of us. We nodded, and watched as the hearse was reloaded onto the truck and then driven off behind the police car to wherever it would be examined. After the officials had left, there was nothing for us to do but go back inside. A small group of interested onlookers had gathered on the sidewalk out front, but as we had nothing to tell them, they soon departed as well.

I wasn't particularly in the mood to answer the questions I could sense were brewing in the minds of the staff, so I merely smiled and said that I had developed a sinus headache and thought I'd better head for home. Fortunately they hadn't yet gathered their thoughts in a cognizant way, so they all agreed that I should rest and hoped I'd feel better soon.

I didn't go home, of course. Instead, I headed west toward a familiar watering hole where I'd not been in some time: Bacio Divino or the Divine Kiss. Tony, who now ran it, had tried to tell me once that he'd thought of me, and that was how it got it's name, which I knew was total bull, since Tony's father Louie had opened and named it long before I came in to the picture.

And how, you may ask, does a straight-laced old cookie like me get connected with a place like that? Well, even the Amish youngsters are known for Rumspringa, which is burning of the wild oats before they join up with the church for life.

For me, it was more of a rite of passage from a dignified upbringing and a stuffy education. I wanted to experience the opposite side of life for a brief encounter or two, so when I was 25, I rented a small furnished apartment in the next town, although as far as my parents were concerned, I was still living at home. There I kept my so-called wild-child apparel and occasionally slept over when I wasn't in any shape to drive home.

I even called myself "Fanny Favor," and pretended to be taking a year off college to find myself. So, that was when and how I met Tony, at a bar, of course. Rye was my "imbibement choice," along with very salty bar popcorn. I was a cheap date.

Tony tended bar at a couple of places other than the one his father Louie ran. Louie believed that a son should go out and learn the hard way off somebody else's dime. So, for all the time that Tony and I were a item, I only saw Louie a few times, when Tony and I would stop in for a quick drink on the way somewhere else on his nights' off.

Louie always eyed me with a rather piercing stare, as if he wasn't believing I was quite as advertised. Those eyes of his could see right through me, especially if I had my back to him. I'd feel this creepy feeling on the back of my neck and turn around, and sure enough Louie was giving me the gaze. I never said anything to Tony about it. He absolutely adored his old man, no matter that any mutual affection wasn't apparent in the way Louie would hassle him.

Tony and I even got engaged one New Year's Eve. It was kind of a lark; we'd only known each other about 3 months, and it was a kid-crazy kind of thing to do. I'd always made sure when I was in my Fanny disguise that we never went anywhere someone who might know me from my other life would recognize me.

Everything went downhill the night that strategy went south. Tony insisted on taking me to a classier restaurant than we ever went to: a new Italian place opened by some friends of his father's from Chicago. It was a big deal to him, so I said O.K.

We got through appetizers, the main course, and were perusing the dessert/drinks menu, when I looked up to see a friend of my father's come in with his wife and sit at a table right in our line of sight. Unfortunately, both he and the wife knew me and my parents quite well, and from the horrified looks on their faces, I knew I was busted.

I didn't say anything to Tony at the restaurant, but when he dropped me off at my apartment and wanted to come in for a nightcap, I decided it was time for the charade to end. I'd never really intended for it to go this far. Poor Tony had never even gotten to second base, because I'd told him that although I might be a bad girl in public, I wanted to be a virgin until I got married. Catholic, of course, he fell for that one, too.

So, I just told him that I had thought it over, and that it wasn't his fault, it was just that I wasn't ready to be tied down yet, and that I was leaving town for a job far away. I gave him back his ring and sent him on his way.

After he'd left, I packed up what I had at the apartment, left a note for the landlady telling her that although I was paid up for the month that I was moving out now, and I went home. I never heard a word about it from my parents. Likely the other couple was so horrified that they never followed up.

It took a few years for Tony to figure out who Fanny Favor had really been. He was hot under the collar when he tracked me down one afternoon at the local library where I was volunteering. Seeing me as Florinda Fletcher Waycross in my sensible shoes and proper attire was almost enough to give him a coronary. I took him into a small back conference room and let him spout off.

But in the end, he realized that it would never work out between us, and we both went our separate ways. I've followed his life in the papers, and knew that he married a nice Italian girl and had a passel of kids. Occasionally, our paths have crossed, and we've exchanged a few pleasantries. I even sent him a card when his father Louie vanished.

That was quite the front-page news for a while and was even

compared to the disappearance of Hoffa, the union boss. But eventually, after a few unexplained bombings at several other local Italian establishments took media precedence, and there were lots of leads on Louie's disappearance, but no solid evidence of what had happened to him, the story fell out of the news.

I always figured it might have been one of the other syndicates taking him out to prove a point, but once Tony took over as the local Don, things quieted down. Tony was a "live and let live" kind of guy, most of the time. He'd never really been a fighter.

Now, I was on my way to see him, my curiosity in high gear. I should probably have let sleeping dogs lie, but at my age, when the urge strikes, it's hard to suppress it. Who knows if one will have tomorrow or not, and if you want to do something, it's better to do it now.

I wondered if the cops had told him yet, and I switched on the car radio as I drove to see if any word had leaked out to the news media. But although the broadcast included local headlines, the discovery of the body was not yet being reported.

There were only a couple cars in the parking lot at the Bacio Divino. I sat for a couple of minutes deciding if I should go in or not, but having come this far, I threw caution to the winds and headed inside.

After the sunlight outside, (the rain had never materialized), it took my eyes a couple of seconds to adjust to the lowered light, but I spotted Tony behind the bar, having a solitary drink. At the other end of the room, there were several couples in sitting in booths, and a "somebody done somebody wrong" song was playing in the background.

I walked quickly to the bar and sat on the stool not far from where Tony was standing. He barely looked up, but walked over to me.

Then as our eyes met, I said. "Long time no see; how'ya doing?"

"Didn't expect to see you here," he said. "Slumming?" he asked in an amused tone of voice.

"Not really," I told him. "Anything new?"

"Like what?" he said. "Gas prices are up; taxes are through the roof…"

Then he didn't know. I wasn't sure if I should be the one to tell him, and frankly, I expected cops to come through the door any minute, but I thought it would be better for him to hear it from me.

"Want a drink?" he asked.

I thought for a minute. These days, lips that touch liquor never touch mine, and I'd not had a drink in years. I figured I needed to keep a clear head.

"Got a diet Pepsi?" I asked. "With a lime?"

He made a scoffing sound, but went to get it.

He handed it across the bar, and I squeezed the lime slice and then took a long drag on the straw. Now I was ready.

"I've got some, well, sad news for you," I began.

"Yeah?" he said. "You run into my truck in the parking lot? It's the one with the shotgun in the back window."

"No," I said. "Seriously, I wanted to tell you about what happened at the museum this morning."

"Oh yeah, that's another of your volunteer gigs, isn't it?"

"It is," I said and launched into telling him about the donation of the funeral hearse and the finding of the body: his father's.

His gaze narrowed. "Is this a joke?" he asked.

"Hardly," I told him. "I think the cops will likely be by soon, and I don't want them to find me here, but I wanted you to be prepared."

"Why? You think I offed my own father?"

"Of course not," I said. "But if something like this happened to me, I'd want to know before the cops came to my door."

"O.K., O.K., you're right. I'm sorry, but it's a real shock. I guess I always hoped he just took off and would be back someday. Stupid, but that's what I wanted to believe."

I never really thought Tony capable of such doing any harm to his father, but I knew from rumor that some people felt he had been involved, and that the cops at one time looked at him as a suspect in his father's disappearance. At least now he was warned to be careful what he said.

"I gotta go," I told him, handing him my card. "Call me if you need anything."

"Like a good lawyer?" he said, and sounded serious.

"I'd be glad to help you out with that," I told him.

"I'll remember you said that," he said, as I got up and left.

Driving home, I wondered if I'd done the right thing. There were people in the bar who saw me, and although I didn't know them, if the police started asking questions, they were bound to figure out I'd been there. I hoped it didn't matter, after all, it was only a weird coincidence that I was on the scene when that particular dead body turned up at the museum. At least I hoped it was.

The next morning I decided to go to the museum to see how the staff was faring. At least the sun was shining, and I remembered that Liam was having a special history program for some visiting elementary school kids. They could probably use a little extra volunteer help today.

Mason met me with his usual friendly smile and greeting, but I could tell he was a bit distracted when I saw him lay his day's agenda on his desk and couldn't seem to find it five minutes later.

I tried to put him at ease. "Have you heard from the museum's board of governors yet about yesterday?" I asked.

His smile faded but his voice was steady. "A couple of them stopped in late yesterday afternoon and offered their support. Fortunately, they agreed we were just the receiver of an unfortunate mix-up at the funeral home. We did discuss closing the museum for a while, but decided it was best to just carry on as usual."

"That was a good decision," I assured him. "People have short memories, and this really had no connection to the museum at all."

Mason took a deep breath. "I hope that's the case."

I could see he was anxious to move on with his plans for the morning, so I asked what I could do to help.

"Lily is getting together an exhibit of working women's apparel through the years," he said. "She's in the annex storage area and she could probably use your help."

"Sure, I'll go right over there," I told him, and smiled goodbye as I left his office.

I went into the specially climate-controlled area where the historical assets are stored, and found Lily laying out garments on a table and referring to a book open to a page on fashion of the 1970s. She looked up and smiled as she saw me.

13

"How's it going?" I asked. "Mason said you could use some help." I glanced at the open page in the book. "The 70s - now that was when I was in my prime," I told her.

"Great," Lily replied. "Then you can help me find some outfits to represent what the typical woman of the era wore to work."

"I remember very well what the office set wore," I said. "But back then, I volunteered in a library that stayed quite reserved for longer than most places. Every day I wore a blazer, blouse (no cleavage of course) and a conservative slightly-below-the-knee skirt with a kick pleat in the back. The other staff and I groused among ourselves that the head librarian was stuck in the 50s. She was a real stickler - even hid the erasers and white-out and allowed no mistakes when we typed. What a tyrant."

Lily laughed. "So what was it that you all wanted to wear?"

"Pants suits," I replied. "That was the big thing for office wear - they had finally let women wear trousers to work - but of course, very conservative ones. They could wear real high heels, while for us, what we called old-lady-tie oxfords were preferred, but we later were able to wear a one and a half inch heel - and no open toes, of course."

"You never rebelled?"

"Well... ." I paused realizing I couldn't let her know about Fanny and her outrageous outfits. "I did own a really cool Carnaby Street-style watermelon green and sky blue pants suit with bell bottom pants in a big diagonal stripped pattern. I only wore it when I went out with a few friends and always carried it in a bag from home and put it on at a girl friend's house.

"Your parents were strict as well?" she asked.

"Kids of today would definitely think so," I told her. "But back then, a lot of my friends had the same sort of upbringing, and we thought it was our duty to mildly rebel. We got over it, eventually."

Lily's eyes were wide, and I realized that I needed to change the subject before it got into territory that I'd rather not visit.

Saved by the bell. My cell rang.

"I'd better take this outside," I said. "I'll be right back."

I went up the back stairs and outside just in time to catch the last ring.

"Yes," I said. "Who is this?"

"It's Tony,"

I was shocked to hear his voice. Before I could say anything else, he hurried on.

"Don't hang up, for God's sake. I can only make one phone call, and you're it. They've just arrested me. Did you mean it about getting me a lawyer?"

"You made your only call to me?" I burst out. "Of course, I meant the offer, but don't you have someone that your, your family retains?"

"I don't have time to explain," he said. "I'm at the central station over here and I'd appreciate it if you'd get one quick."

"All right," I agreed. "I'll bring my lawyer as soon as I can find him."

"Hope he does criminal cases," Tony said.

"We'll work it out," I said, hanging up.

It only took one phone call to my lawyer's cell phone, and he agreed to meet me there at the police station there in the next biggest city between here and Chicago, and where both the Bacio Divino and the funeral parlor that had donated the hearse were located. It would take me about 45 minutes, but the lawyer was closer and should arrive within half an hour. People knowing you have a vault full of money behind you often provides more immediate access to any required assistance, I'd learned long ago.

I went back inside and found Lily still sorting garments.

"Sorry," I said, "but something's come up and I have to go. If you'd still like my help, I'll come back either this afternoon or tomorrow."

"No problem," Lily told me. "This exhibit isn't going up until next month, but I like to get organized early, and it helps keep my mind off of other things."

Bidding her goodbye, I retraced my steps out the back entrance and got into my car for the trip west. The noon-time traffic hadn't yet become a traffic jam and I made better time than I thought and pulled into the station parking lot just as my lawyer did. We stood by my car as I filled him in on the details and offered a retainer for Tony.

"I'll just bill you as we regularly do," Justin Enoch told me. "You may as well go on home. I'll call and let you know how it goes. They aren't likely to let you see him."

I nodded, as I realized that he was right. I got in my car as he went inside. I didn't really feel like going back to the museum today, and I'd covered my absence for the day with Lily, so I drove home.

On the drive, I thought about how I hadn't really expected to get this involved with Tony. My offer was made, I decided, mainly because of nearly 40-year-old guilt over how I had treated him back then. If I were honest with myself, I'd have to admit that I really did once have a yen for him.

If things had been different with my background, maybe I would have been the wife with a passel of kids. I shuddered and thought of Switch, my cat. Now that was the kind of family to have. Other than food, water, litter pan monitoring and a pat or snuggle now and then, he made few demands on me.

No sense crying over spilled Rye, or that I'd lost a yearning for extra-salty bar popcorn. The past was the past. But ah, there was the rub. My preference for nosing around in the past was primarily built on the fact that it just stayed past, subject to my whims of discovery on my time frame. This bit of my past, however, was bubbling to the surface most inconveniently without my cooperation whatsoever.

I liked Tony; always had. But other than feeling sorry for him and hoping that he wasn't guilty, I didn't really think I wanted any future relationship with him. I shook my head. There I go, worrying about a problem that doesn't really exist. Tony doesn't want to marry me - he already has a wife - and kids. He just wants the use of my money. Fair enough.

When I got home, I had a desire for the first time in a long time to have a stiff drink. Fortunately, I don't keep any alcoholic beverages in the house, so I settled for a diet Pepsi and wastefully cut open a whole lime just to have a slice for my glass. I put the rest of the lime in a plastic bag and stuck it in the refrigerator. Still couldn't get over that waste-not, want-not upbringing.

Not a proponent of the evening television news, I nonetheless found myself in front of the wide screen T.V. hidden away behind a panel in my computer room. I usually check out the news on the Internet, but tonight I wanted to see full screen video footage of the arrest, if there was any. I wondered there was a perp walk, or how big the story would be. I still hadn't heard anything on the radio, and the overnight Internet news hadn't yet caught the buzz, if it was out there.

The six o'clock local nightly news led off with the story. Apparently, the media was in hyped up over the finding of the body of the former godfather. Since the reporters didn't get a chance to watch the hauling away of the hearse, they tried the next best thing, going to the museum.

But all they got on video was Mason walking out the front door and putting the closed sign out in the yard. He only shook his head as the cameras rolled and caught him retreating back into the museum, as it recorded the shouts of the reporters as they called out questions he didn't acknowledge.

It had been hours since I had met with the lawyer, and there were only sketchy details of Tony's arrest on the broadcast. I was about ready to call the lawyer myself when my cell rang. It was him, with an update. He told me that Tony was being held for questioning and that most of the so-called evidence appeared to be circumstantial.

Several informants had come forward to tell of suspicious activity on Tony's part after the disappearance of his father. One informer had said that he knew for a fact Tony had made a deal with the funeral parlor owner to pick up the dead body back then from an undisclosed location and "deep six it."

"Not releasing him yet, I'm guessing," I said, more to comment than to ask a question.

"No," the lawyer said. "With your O.K., I'm assigning a crew of litigators to handle this one at another firm. It's high profile for us, and frankly we don't do criminal law. That work for you?"

Money was no object for me, and having it taken care of at arm's length worked for me. I agreed.

"We'd like to hire an separate investigator to have the background of these witnesses checked out," the lawyer told me. "Something really stinks about this whole thing."

"Do whatever you feel necessary. Let me know if I need to do anything on my end. Do you think they'll let him have visitors?"

"Not yet," he told me. "Let me get back to you on that," and he hung up.

My immediate concern was how I was going to be able to help the museum regain any semblance of normality. I decided that they needed to have a crisis coordinator to handle the PR of this whole thing. I knew that the museum board of governors wouldn't have the funds for such an undertaking, so I called a friend from some years ago, who ran a public relations agency now, specializing in handling sticky situations and set up an appointment with her for tomorrow morning.

Then I called Mason on his cell explained my plan and told him where to meet me at 8am sharp. I'd done all I could do, so I turned my attention to Switch, who was swishing his tail back and forth as a signal that he'd been ignored long enough. I took care of his immediate needs, and we snuggled up on the couch together to watch a funny video. I had no desire to see a repeat of the news at eleven. By then Switch and I were fast asleep.

When I rolled out of bed the next morning, I was pleased to see that it was a dark, damp and stormy day, that would likely keep the reporters at bay until Mason and I could meet with Vickie Brewer, my P.R. friend. Mason was already sitting in Vickie's office with a cup of tea, calmly chatting when I arrived. Vickie got up to give me a hug.

"Great to see you again, Flo," she said. "Sorry though it had to be under these circumstances, but as I've been telling Mason, this is a situation that can be handled and even made to provide positive end results. He and I have already had a conference call with the museum board of governors, and they're very thankful that you are funding this program. They'll do whatever we need them to do or say."

"Making lemonade out of lemons, eh?" I asked Vickie with a smile. I knew she'd be just the person to handle this. I was relieved.

She gave me a big thumb's up.

"Then you probably don't need me anymore," I said. "Just send me a bill, Vick."

Mason spoke up, "We really do want to thank you, Miss Waycross," he said. "You will still be volunteering, I hope?"

"Wild horses couldn't keep me away," I told him. "See you tomorrow - or will the museum be open tomorrow?" I directed my question to Vickie.

"Oh, they'll be open, right after the press conference," she said. "Mason and I are reviewing the details now."

"Excellent, then I'll be off. See you tomorrow, Mason. And Vick, let's do lunch. Have your people call my people."

She laughed. "You'll call me yourself, Florinda Fletcher Waycross, like you did yesterday."

Vickie had taken charge, just like she always had when she worked at the library. I knew I could count on her to make this mess for the museum go away as quietly as possible and become a benefit in the end. Clever girl.

True to her word, Vickie had gotten the word out to the media about tomorrow's eleven o'clock presser. I got there at ten and parked in the lot behind the museum where my car would be out of the way. Already T.V. trucks and newspaper cars were pulling into the front lot.

I went to the back door and pushed the buzzer. Liam opened the door. He was looking a little flushed.

"I hope this goes O.K., " he said to me, as we walked down the steps into the basement area where he and Lily and any interns had their offices.

Vickie was already there, conferring with Mason and the head of the board of governors of the museum. She looked up and smiled at me, and then continued her conversation. After a final review, at 10 minutes to eleven, the three of them went upstairs and waited in the upper lobby. Lily, Liam, and I headed out the back door to stand off to the sidelines away from the milling crowd of journalists.

At precisely eleven, Mason opened the doors, and he and the board member went out to greet the crowd. Vickie came to stand next to me, Lily and Liam where we had moved beside the steps out front where Mason was speaking.

Mason introduced the board member who gave a brief speech offering the museum's condolences. Vicki had selecting the one board member who spoke best on his feet and wasn't rattled by the cameras and microphones. He then gave a brief history of the museum and touched on its achievements over the last few years. He even took a few questions and managed to show the proper amount of concern without revealing any new information. As he told the audience, he could only speak to the fact that the hearse and its unexpected cargo had been delivered to the museum. Any other details would need to come from the police.

Then Mason stepped forward and invited anyone who cared to join us into the auditorium for refreshments. A few, especially those who manned the T.V. trucks left, but a number of the reporters who had never been to the town before, let alone the museum, trooped inside, led carefully by Mason, who like a tour guide, pointed out the various exhibits they passed by on their way to the auditorium on the lower level.

Vickie had outdone herself, on very short notice, pulling together, with the staff's help, a catered buffet lunch at the rear of the room, from an exclusive area restaurant. with tables and chairs set up for the guests to use as they indulged their appetites. I had, after all, told her to spare no expense.

So the feeding frenzy that began on the front lawn, turned into chatty grazing as those in attendance filled their plates and cups and made small talk with both their friends and competitors. Bellies full, they all left in a much more mellow frame of mind than when they arrived. We hoped that any stories they wrote would reflect a more positive spin than might have been expected previously. After the crowd had gone, I helped the others clear the tables.

"Want some cake?" Lily asked me. "We still have some left in the extra frig."

Liam grinned. "Yeah, Vickie thought it wouldn't be appropriate to serve several-day-old cake to our guests, especially when it had a drawing of the hearse on the front."

"Chocolate?" I asked.

"Or yellow," Lily answered.

"Chocolate, and you're on," I told her.

Mason went upstairs in case there were any visitors or stragglers, but the rest of us sat around the table, munching on cake, and talking to Vickie. I was pleased to see that Lily and Liam were at ease around Vickie, but then, she was a real people person.

"Do you think the worst is over," Liam asked. "I mean for the museum," he added.

"I should think so," Vickie said. "They've satisfied their curiosity and gotten all they can get here, so they'll go now for more promising targets. I pity the son, though. The vultures are likely circling around his head."

Vickie had no idea of my connection to Tony, and I wasn't about to reveal it, unless for some reason I needed her further help. I hoped I wouldn't. After all, I was hiring the best lawyers and investigator that money could buy, at least between here and Chicago. And if need be, we'd import a big name. I couldn't let Tony go down without a fight. I didn't really think he was responsible.

I caught the evening T.V. news, with dear Switch purring on my lap, or rather as much of him that still fit on my lap. At least his front half fit; the rest was behind him on the sofa cushion.

I watched the news video of this morning's event and heard the board member's speech. The reporter on the channel advertised as the news leader of the area, spent more time telling how the museum was a positive influence in the community, and that the finding of the body there had been unfortunate and entirely unrelated.

I drew a relieved breath. If the other stations followed suit, then the crisis had been truly handled. The next hurdle would be if and when the hearse was returned to the museum, but that would be much later. I hoped things wouldn't go so far as Tony actually facing a jury of his peers. None of the other families were likely to step forward to help him, so Tony was on his own, except for whatever support the team I'd hired could muster.

The followup stories about Tony in the next few days were lean, as well. Apparently nobody was talking off the record, the cops were stonewalling the press, and the story disappeared from the front pages of newspapers, or as the lead story on the news.

There was a lot of speculation, but not much hard information. The new lawyer team deferentially gave me updates; they too, were smart enough to know who was paying the bills, but there was not much to tell.

I went back to the museum to help out, as the normal schedule was maintained, and other than a few curiosity seekers who stopped in hoping to see the hearse, the attendance remained steady. Mason had to explain to them that the museum had no idea when they would actually get the hearse back for display. Secretly, I wondered if they ever would.

Finally, tired of the excuses I got when I asked about seeing Tony, one of the new lawyers finally conceded that to let me pose as a researcher and accompany Tony's main counsel on his next visit.

I dressed carefully the morning to meet the lawyer at the facility whereTony was being held. My usual museum attire was low-key enough, and I wore eyeglasses that made me look quite scholarly. I arrived on time, and joined the lawyer as he got out of his car to go inside.

"Mr. Carlson?" I inquired. He certainly looked like a lawyer, all thousand-dollar suited, and hair carefully coiffed.

"Miss Waycross," he said and held out his hand to shake mine. I was pleased that he had a firm grip. He handed me a small folder and a notepad and pen. "You can take a few notes if you like."

I nodded, and we went into the facility, signed in and were taken to a small interview room, where Tony was soon brought in. The lawyer nodded to the guard, who stepped outside.

"Flo," Tony cried. "I can't begin to thank you enough… "

"Not necessary," I told him. "We just want to ensure you have adequate defense."

"Mr. Lamorata," the lawyer began, "do you want to tell Miss Waycross what you have told me."

"O.K., look, Flo, I didn't kill my father. He left home about 10 days before I filed the missing persons' report. He had a doctor's appointment in Chicago, and he wasn't expecting good news. He'd already prepared me for his eventual retirement by giving me access to all the necessary accounts, etc. in case something ever happened to him. He called me late that night, I guess from Chicago, and said that he was going away, but not to do anything about it, unless he was gone more than a week. I agreed, because I'd learned early on never to disagree with him." Tony stopped talking and took my hand. "You do believe me, don't you."

"Yes, but go on," I said.

"Well, I figured he'd be staying with one of his friends to kind of pull himself together to face whatever it was he learned from the doctor. But once a week went by, I began to worry, and it was 10 days before I filed the report. The cops took it without a lot of questions, I guess supposing that someone his age of late 70s could have been senile and just wandered off. They didn't do anything to look for him; he was an adult and could certainly drop out of sight, if he wanted to. But by giving me that one week deadline, I figured he did want me to make an attempt to find him."

"Mr. Lamorata did contact a private investigator to look into the matter," the lawyer said to me. "We checked. But the trail went cold."

"Truthfully, I ran out of cash to keep up a search," Tony said. "The bar wasn't doing so hot, and frankly, we've been out of the protection racket and those sorts of schemes for decades, so there wasn't a lot of money coming in."

"So, you gave up looking?" I asked.

"Officially, yes. But I looked in the out-of-town papers to see if any unidentified bodies had been found, because I knew that there was the possibility that some other family head had actually been responsible for his disappearance. There's not a lot of love and brotherhood among the families - never has been."

"Any real suspects?" I asked.

"Lots," Tony said shaking his head. "But nothing substantial enough to give the cops to follow up on. To tell the truth, they really didn't care one way or the other."

"There must be something," I told him.

"Only one thing sticks out in my mind," he said. "Tommy Belofina was my father's oldest and closest friend. I thought maybe he'd reached out to him. He was the original owner of the funeral parlor that donated the hearse to the museum. by the way. But by the time I'd tried to contact him, maybe six months later, he had vanished into thin air, too, and nobody else was talking. They just said the old man had retired to somewhere or another and wanted to be left alone."

"You think this man might know what happened to your father and how he ended up in that coffin?" I asked, staring at him, trying to get him to meet my eyes, something he'd avoided the whole time we'd been talking.

The lawyer who had been sitting quietly during our conversation spoke up. "We're following up that lead with our investigator," he told us. "But so far, no luck. Now our time's

23

about up."

"Will you come back Flo?" Tony asked me in what I was surprised to hear was a pleading voice.

"Later on, Mr. Lamorata," the lawyer said.

"I'll see you again," I told Tony. "Take care of yourself."

I looked back once to see Tony sitting with his head down in his hands, as the guard came in to take him back to his cell.

I wanted to help him, but there really wasn't anything else I could do, and I was glad to leave that most depressing facility. I hated to think how Tony was able to face it day after day.

The next day, after a restless sleep in which I had dreams of Tony being tortured in prison, I came up with my wildest idea yet. Something smelled about that funeral home and the management, and their haste to give the museum the $50,000 of what I considered hush money. That situation could bear some further investigation, but from someone outside the legal profession.

So, I hired Vickie to go to the funeral parlor and pretend to make some prearrangements for her mother, supposedly deathly ill. I gave her a fistful of cash, supposedly from her mother to pay for it. I figured that cash might loosen the tongues a bit on the part of the owners. We concocted the story that her mother hated banks and and that's why she brought the money for the advance arrangements in cash. I also cautioned her to only speak with a Belofina family member, preferably the owner to see what kind of information she could get on the operation. Just nosing around, she might find out something.

I paid Vickie in cash, too, for her services. I've found that although most people do pay taxes, they aren't averse to getting under the table money every now and then, no matter how honest they think they are.

I waited for Vickie's call that evening, but none came. Only an odd text I'd received from her, about the time I would have expected her to be on her way home.

"It's a coverup, I'm sure. They knew more than they've said. More later. Vick."

I tried calling her, but she didn't answer. Finally, I went to bed, wondering what had hadn't called me, but I figured she'd call in the morning.

The next morning's early news gave me the answer of why

I'd not heard from her. A body had been found floating in the river, and a car was found parked just a bridge in a park I realized was not far from the funeral home. She was identified as Vickie Brewer, since her purse with her driver's license was in the car with her. The keys were still in the ignition. They speculated she had jumped from the bridge and committed suicide.

Oh, my God, I thought. I had sent Vickie into a nest of vipers, and she hadn't survived it. I knew for certain that Vickie, whose love of life and vitality was so strong that she would have never, ever have taken her own life.

What had she stumbled into? What had she overheard that made her someone that had to be eliminated? Had someone identified her with me and through me to Tony? Was the cash the tip-off? I pulled out of my wastebasket the previous few days' newspapers. There was a photo with the coverage of the press conference at the museum. Looking closely at the photos, I saw Vickie and me standing near the steps, caught in the angle shot of a photo of Mason and the board member.

It wouldn't have been hard for someone to figure out that the money for Tony's defense had come from me, and that Vickie was connected to me as well. As my lawyer said, there was something about this whole thing that didn't smell good, and it wasn't just the old man's corpse. The police were still withholding the cause of the old man's death. There was something rotten going on..

I'd been under the mistaken impression that money could buy anything and that I was infallible. That hadn't been the case, and Vickie had paid the price. I knew Vickie had no family, was an only child and parents and other relatives were were long dead. My lawyers would have to step forward and take care of arrangements. I owed VIckie that much.

Somehow I felt that Tony knew more than he was telling me. I'd press the lawyer to get me back in one more time to get Tony to tell the whole truth. Once again the lure of my money came to the forefront, as the lawyer agreed to let me accompany him again the next day.

We went into the interview room to meet with Tony. I'd already warned the lawyer not to interrupt me. The lawyer was only there so that I could talk to Tony without being recorded.

Not in the mood for small talk, I got right to the point. "Let's have the real story." I told him. "I know there's more to it than you've told us. Vickie was killed for some reason connected to this case, and so help me, if you don't let me find out why, you'll wish to stay in prison, so I can't get my hands on you."

Tony sighed. "I heard about her, and I could never wanted that to happen."

"It all revolves around that funeral home, doesn't it, and your father's friend?" I demanded.

Tony sighed before he replied. "It was bound to come out sooner or later. What I told you was true to a point. My father was sick and not expected to last more than a few weeks. After he got the final word from the specialists, he wanted to drop out of sight, retire quietly. He didn't want to become a spectacle in the press, and definitely didn't want pity, from anyone.

"So, he went to stay with the old man, Tommy Belofina, in a lake cabin up north. He called me with instructions once he got there. I was to say nothing for at least 10 days, then put out the word that he'd disappeared, even file a missing person's report, which would amount to nothing, and eventually he'd fall out of the news, and I could just quietly take over what was left of our family organization. Like I said, it isn't the same as it was years ago. I'm just not into that stuff, and avoid it as much as I can."

He finally looked me in the eyes and continued, "So, when the old man died a few weeks later, Tommy called me and said he was taking care of things. Apparently he took my father secretly back to the funeral home and had him secretly embalmed and put into storage there.

"As I learned later, his plan was to have Dad, who was much smaller than he, put into one of those special double caskets along with Tommy, who apparently didn't expect to last long, either.

"But obviously when Tommy died later, it didn't come off the way it was planned. I don't know if Tommy was the one who had my father stored in the old hearse, although it would have been the kind of joke they both would have enjoyed, but when the hearse was donated to the museum and the coffin was opened, it presented a real nightmare issue for the present funeral home owners.

"Are you sure they didn't know it was there? After all they were giving the museum a $50,000 donation to take the hearse into their collection."

"I really don't think they knew," Tony said. "Money is no problem for them. There always seems to be a lot of activity going on in that place that generated a cash flow: ordinary funerals, pre-planning, upscale caskets and the like."

"But I think the donation was likely just a gesture to maintain public good will, and get rid of an old relic they didn't want around anymore. But having to explain how that body got there, and why. Well, that was likely publicity they didn't need," Tony said.

"So why do you think they had Vickie was killed. She sent me a text afraid that someone was on to her. Do you think that someone there is capable of murder to keep it quiet?"

"Don't expect it was planned; more likely, somebody panicked," Tony said.

Then I remembered the nervous guy who delivered the hearse. He was definitely afraid of something. At least I figured now that I'd gotten out of Tony all that he knew.

"So, if Tony had nothing to do with his father's death, why did they arrest him?" I asked the lawyer.

"LIkely all they might have on him is filing a false missing person's report that might be grounds for a misdemeanor charge," the lawyer speculated. "He's actually being held as a material witness. Looks like the cops are gunning for bigger game, though."

"Can you get me out?" Tony asked.

"All in good time," the lawyer told him "The wheels of justice grind very slowly."

We left, and I filled the lawyer in on the delivery guy as a possible suspect. I figured the guy could have been following the publicity on the discovery, and saw the photo of me and Vickie at the press conference. He must freaked out when he saw her again at the funeral home where I had sent her. She was targeted because she was in the wrong place, seen by the wrong person.

Not surprisingly, our investigator was able to soon get a background check on the delivery guy, also a driver for the funeral home in a number of capacities, including some more questionable odd jobs. He had worked there for nearly twenty years. Arrested at various times for petty crimes, he had continued to be employed there, and was likely considered a useful idiot. But whether he had killed Vickie on his own, or was directed to do so would be a more difficult thing to prove.

But one thing he didn't have going for him, from the outset, obviously, was being so dumb that he wasn't aware of the sheer numbers of surveillance cameras in places one would never expect to see them. Once our investigator was able to find out that a business not far from the bridge where Vickie's car was found had recorded the whole thing, showing that it hadn't been Vickie driving or parking her car that night, the truth was revealed.

The delivery guy, whose name was Denison Forder, had gotten out of the car with an unconscious Vickie across his shoulder and pitched her over the rail, then left the car and walked away, not even bothering to steal her purse. Once he was identified, it didn't take long for an arrest to occur, and for Tony to be set free.

How the funeral home managed to escape a major investigation, is one for the history books; but again, big money has deep pockets, and the place had for years been a major donor and sponsor for city projects.

Once the current third-generation front person owner was proven to be squeaky clean (nothing could be pinned on him) - anything of the prior regimes was considered in the past, and the poor delivery guy was determined to have acted solely on his own, afraid that he indeed would be blamed and finally lose his job for not checking that the coffin in the hearse was really empty. Targeting Vickie was one more stupid decision in the sordid tale of his life.

I watched on T.V. as they released Tony from jail. The T.V. cameras were on him and the reporters were screaming for quotes, as he went into the waiting arms of his wife, surrounded by his kids and grandkids.

He only turned to the cameras, and it seemed as though he was looking directly at me as he said: "I just want to thank all those who supported and believed in me." Then he turned back to his family, got in a car and drove off. It almost brought a tear to my eye, O.K., almost, but not quite.

Now I had to make things right for Vickie - and clear up any distressing hint of scandal for the museum. First of all, I had Mason confirm that the hearse would be returned to the museum once it was released from evidence. Vickie and Mason had already planned the presentation for that eventuality, and I wanted to make sure that this would be done her way.

Then, I set up two scholarship grants for the museum. One a special recurring yearly promotional and public relations intern position to honor Vickie, and the second, set up on the same basis to be known as the Lamorata award for heritage exhibits intern position, especially focusing on history of early County settlers.

It was some weeks later, that we all gathered once again in the front yard of the museum as the horse-drawn hearse was finally re-delivered to the museum. This time the coffin inside was really empty. In fact, when the vehicle was taken off the delivery van, the coffin lid and lid were separate, and I helped Lily and Liam place the assembled coffin inside inside the hearse. Just before we closed the lid, Lily with her flawless sense of style, tucked a lovely bouquet of silk flowers inside.

Although Mason thought that not much attention would be paid to the event, since it was no longer in the news, we were all thrilled to see a crowd in attendance for the presentation, who came inside to tour the museum afterward.

I wasn't surprised that among them were Tony and his family. I went over and welcomed them myself. After all, I was thankful that she had been the one to have married him and not me. I didn't think that I could have been so gracious with six children, and fourteen grandchildren all in tow.

Later that afternoon, when I went home, Switch was waiting for me, along with some peace and quiet, which at my age and inclination can be considered a blessing. But I'll be back at the museum in a few days for more historical probing, and who knows what might turn up?

THE END

April Fools

RoseMary McDaniel a.k.a. Amy Hayle

In the Fruithills, a place that has never lost its ties to a spirit-filled past, a century old theatre was refurbished by a hardy group of performers who respected the history, including the resident Ghost, but when teenagers played a cruel April Fool prank, the joke was on them.

Author's note: Although the stories have been inspired by some actual places and events in history, they are all a product of the author's imagination and not intended to represent any persons, living or dead.

April Fools

Never underestimate a resident
ghost. After all, he's still there..

RoseMary McDaniel

April Fools

RoseMary McDaniel a.k.a. Amy Hayle

It was dark as midnight, but the path was a familiar one that led down the old wooden stairs to the basement dressing room. No need for sight, memories were what he was made of, and driven by the deep instinctive longing to repeat the familiar journey upstairs and down, he made the rounds that had been done for year after year. Not a sound betrayed his journey and the stillness of the theatre soothed his restless spirit. Alone at last until the next disruption. But all was controlled by his indestructible will and in the end, he alone would remain as he had for generations past.

******

"I don't know how you let your mother talk you into this," Fawn said. "And then you drag us into coming with you." She rolled down the window of the car to get some air.

"Oh, come on," Audrey, the driver, told her friend, as she put on the signal to turn the corner. "It's going to be fun. We can dress up and be on stage like famous actresses."

"Yeah," echoed Dara. "We might even be seen by somebody famous who offers us a screen test or something."

"You've been reading too many of your grandmother's old movie magazines in the attic," Fawn replied. "Besides, the word actress is so yesterday, and who of importance would come to this stinky little theatre to see anything."

"That's just not fair, Fawn," Audrey said. "My grandparents and a lot of other people around here did a heck of a lot of work to make this place fit to put on their performances back in the 1960's. I, for one am really proud of them."

"Well, I wouldn't be looking for any talent scouts in the audience," Fawn replied. "And I'd watch where I sat. Who cleans that place, anyway?"

"They can't afford to hire it out," Audrey said. "Everybody pitches in. There are lots of volunteers who do it just for the… "

"I know, for the love of it. I've heard this speech half a dozen times before. I've even driven by there. I just think it's a pretty dumb idea," Fawn told them.

"I'm excited about the chance to sing on stage," Dara said. "The whole idea of being in front a real audience is so exciting."

"You were too scared to try out for the junior class play," Fawn reminded her. "So why's this so special?"

"I was asked to take part and I mentioned it to Dara, who was thrilled," Audrey replied, answering for her. "We needed a third singer, because we're supposed to be one of those girl groups from the 1960s, so we asked you."

"What's the name of this extravaganza?" Fawn asked.

"It's an original musical comedy written by an old classmate of my grandmother's," Audrey answered. "It's called "Ghost of Elvis and Friends Have Not Left the Building.""

"That is so cool!" cried Dara.

"Oh, please," Fawn broke in. "That is so corny."

Audrey pulled into the parking lot beside the old Opera House, painted a pale gray blue with large gold colored metal letters spelling out its name on the front of the building.

"We're here now, so please try to show a little enthusiasm," Audrey said to Fawn.

"Why'd you pick me, anyway?" Fawn asked, as they got out of the car and walked to the entrance.

"It sure wasn't for your sparkling personality," came a voice from behind them.

The trio of girls turned to see three of their high school classmates walking behind them.

"Thanks for the compliment, Cody," Fawn said in a sarcastic tone. "What are you doing here?"

"You don't recognize Mick Jagger, Frankie Valli and Bobby Darren?" Cody asked in mock surprise.

"Wow," said Dara. "That is just so cool."

"To you, everything is cool," Fawn said to Dara. Then she turned to the boys. "You aren't serious, are you? Whoever told you that you could sing?"

Connor, Cody's friend gave an amused shrug in the direction of the girls. "Whoever told them that they could sing?"

"Yeah, and we didn't even have to try out," Vince, the third teenager said.

Audrey laughed. "They've got a point, Fawn. To answer your question, we picked you because we needed a lead. And although I hate to admit it, you really can sing."

"Faint praise," Fawn sniffed.

The group went inside and were met in the lobby of the theatre by Mrs. Branson, the current production director.

"Glad to see you," she said as she wrote down each of their names on her clipboard. "If you all just want to sit in the coffee room through the door on the right, I'll come and get you as soon as we're ready to start. Help yourself to refreshments."

The six went into the other room, picked out sodas from a cooler and sat on the various sofas and chairs about the room.

"They've really done a great job decorating," Dara said. "I really like the wallpaper and the color scheme. I was here a few years ago, and this room didn't look anything like this."

"They've still renovating, even after all the years they've owned it. It's their 50th Anniversary this year. That's why they're doing the retrospective 1960s play." Audrey said.

"Wonder where Percy's hanging out when a play's going on?" Connor remarked.

"Who?" Fawn asked. "Did you say Pervy?"

"No," Audrey replied. "He's talking about the resident ghost, who's called Percy."

"No kidding," Dara said. "Who was he?"

"Oh, he was some sort of a handy man here, years ago, and when he died, he never left. He just likes to borrow things, or move them around or play jokes on the players." Audrey answered.

"Oh, great. Not only likely rats and spiders that we have to look out for; there's also a perverted ghost on the premises," said Fawn.

"I'm sure he'll like you," Cody laughed.

"More than I like you," Fawn replied.

"O.K., children," Audrey cut in. "Let's try to keep it civil, all right?"

"So when does the play open?" asked Dara.

"We start rehearsing Sunday afternoon, and our first performance is April 2.

"That's pretty quick, only a few weeks," Cody said.

"Obviously some people have more trouble than others with learning their parts," Fawn replied.

Audrey ignored her remark to answer Cody. "Well, those

with the speaking parts are seasoned actors and quick studies. All we have to do is learn our one song each and that should be pretty easy, since we've all had choir, and even done some other performing."

"Sounds simple enough," Connor agreed.

At that point, Mrs. Branson returned to usher them into the auditorium where she gave out the scripts and other information, and a suggested costume list.

"We've got quite a few costume pieces, both from older plays and from donations in the basement dressing room," she told the group. "Feel free to check that out before you go out and buy or rent anything. Unfortunately, we don't have much allotted to buying new ones, so we ask that you try to beg, borrow or steal - hypothetically, of course, whatever you can. Bring your costumes to our first rehearsal, or contact Mrs. Davis, the wardrobe lady before that, if you have any questions. See you all then."

Most of the older performers left, apparently already decided on their costumes, but the teens followed Audrey, who knew the way to the basement storage room. The boys headed for the other dressing room, where the male costumes were kept.

It didn't Audrey and Dara long to find some possible outfits.

"Look at these three dresses - complete with sashes, all alike, just different colors. They look like they'd fit us with a few alterations that Mrs. Davis could do. And here are three wigs, a blonde, brunette and redhead, perfect. And we can wear flats," Audrey's words came out in a rush.

"They look like prom dresses," was Fawn's appraisal.

"That's more or less what they wore," Audrey replied, pulling a folded piece of paper out of her pocket. "Here's a picture of the Shirelles I printed off the internet last night."

"How about wearing white boots, they're so… "

"Yeah, I know, cool," Fawn said, cutting Dara off. "Even they weren't dumb enough to wear those boots with prom dresses." She took the blonde wig out of Audrey's hand. "I'll be the blonde, if I have to be anything," she said.

"Can I have the red one?" Dara asked.

"Sure," Audrey agreed. "The brown one suits me just fine."

"OK, can we go now?" Fawn asked. "I've had enough drama for today."

"Just let me put these things into this big shopping bag and leave a note for Mrs. Davis that these are the costumes we picked and that we'll come to her for fittings after the first night's rehearsal," Audrey told her.

It took her only a few minutes for the task, and the girls headed for the stairs. At the sound of laughter from the other dressing room, they went over to peek inside.

Connor and Cody were wearing 60s sport jackets and button down shirts, and were affixing snap on ties. Vince had on a wide brimmed hat with sequins and a matching jacket. They were all snickering as they looked at themselves in the floor length mirror.

"You guys look great!" Audrey said.

"That's a matter of taste," Fawn replied. "I presume your singing will match."

"Just wait and see," Connor told her. "You'll be shown up, that's for sure."

"Yeah, maybe by Elvis," Fawn replied.

"Who's playing Elvis, anyway?" Cody asked.

"I really don't know," Audrey said. "I guess we'll have to wait and see at the rehearsal."

The girls left, and the guys continued their costume search.

******

It was a rainy March evening for the first gathering of the performers at the old Opera House. Audrey had to park a block away because the other spaces were filled.

"Nice," Fawn said. "We get to walk in the rain."

"Gee, Fawn, it's because we're late that we didn't get a good parking space. Audrey wanted to leave earlier, but you said… " Dara put in.

"Who asked you?" Fawn said in a sharp voice, and opened the front passenger door to get out.

"I've got an umbrella," Audrey offered.

"Forget it," Fawn said and sprinted off down the block.

"Is she always this grouchy?" Audrey asked Dara, who was more or less Fawn's best friend.

"Mostly," Dara replied cheerfully. "But I'm OK with it. I think she has a bigger bark than bite, really, and she has helped me a lot. I'm just not as good at math as she is, and if it weren't for her, I'm not sure I'd have done as well last year."

"Everyone has their good points, I guess," Audrey agreed. "I just hope she doesn't drop out of our trio."

"I'm sure she won't," Dara replied.

The first run through was mostly for setting the scene, reviewing the stage directions blocking out all the stage activity and marking the places for the scenes for each performer. Everyone was there, but one.

"Where's Elvis?" someone asked.

Mrs. Branson smiled, "He's our best kept secret," she said. "Actually, I don't know him personally, but he was highly recommended by a friend of a friend who knows a show manager in Las Vegas. Unfortunately, he won't be able to be with us for most of the rehearsals, having previous commitments, I understand. But with his talent, that shouldn't be a problem."

When the group broke for ten minutes, the teenagers drifted together at the refreshments table.

"Wonder when the big star will show up," Cody said to no one in particular.

"He'll probably at least make it for the opening," Vince replied.

"He likely doesn't want to spend any more time among the common people, than he has to," Fawn put in. "Maybe he heard about Pervy. Those Los Vegas pretenders don't like competition."

"It's Percy," Audrey corrected her again.

"Whatever," Fawn replied. "Doesn't scare me. I'd be able to handle a ghost - but then, there isn't such a thing, anyway."

"Don't be too sure," Mrs. Branson came in and broke into their conversation. "Percy is a documented phenomenon around here, lots of people will swear they've had an encounter with him."

"Really! How... curious," Dara said, quickly substituting her usual "cool" reply.

"Absolutely," replied Mrs. Branson, smiling. "But now it's time to get back to our rehearsal."

The teens, except Fawn, exchanged speculative looks and all followed Mrs. Branson back into the auditorium.

Several more rehearsals went by over the next week, but Elvis still hadn't shown up. Late one afternoon, Fawn and Dara had stayed after rehearsal to wait for Mrs. Davis to come

37

downstairs so they could get some alterations to their costumes, while Audrey was helping Mrs. Branson and the crew with some changes on the set.

Fawn, bored with waiting, poked her head through the curtain that divided the women's from the men's dressing rooms.

"Hey, Dara, come here," she called, once she had gone into the other room.

Dara followed to find Fawn holding a gray garment bag from which she had removed a flashy sequined white costume. She placed the hanger over a wire strung across the corner, and opened a shoe box containing a pair of shiny white boots.

"Elvis may not be here yet," Fawn said. "But his costume is."

"It looks very authentic," Dara said, reaching out a hand to touch it.

"Yeah, too authentic. Let's alter it a bit." said Fawn, reaching for a pair of scissors.

"What are you going to do?" Dara asked in alarm.

"You'll see," Fawn said, and turning the suit around, she whacked at the decorations and made half a dozen jagged cuts on the back of the jacket. Then she replaced the scissors where she'd found them, and picked up a small bottle of glue and a package of straight pins which she poured into the boots. Then she turned the suit around, replaced the garment bag over the suit and put the boots back in the shoe box. Nothing was visible of her nasty prank.

"That's pretty mean," Dara told her.

"Serves him right for thinking he's better than the rest of us," Fawn told her and took off back to the other room.

When Mrs. Davis finally came down to help with their costumes, Fawn was casually leafing through a fashion magazine, and Dara was sitting next to her with a worried look.

"Don't fret, dear," Mrs. Davis said, sensing concern, but for the wrong reason. "We'll get your costume fixed in a jiffy."

When Mrs. Davis had finished the alterations, Fawn and Dara went out front to sit on the bench in front of the theatre and wait for Audrey.

"Not a word of this to anybody. They'll never believe that you weren't in on it," Fawn told her.

Dara merely nodded.

******

On the day of the final run-through the evening of April 1st, Audrey, Dara and Fawn got their turn at the makeup tables in the dressing room. They applied eyeliner, lipstick and blush before they got into their costumes and donned their wigs.

"How do I look?" Dara asked, fluffing up her red wig. She turned to Fawn. "Hey, I thought you were wearing the blonde one?"

Fawn had settled a bright red pageboy style over her short haircut. "I bought this one instead, and I look better in red than you do, anyway."

She picked up the blonde one laying on the table and tossed it to Dara. "Here, put this one on."

Dara took it without another word, removing the red one and replacing it with the blonde curls.

"That really looks cute on you," Audrey told Dara, attempting to smooth things over.

"Do you really think so?" Dara asked doubtfully.

"Yes, I do." Audrey smiled at her. "Come on, I'll help you with your dress."

Finally, the company was assembled on stage for the opening number, when Mrs. Branson announced that Elvis had arrived, was parked at the rear door of the theatre and going down to get ready. There was a murmur of excitement among the performers, and Fawn gave Dara a warning look.

"Everyone stand by," Mrs. Branson called. "Elvis will join us shortly."

Not five minutes passed until a figure in a sparking white suit and boots wearing sunglasses appeared from stage left and joined the rest. The other performers clapped a welcome, and Mrs. Branson held up her hands for silence, signaled the curtain to be dropped, and the run-through to begin.

While the curtain was being lowered, Dara turned to Fawn and whispered "What happened?"

Fawn didn't reply, and Audrey's look from the other side of Fawn silenced Dara, as the curtain was raised to begin the performance.

******

To Fawn and Dara's surprise, the run-through was flawless. Even Dara managed to forget her anxiety and perform well. But the biggest success of the rehearsal was the performance by Elvis. Afterward, everyone wanted to congratulate and meet him, but he had disappeared off stage and was gone before Mrs. Branson released the rest of the crew. She assured them that he would return for the performance the next night.

They all trooped downstairs where they took off their costumes and prepared to leave.

The girls went back up to the auditorium, and Audrey asked Fawn and Dara if they wanted to go to an informal cast gathering at a local restaurant, but Fawn said she'd call her father on her cell to pick up her and Dara, because they were too tired to go with the group.

After Audrey left, Dara looked at Fawn. "Aren't you going to call your father?"

"Not yet," Fawn said. She picked up a play program from a nearby table, opened it and looked through the cast list. Where the name of the person who played Elvis would have been printed, there was only the cryptic "Special Guest Star."

She threw the program on a nearby seat. "Come on, we're going back downstairs."

They slipped down the back stairs, and Fawn pretended to be making an adjustment to her costume that was folded on a shelf by the makeup mirrors against the wall between the two dressing rooms. Once everyone else had left the room, she grabbed Dara and pulled her behind one of the curtained areas used for changing. She held up her finger to her mouth to signal to Dara to keep quiet.

Finally, the lights went out, and they could hear the final footsteps as everyone left.

"Come on," Fawn said to Dara, "We're going to find that costume and see why it wasn't the one we altered."

"Not we," Dara protested. "You."

Fawn shrugged and pulled Dara into the adjoining room, which was also dark.

"I can't see a thing," Dara said.

Fawn reached over and switched on a makeup light on the nearby table, which shed a faint glow in the darkened room. Fawn pawed through the line of garment bags lining the wire stretched across the room. "Nuts," she said aloud. "I don't see it. He must have worn it out of here."

Dara let out a squeal and Fawn turned around angrily.

"What's wrong with you… " she began and stopped as she saw what Dara was staring at. Standing just inside the rear door of the dressing room that led outside, was the man in the white Elvis costume.

"So, you never left at all," Fawn accused him. "I suppose you had another suit and wore it instead of the one you left here."

The figure shook his head, stepped out of the shadows and removed his sunglasses.

Fawn and Dara stared into darkness because the man had no face, but laughter poured from where his mouth should have been.

"Oh my God," cried Dara, "It's Percy, dressed as Elvis."

"It can't be," Fawn said. "It's just a joke, an April Fool joke. Who are you?" she demanded as she approached him.

The laughter continued as the figure shed the white spangled coat: there was nothing, no body beneath it, like the invisible man from horror movies.

By now, Dara had hurried to the door and felt for the door knob to open it and get away, but Fawn suddenly pushed in front of her, flung open the door and ran out into the yard.

With a final look at the figure only visible by the pants and the boots, Dara quickly followed. But by the time she got outside, somehow the figure had gotten ahead of her and was chasing Fawn across the yard toward the high bluff over the river that stretched behind the old theatre.

Fawn only looked back once, and as she did, she tripped on a root and unable to restore her balance, plunged over the edge down onto the rocks along the river far below. She lay very still.

The ghostly figure turned away and headed back toward the theatre, breezing by Dara like a cold wind. She stood there frozen.

He spoke in a low voice as he passed close by her ear. "April Fools! Elvis has left the building, but I have not."

Then Dara began screaming.

THE END

41

The Christmas Jester

RoseMary McDaniel a.k.a. Amy Hayle

In the Fruithills, a place that has never lost its ties to a spirit-filled past, Fiona and Lindy renovated a 100-year-old home for their gift shop. It was a dream come true, until Fiona learned that the former owners had left behind much more than dust bunnies, including the strange little jester doll she discovered among the Christmas displays.

Author's note: Although the stories have been inspired by some actual places and events in history, they are all a product of the author's imagination and not intended to represent any persons, living or dead.

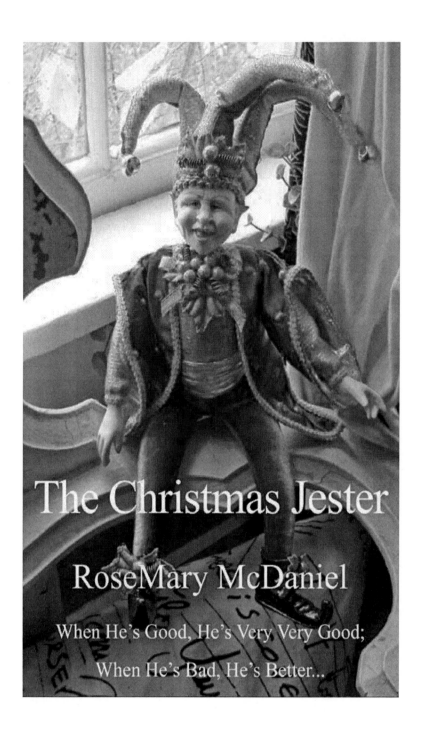

The Christmas Jester

RoseMary McDaniel

When He's Good, He's Very Very Good;

When He's Bad, He's Better...

The Christmas Jester

RoseMary McDaniel a.k.a. Amy Hayle

Early Morning:

Draperies rustled as a nimble little figure suddenly appeared and hopped up to sit on the edge of a shelf beneath the window. He shook himself, causing the golden bells on the tips of his pointed jester hat to jingle softly. He wore a festive red and green velvet suit trimmed with holly, and he blended into the decor as he settled on his perch next to the evergreen trimmed fireplace on his right and a twinkling all-red decorated tree on his left. His blue eyes crinkled above the broad grin on his face as he sat silently peering into the room.

Late Afternoon:

Fiona was tired, but it was a good kind of tired. She and her business partner Lindy had finally finished setting up the displays in every room of their new shop. She paused by the bookcase full of Christmas candy, straightened a few boxes of chocolates and absent-mindedly plucked a miniature candy cane from the container they kept for the visiting children.

Tomorrow would be the grand opening of Fiona's Gift & Florals for their first Christmas season. Lindy had already gone home for a bowl of soup and an early night before returning in the morning to handle any last minute details.

Lindy was the business end of the partnership who kept tabs on the practical matters, nailed down the finance plans and put them in place. She also handled all the outside work. Fiona was the creative partner who had the eye for color and style and managed the Floral end of the business and worked on the PR. They both collaborated on the selection of gift items to offer and described themselves as eager children in adult bodies when it came to a knack for spotting just what would appeal to their customers.

Fiona unwrapped the candy treat and stuck it part way in her mouth to let it slowly melt, just like she'd done when she was a five-year-old who'd sat on Santa's lap for the first time. She'd been scared to death of the jolly old man for the first four years of her life, refusing to go near him when her mother visited the mall on a shopping expedition. But it was the costumed little Elf who always stood beside Mrs. Claus and handed out the candy canes that really freaked her out. Some people hated clowns; Fiona didn't like elves, or anything that resembled them.

She wasn't sure what had tipped the scales the year she turned five, but the bragging of her kindergarten friends of all the gifts they'd gotten after whispering in Santa's ear was enough to convince her to get in line, climb onto Santa's lap to tell him exactly what she wanted for Christmas, and bravely collect her candy cane from the Elf at the end. And it seemed to work.

That year she got everything on her list that she'd recited to Santa. In retrospect, of course, she realized that her relieved mother had been listening and made sure that she got everything she'd asked for.

Fiona smiled at the memory of her younger self, who loved the holiday season as much then as the older Fiona did now. This store that she and her friend Lindy had opened was the culmination of a dream business venture for both of them. It was not only a gift store that offered the unique and the unexpected, it included a floral shop to provide flowers for weddings and special events as well as offer ready-to-go bouquets for the last-minute shopper.

After months of effort by herself, Lindy and many others, the more than 100 year old house in the small downtown area had truly become a work of art. Sadly neglected by the past owners, who had been overwhelmed by illness, the building seemed to be a great bargain. But once they had began the restoration, the partners realized that they had greatly underestimated the amount of funds and labor that it would take to transform it.

Finally after nine long months of work, it was a sight to behold. From the newly landscaped yard to the uniquely painted and decorated rooms that held a pirate's treasure chest of amazing gifts to the bloom-bursting floral shop at the rear, a lot of hope and an artist's vision had brought beauty to the tired old home. It had become an endless trove of whimsical gifts and practical items that truly offered something for everyone.

Attracting trade to the tiny town nestled at the edge of the Fruithills was thought to be by some a difficult task, but Fiona came to the business with a history. Well known by many in the community for her wizardry with floral design over the years as she worked at several other businesses, it didn't take long for the buzz to circulate that Fiona was back. She just hoped that all the talk equaled customers.

But now Fiona's eyes were burning with the need for sleep. She knew it was time to head for home because she must be back bright and early tomorrow long before the hoped-for-hordes of visitors on the official Fridays sale day.

She made her way slowly through each room, checking out the displays, tweaking an ornament here and there on the dozen floor-to-ceiling decorated Christmas trees, and straightening a fat Santa statue here and a dancing polar bear there. She stopped for a moment to adjust a bit of tinsel on the mantel of the fireplace in the dining room.

"Hello, who are you?" she said, addressing a colorful Christmas jester in red and green, perched on a nearby window shelf.

He wore a bright red and green outfit topped off with a jester's hat with bells and holly. She didn't remember putting him there, but he certainly looked at home. Although he had a broad smile, frankly she found him creepy, and in his seasonal outfit he reminded her of that long-ago elf.

She certainly hadn't picked him out of a catalog, nor unpacked and put him there. But so many friends had helped them get ready for the holiday opening, that she must have just been unaware that someone, perhaps Lindy, had ordered it.

"Ok, Mr. Jester," she said. "You can stay. But, I'm watching you," she said and paused, feeling a bit foolish talking to a doll. But he was compelling. It was those eyes, or that open mouthed grin, perhaps. She really had to leave and get some sleep before she imagined him answering her.

She paused again in front of the mantel mirror and stuck her tongue out at the sight of her tired face with a half-eaten candy cane sticking out. Then she gathered up her purse and keys, locked the door, set the alarm and left.

The next morning, Fiona, Lindy and their helpers arrived early to make sure everything was ready and set out the cookies and punch for the planned-for shoppers. They even shooed Lizzie, the shop cat outside so she'd not be underfoot for the day.

The parking lot and even curbside parking filled up quickly when the store opened. A surge of guests admired each of the rooms that were decorated in a distinct and different color scheme and held gifts of all kinds from warm scarves, mittens and hats to playful purses and colorful mugs and imprinted gifts of every description that filled the tables and walls and even nestled on the floor.

There was something new to see everywhere one looked, and the crowds moved from room to room, admiring the tasteful items that filled every available space. Gorgeous wreaths hung from doorways tempting shoppers to buy for their own home. Ornaments of every variety hung from trees in each room, tempting that impulse buy for relatives, friends, or the fireman, teacher, or other important person in everyone's lives with fun or even gag gifts.

Lindy had been pressed into service dipping out the punch and encouraging shoppers to try the home-baked tree and bell and Santa-shaped frosted cookies as they entered the the little room where the refreshments were served. Fiona left her post at the floral counter to get from Lindy a cup of punch and a cookie for a favorite friend of hers.

"Mrs. Morrison came in today with her daughter, " she remarked to Lindy. "But she really looks tired, so I made her sit down in the back and said I'd bring her a treat."

Lindy filled a cup and put a couple of cookies on a plate and handed it all to Fiona with a napkin. "Give her my best," she said.

Fiona had met Mrs. Morrison when she'd attended an autumn craft fair held at the church across the street, where the older woman had been sitting with a friend selling crocheted doilies. Mrs. Morrison had been delighted to learn that Fiona and Lindy had bought the old house for their shop.

As a child, Sylvia Peters (later Morrison) had actually lived in the house with her grandparents, years ago, after her parents died. But sadly, the grandfather had died just a few years after she'd come to stay with them, and the house had to be sold. Fiona had bought several of the friend's delightful handicrafts to use in the gift displays at the shop.

Fiona returned with the punch and cookies and sat up a wooden TV tray to hold them. She'd finished her floral work for the minute, and was free to spend a few minutes chatting. Mrs. Morrison always contributed some delightful stories about the house, since once she and her grandmother had moved to a much smaller house in the town, little Sylvia had been a frequent welcome visitor to the new family who had moved into her grandparents' old home.

Mrs. Morrison took a sip of the punch and declared it was the best she'd ever tasted. Looking out to the rooms beyond, she smiled. "You've been a real blessing to this house and all the people who ever lived here," she told Fiona. "It was old and worn out, like me, but you've worked hard to give it new life, and you'll be rewarded for it."

"Seeing the smiles on the faces of people like you is enough of a reward," Fiona replied and then laughed. "Of course, having them like the things we offer enough to actually buy them is very reassuring as well."

Mrs. Morrison smiled again and then her face grew serious. "You've not had any, well, any unusual visitors, have you?" She took a bite of her cookie and then looked up to meet Fiona's questioning look.

"All our clients are pretty individual," Fiona answered, puzzled.

"I don't mean the customers," Mrs. Morrison said, her voice low. "I mean the spirits, of course."

"Spirits?"

"Ah, well, perhaps I mis-spoke," Mrs. Morrison said.

Fiona was taken aback. "You mean like ghosts?"

Mrs. Morrison patted FIona's hand with her own. "Not exactly like that, but well, a house this old has seen many things happen inside its walls, and sometimes echoes of those times can be heard or seen again. But perhaps the new paint and the noise and workmen have covered over all that in the renovation."

But Fiona wanted to know more. "Did you ever experience anything like that, here?" she asked.

Mrs. Morrison paused and took another sip of the punch. "Well, when I was a child, my room was upstairs, the one with the little closet and I had a very active imagination that kept me looking for monsters under my bed. And of course, there was Emily.

48

"Emily?"

"The little girl spirit who lived in the attic. I saw her shadow on the stairs sometimes. She mostly stayed in the attic, and I was too afraid to ever go there. I once overheard my grandmother talking about her, saying she'd died of a fever when she was about 8 years old, long before my grandparents lived there. She didn't mean any harm, of course. She just loved dolls, and I thought sometimes she'd borrow mine. But I always found them later, so perhaps I'd just misplaced them. If you've not seen her, then likely she's gone."

Fiona's heart stopped for a moment. Beau, one of their friends who redid their wiring had never liked working in the attic, but never said why.

And what was it that Kallie, their number one assistant, had said about noises in the house when she was alone? Fiona had figured it was just the wind or Kallie's super sensitivity and hadn't paid much attention to her complaints.

"I was very sad when I came to live with my grandparents," Mrs. Morrison went on. But everything was better when Giles came. He was what they would now call an imaginary friend, and he helped me adjust to my new home here and made me feel safe.

"But when my grandmother and I moved later on, Giles wouldn't go with me. Perhaps I just outgrew him or didn't need him anymore."

"So you never really saw this little girl?" Fiona asked.

"In dreams several times, I did. And as for the others.."

"Others?" Fiona asked.

Mrs. Morrison polished off her last cookie and smiled. "Giles said there were others, but he kept them away."

"And this Giles, what was he like?"

"He had what I supposed was a French accent, and I pictured him in a pointed hat with little bells on it and funny shoes, like something I'd seen in a book, I guess." She paused and sighed.

Just then, a customer came up to the floral counter to pick up an arrangement she'd ordered, and Fiona excused herself to take care of her.

By the time she'd finished, Mrs. Morrison's daughter was done shopping and Fiona helped her get Mrs. Morrison settled in their car. Fiona gave her a big hug.

"Thank you, dear," Mrs. Morrison said said. Then she whispered to Fiona so her daughter who was putting her purchases in the trunk wouldn't hear.

"Don't mind silly old me going on about the past. You've done a fine thing and brought new life into this old place and that's what it sorely needed. It will all work out; you'll see."

Fiona bid her and her daughter good-bye and returned to her floral work.

She tried to put their conversation out of her mind for now. But Mrs. Morrison's mention of her "imaginary friend" Giles couldn't help but make her think of that jester doll in the dining room. Once things calmed down a bit, she'd have to ask who had ordered it and put it on the shelf.

But for now she had work to do, and reluctantly she returned to filling floral orders that needed to be delivered later that day.

By the end of the weekend, Fiona was even more tired, but extremely pleased at the number of customers that had poured through the doors and the amount of purchases that left with them. She not had a second to think about the jester or her conversation with Mrs. Morrison.

She, Lindy and their help, had gone home on all three nights too tired to linger for conversation, so she'd had no chance to ask about the mysterious appearance of the doll.

But by Monday morning, when both she and Lindy arrived early, Fiona made coffee, poured them both a cup and urged Lindy to sit down with her at the table where they had served the open house refreshments.

"Did you put the little red & green jester in the window in the other room?" Fiona asked.

"Huh?" said Lindy. "What jester?"

"That's just it," Fiona told her. "I didn't order one. "

Just then the ringing of the phone in the little office interrupted the conversation as Lindy went to answer it. In a few minutes, Lindy returned with a sad look on her face.

"That was Kallie, she'll be a little late. She told me she talked to her mother, you remember, she's a nurse at the hospital. She said Mrs. Morrison was admitted last night; she and her daughter were in an auto accident on their way home from church. The daughter is O.K., but Mrs. Morrison is hurt pretty bad, and they don't have much insurance."

All thoughts of their previous conversation vanished as Fiona thought about what they could do to help out.

"Kallie says they're setting up a fund to collect donations at the bank and I said we'd be sure to contribute," Lindy told Fiona.

"Of course," Fiona said. "And once we find out how she's doing, we'll take her a special bouquet."

"I'm sure she'd like that," Lindy said, glancing up at the clock in the corner. "Oh, just five minutes left till opening, so I'd better get ready for the the day."

Fiona nodded, but sat quietly at the table for a few minutes. Cyber Monday probably meant fewer customers today, but she had orders to fill from the busy weekend and put on her apron to begin.

The news about Mrs. Morrison was just the beginning of a disturbing week. First, Lizzie the cat ran away, or at least was nowhere to be seen. The cat had suddenly appeared at their door their first week in business, and hadn't been inclined to leave since. She'd established herself as head security cat and fortunately her manners improved as she accepted visitors to the shop as normal occurrences.

Fiona couldn't recall when they'd last seen her, sometime on Sunday afternoon, Lindy had said. Everyone who worked at the shop had learned to love that crabby little fur ball and hoped she was just taking a little time off, after the holiday rush.

Then on Tuesday afternoon, Kallie tripped on the stairs and sprained her ankle. Fortunately, she just needed it taped up and came back to work the next day. But she swore she had seen shadows on the steps that tripped her up, just before she was hurt. Fiona wrote it off to Kallie's very alert imagination.

But the crowning touch of the new week was the number of broken ornaments that they found scattered under the decorated trees. First, the tree in the red room, and then more under the tree in the green room, and so on through the week. On Friday morning, Fiona arrived to the shop first and because of the damage, made her way through the shop to find not only several broken ornaments but a whole table arrangement tipped over. They might have blamed Lizzie ordinarily, but Lizzie hadn't been seen all week. Although there were only a few things damaged each day and not valued at a lot of money, but it was very disconcerting.

Fiona stopped short in the dining room in front of the jester who was still sitting in the same place, but surrounded by fat little skating penguin statues. She hadn't moved them there, and she hadn't even had time to ask anyone who'd ordered that odd little guy.

Shaking her head, she straightened the mess on the tables, picked up the pieces of some shattered decorations and piled them on a plastic dustpan. Just as she finished Lindy came in, carrying a white sack.

"Cinnamon rolls with sticky frosting," Lindy declared. "I figured we needed a morning pick-me-up." She glanced down at the dust pan that Fiona held. "Damage, again?" she asked.

"More of the same," Fiona answered.

Lindy turned to take the rolls to the workroom, but Fiona called her back. "Did you order that Christmas jester?" she asked.

"Where?" was the reply.

"There," Fiona said pointing to the window shelf. To her surprise, the shelf was empty, except for the little figurines.

"Those are penguins," Lindy said.

"But there was a jester there, just a few minutes ago," Fiona replied.

"Come on, you need coffee and carbs," Lindy said, heading off for the back of the shop. Speechless, Fiona followed.

Later, on Friday afternoon, Lindy met with the bookkeeper, and she was smiling when she came out into the floral workroom to talk to Fiona afterwards.

"We're golden," Lindy said, "and in the black already. So I asked the bookkeeper to send a check to Mrs. Morrison's insurance fund for $500. I didn't think you'd mind."

"Of course not," Fiona replied. "Have you heard how she's doing?"

Just then, Kallie appeared in the the doorway. "I just talked to my Mom at the hospital a while ago, and they said she's recovering nicely. And Laura, who works at the bank says the donation fund is almost at $5,000.00 now."

"That's good news," Fiona said. "And we could sure use some. "I'm really worried about Lizzie, it's been too long since we've seen her."

"I'm sure she'll be back," Lindy told her. "Why don't you

take a bouquet up to Mrs. Morrison at the hospital this afternoon. I'm sure she'd like to see you, and you need to get away from here for a little while."

Fiona shed her apron. "You don't have to tell me twice," she replied, opening the cooler and picking out a deep red vase filled with white pom pom chrysanthemums, red roses and red and green sparkling fern leaves. She placed it in a small box and wrapped it with colorful holiday paper.

She put on her coat and hat, and then she looked around uncertainly. "Sure you don't need me?"

"We can handle it," Kallie answered. "Go see her and then go home and get a good night's rest. Things will look better in the morning."

"But there are some more deliveries, I think," she began, but Lindy literally pushed her firmly but gently toward the door.

"I'll do those. Now go on and get out of here," Lindy finished as she opened the door and bowed low for Fiona to pass through.

So, before she knew it, Fiona was sitting beside Mrs. Morrison's bed, pouring out her heart about all the things that had gone on the past week.

"Oh, dear," Mrs. Morrison said, "I knew I should have told you more about the others, but I really had hoped they were gone."

"Who are the others?"

"A couple of naughty little boys who like to pull cats' tails and play tricks on any unsuspecting person in their reach. Boy spirits, I guess you'd say, and they liked to play pranks on our cat and Grandfather and me. I never really saw them, just what they did. But once Giles came along, they stopped."

"For being an imaginary friend, Giles certainly took care of you," Fiona said.

"Well, I don't want people thinking I've gone dotty or anything," Mrs. Morrison said. "So I don't mention Giles or how helpful was to me when I was all alone at night in my room, crying my eyes out. when I first came to live with my grandparents. I didn't want Grandmother to know because she'd feel bad that she couldn't help. But I guess nobody could have, really, because I had to work it all out for myself. Those two naughty spirits took delight in teasing me, hiding my things and even breaking my favorite doll. I'd thought it might have been Emily, but it wasn't. Then once Giles took over, he made sure they left me alone.. He was kind to Emily, though, and she came to me in dreams where we'd play together so I wouldn't be so lonely." She stopped and looked over at Fiona.

"You must think I'm crazy," she said. "And maybe I am."

"No, please," Fiona protested. "I need your advice. Do you think Giles might be able to help me too? I'm afraid someone has frightened Lizzie our cat away, and every day this week something new has been damaged in the shop."

"Oh, dear, it's happening again," Mrs. Morrison said. "But it's been so long, do you suppose Giles' spirit is still in the house?"

"Maybe," Fiona replied, not going into details. "Thank you so much, Mrs. Morrison, I'd better go now, visiting hours are almost over."

"Come back soon, dear," Mrs. Morrison told her. "Let me know how things work out."

Fiona hugged her goodbye and left the hospital for home. She'd go back to the shop tonight, after she was sure everyone was gone and get to the bottom of this.

Fiona's intent to take a short nap when she got home stretched out longer than she'd planned, and it was nearly eleven o'clock when she awoke.

"Well," she said to herself, "at least everyone has left by now."

She drove through nearly deserted streets to the shop. It had grown colder and light snow flakes blown by the wind danced across the windshield between sweeps of the wipers. She drove into the parking lot of the shop and switched off the engine and the lights.

Lindy had left some of the decorative outside lights ablaze and the festive colors gave a friendly look to the old home. She hurried up the back steps, disengaged the alarm and unlocked the door to her floral shop.

Although she'd left it a bit of a mess, someone, probably Kallie, had picked up the discarded stems and leaves, deposited them into a trash can, and swept the floor.

Slowly Fiona walked through the shop toward the front door, and then turned and headed back toward the floral shop. She felt a cold chill.

Something wasn't right. Then, she stopped short at the doorway into the dining room. Ahead she could see clear to the back of the shop and to her horror there was a large black shadow in the doorway by the floral counter. The shadow began to move and suddenly split in two and slowly made its way toward her. Frozen in place, she glanced over at the dining room window, illuminated by a yard light next door.

There just under the window on the shelf was the Christmas Jester, sitting just as he had the first day she had seen him. Where had he come from?

She heard Mrs. Morrison's voice in her head. "Giles, Giles, please help."

As Fiona watched, a blur of red and green swirled together from the elf on the shelf, growing larger and larger with each second, as the dismal dual shadow continued edging slowly toward her.

Then, the spinning orb of red and green light surged forward and cut through the shadows like a saw, and she saw the shadows vibrate, osculate and fade away. They had disappeared. The swirling ball of color spun faster and faster and as quickly as it had appeared, it was gone.

Fiona watched in the darkness for a few moments, but there was nothing to see. She walked over to the shelf. It was empty again, except for the penguins that she'd seen earlier with Lindy.

She felt a peppermint-scented breeze pass over her. It smelled just like a candy cane tasted, and now she was alone but unafraid. There was nothing to do but lock up and go home.

Fiona again arrived at the shop early on Saturday morning, wanting to check out the shop and walk through it just as she had the night before. But there was nothing out of place or broken, and the jester was still gone.

But something else troubled her; Lizzie was still missing.

It wasn't until Kallie arrived, and Lindy was off on an early delivery that Fiona grew attentive, aware of something just beyond her conscious hearing. She kept listening to what, she wasn't sure.

"Kallie, do you hear anything, or well, feel anything different in the house?" she asked, trusting that Kallie's super sensing ability might pick up something she was missing.

Kallie listened for a long moment, and her face broke into a big smile. "Yes, I do hear something," and she headed off up the stairs to the second floor.

Fiona waited at the bottom of the stairway. She could hear Kallie's footsteps and then heard her exclaim "Lizzie, whatever are you doing here?"

Then Kallie literally ran down the steps to where Fiona stood, holding a bundle in her arms, trailed by the cat. Fiona could have sworn the cat was grinning, as Lizzie came to the bottom of the stairway and twirled around Fiona's legs. Fiona reached down to give her a pat.

"Somehow she got shut up in the attic, but I don't know how," Kallie exclaimed. "I always keep the door shut, and she sure wasn't in there a few days ago when I went to get boxes."

Then Kallie shifted the bundle of red and green fabric she held in her arms.

"And look what I found up there, Lizzie was laying on it for a pillow, I guess. It must have been somebody's old toy, and it's all dusty and full of cat fur. Shall I toss it?"

"No," Fiona cried, recognizing it and held out her arms. "Let me have it. You'd better get Lizzie some food; I'll bet she's hungry."

Lizzie, hearing her name, bumped her head into Kallie's leg and meowed.

"Ok, chum, we'll get you fed." Kallie told Lizzie. "Doesn't look like you're exactly starving though."

Kallie and Lizzie set off for the closed-in side porch where the cat food bowl was, and Fiona brushed dust and hair from the bedraggled figure she held.

"Good job, Giles, even if you did get a bit mussed up. I think we'd better find a spot for you to keep up the good work."

She took him back to her work table, and was still brushing the velvet suit at her work table when Lindy came in, returning from the delivery.

"I thought you hated elves," she said to Fiona.

"This is no elf," FIona told her. "This is our new shop mascot: the Christmas Jester, and he's going to keep an eye on things around here."

Just then, Kallie came out of the side porch with Lizzie in her

56

arms.

"Hey," said Lindy, giving the cat an ear rub that brought a loud purr. "Look who's here. I'll bet if she could talk, she'd probably have some good stories to tell."

Lizzie jumped down from Kallie's arms and went over to hop on Fiona's lap. She rubbed her head against the jester's pointed hat and purred loudly.

"Are you really keeping that old thing?" Kallie asked, looking pointedly at the doll.

"Beauty is in the eye of the beholder," Fiona answered.

"Come on, Kallie," Lindy said, handing her a couple of boxes. "Grab your coat and help me get the rest of this morning's deliveries packed in the truck. We'll never understand the artistic temperament, anyway."

Fiona sat smiling at her work table, watching Lizzie trail out the door after the other two women. She stood up and carefully placed the jester on a shelf over the table, so that his head was turned toward the front of the shop.

She'd visit Mrs. Morrison at the hospital tomorrow. She knew that her friend and former resident of the house would be glad to know that Giles was back on the job, protecting the place they all loved. It was a good feeling, and she hoped the other spirits, or whatever they had been, were at peace at last.

THE END

Death Clock

RoseMary McDaniel a.k.a. Amy Hayle

A small town funeral home closes after 100 years, leaving the community upset over the loss. Suddenly, no one in town is dying, and time stands still in this Fruithills town; a place that has never lost its ties to a spirit-filled past.

Author's note: Although the stories have been inspired by some actual places and events in history, they are all a product of the author's imagination and not intended to represent any persons, living or dead.

Death Clock

Time waits for one man

RoseMary McDaniel

Death Clock

RoseMary McDaniel a.k.a. Amy Hayle

The hands on the old clock that was mounted on the overhang on the front of the building facing the street side stood at exactly twenty minutes until eleven in the morning, when Horace Latham pulled the electric cord and stopped them. Safety first, he reminded himself as he reached up with a small paint brush to whisk away the cobwebs.

He looked over his shoulder at the door that led into the building, as it opened and the owner and his boss, Jacob Addison, called to him from the doorway.

"Horace, can you come in here for a few minutes?"

Horace lay down his brush, got off the small stepladder and left the porch to go inside. To his surprise, the four other employees were seated around the wooden table in the small alcove that served as the office. Addison pushed an extra chair over and motioned for him to sit down.

"I wanted to tell all of you at once," Addison said. "I've just signed the papers and sold the business to Merle Olson. He'll be combining it with his establishment, and we're closing this location as of today and putting it on the market. We've done our last funeral here."

"But this has been a funeral home for the last 100 years," Horace burst out. "You can't just shut it down. People are depending on us." Horace objected.

"We've had less and less business here over the last five years," Addison replied.

Madelyn Morris spoke up. "Many folks prefer to go to a more modern, bigger facility, like Olson's."

"Olson has agreed to consider all of you for positions at his place, and Madelyn has made interview appointments for each of you," Addison told them. "I have checks here for everyone for 6 weeks of severance pay, in leu of notice. You can finish up the day, or leave now, if you like. Thank you for your service."

He handed one to each of them, including Horace, who took his, folded it up and placed it in his work shirt pocket, shook his head, left the room, walked out the door, picked up his ladder and brush, threw them into his pickup, and drove off, none too quietly. The others chatted among themselves as they absorbed the news. Madelyn Morris, who had been the bookkeeper and the only one aware of the financial situation and pending sale, turned toward her friend and co-worker Della Johnson, smiled and tried to smooth over the awkwardness of the moment.

"I've made an appointment with Mr. Olson for all of us to interview. He's really very nice, and I'm sure that we'll all be working together again," she said, handing each of them a printed schedule of appointment times. "If the time isn't convenient for you; feel free to call the number on the page and reschedule."

The other employees solemnly took a schedule and scanned the page for their names. Addison looked at his watch, picked up his briefcase and announced that he was late for an appointment, and left the building.

Madelyn again assumed leadership of the meeting. "There's coffee in the kitchen and rolls, if you'd like some," she said, standing up leading the way to the other room.

Only Della followed her. The other two employees, Fred Metzler and Joseph Stine, who took turns driving the hearse, picking up the bodies from the outsource location who processed them and setting up the viewing for the families, left.

"Is Mr. Addison in financial trouble?" Della asked Madelyn.

"Not now, since he's sold the business," Madelyn replied. "But he had to face facts. Every year for the past five years, we've done fewer viewings. Since bodies haven't been processed here for years, it just didn't make good economical sense to keep the place open for the limited amounts of viewings we had."

"I guess so," Della said, accepting the cup of coffee that Madelyn handed her. "But still, a lot of older folks were pretty keen on having the services here. It's like a tradition. Even the slogan was "100 years of Service to the Community at Addison's."

"Times change and circumstances as well," replied Madelyn. "We can still serve at the new facility, it's less than five miles away, after all."

"That's like the other side of the world to some people," Della remarked and sipped her coffee.

The commercial "For Sale" real estate sign went up the following morning, much to the surprise of the local crowd who met for coffee every morning at the Sidewalk Cafe downtown.

Melvin Shrock opened the monthly Town news sheet that had just come out that morning and read aloud to his table mates.

"Letter to the Community: It is with regret that I advise our clients and friends whom we have proudly served over the past 100 years that we have sold our business to Olson Funeral Home and Chapel and will be closing this location immediately and offering the building for sale. For any information on records of our establishment, please contact Olson's, as we have transferred all our records to them. Thank you again for letting our family serve yours. Sincerely, Jacob Addison."

Shrock looked up at his his companions, none of whom seemed overly surprised.

"Less and less of us old buzzards left around here," Harley Groves said, laying down his fork and wiping his mouth with a napkin.

"There's still a few old-fashioned parlors left like the one in Goshen," Stewart Connant replied. "Gonna tell Bessie I'd rather go to one of them than that new-fangled one."

"Better make an appointment early then," Schrock told him. "Likely most folks around here wouldn't be caught dead at Olson's."

"Very funny," Groves told him. "Maybe I just won't die at all. That'd hit all the Olson types right in the old pocketbook."

"Yeah," Connant said. "Maybe the whole Town will just decide not to die."

The men all laughed and then returned to drinking coffee and changed the subject.

Two weeks later, Madelyn Morris joined her friend Della for a coffee break in the little lounge at Olson's, where they had both secured a job. "Do you think the Town folk are boycotting coming here?" Della asked.

"Well, now that you mention it, we haven't had any Fruithills area funerals here yet," Madelyn replied. "But then, I don't recall seeing any obituaries from there, either. Mr. Olson provides me a list every day with possible clients from his sources. Funny, though. I was sure that a couple of people at the Hightower assisted living facility weren't doing well."

"My aunt lives there," Della said. "She's not from the Fruithills though, she came here from Ohio to be close to her children."

"Well, we'll be sure to see someone here eventually. They can't all live forever." Madelyn told her.

When Della visited her aunt one evening later in the week, she found her enjoying a card game in the large atrium common area where many residents gathered in the evenings.

"Pull up a chair, Della," Aunt Gladys told her. "I'll just finish this one hand, and then we can have a nice chat."

It only took a few minutes for Aunt Gladys to win the hand and the pot. She smiled at her table mates and then swept the pennies into a little gold purse she carried and got up to lead Della to a table in the corner by the refreshment area.

"I'll get us each a lemonade," Della said, having been there before and knowing what they served at the small complimentary juice bar.

"That would be nice, dear," her aunt replied.

When Della returned with the glasses, her aunt took a long drink before she spoke.

"Not as good as homemade, of course," she said. "But much easier than all that squeezing."

Della nodded and took a sip of hers. "So, how have you been?" she asked.

"Better than yesterday, worse than tomorrow," Aunt Gladys laughed. "Or maybe the reverse. I'm not getting any younger."

"I think you look great," Della told her. "Is that a new hairstyle?"

Her aunt patted the sleek white bob. "Do you like it? I took Hennie Johnson's appointment time at the shop. It's really hard to get one because the stylist only comes on Thursdays."

"What happened to Hennie?" Della asked, remembering a tiny wizened woman with flame red hair.

"Oh, she died last week," Aunt Gladys said nonchalantly.

"Is she one of the Fruithills crowd?" Della questioned.

"No, she was from over in St. Joe County, quite a ways from here. She just came here because her sister did."

"Don't you have a few ladies here from the Fruithills?" was

Della's next inquiry.

"As a matter of fact, everybody expected old Mrs. Kurtz to pass last week. She lived in town there until her husband died, and then she came here. She's been quite poorly." her aunt said.

"Anybody else?" Della asked.

"A couple more I guess still live here, and doing well as far as I know. Why do you ask?"

Suddenly Della was embarrassed about her suspicions and didn't reply, but Aunt Gladys wasn't about to let it drop.

"You think they're not dying because that funeral home closed?" Aunt Gladys asked, shaking her head. "The surprise closure was quite the discussion at brunch a few weeks ago, but one thing for sure, most people weren't happy about it."

"You mean they don't like Olson's?" Della said.

"Some don't, but people don't like losing something they were counting on being there when they needed it." her aunt replied.

"I'm at Olson's, you know," Della told her. "I do office work there, and they are somewhat more expensive than Addison's was. But they have a pretty big clientele and do quite a nice job."

"That may well be," Aunt Gladys said. "But some of us old folks are pretty set in their ways."

"Not you, Auntie," Della declared. "You're my favorite aunt."

"Your only aunt," the other woman reminded her, smiling.

Soon afterward, Della left for home, pondering what her aunt had told her. Maybe there was some reasonable explanation for the fact that nobody from the Town had called about using Olson's services. Had no one from there died in the last few weeks? That was certainly possible, although somewhat unusual. She decided to put it out of her mind for now.

Della was awakened early on a Monday morning by the sirens from the local paramedics/fire department building that she could clearly hear from her home in the Town. She opened her eyes to check the illuminated clock face across the room. Only 5am. Not time to get up for work yet.

She turned over, but sleep did not immediately return. She wondered where the ambulance or fire truck was going. Perhaps one of the older residents had taken a turn for the worse. She slipped into a troubled sleep, until her alarm went off at seven.

When she got to Olson's, Madelyn was drinking a cup of coffee and already reviewing the list of over the weekend obituaries that Mr. Olson had compiled.

"Anybody we know?" Della asked.

"If you mean someone from your hometown, then the answer is no." Madelyn replied.

"I heard the sirens from the fire station go out really early this morning," Della told her. "They didn't go far from what I heard. I thought maybe they went to Mrs. Ellison's. I'd heard she's not doing well."

"Well, if it was her, we'll be seeing the obit," Madelyn replied. She lay the list on the table and drained her coffee cup.

"Grab a quick cup, and meet me in the Orchid room as soon as you can. We've got a couple of services this afternoon with a lot of people coming in from out of the State."

It was quite a busy day for Della, and when she drove past the Ellison home after work, she saw no unusual action and noticed only one car in the driveway.

Addison's Funeral Home was on her route to the grocery store to pick up food for her cat Gray Boy, and she slowed as she drove past. It looked the same as always, the big For Sale sign was the only thing that revealed the change.

She glanced up at the old clock, and then looked at her watch. It was nearly six, but the hands of the clock were frozen at 20 minutes to eleven.

They must have shut off the electricity, she thought, but then noticed that the light in the bay window of the building kept on a timer had switched on.

Shaking her head, she continued on to the store. As she pushed her cart through the store in the semi-mesmerized state people often assume when shopping, she was started by a familiar voice behind her.

"Sleeping your way through the store?" asked Horace, as she turned to see him carrying an armful of TV dinners.

She laughed. "I guess I was. I just came in for cat food."

"That doesn't look like cat food," he remarked, eyeing the bread, milk, and cereal and chocolate doughnuts in her cart.

"Actually, I haven't gotten to that aisle yet," she admitted.

"You know how it is, you find things you didn't know you needed. Sometimes I think stores have some kind of a beacon that makes you buy more than you intended."

"Could be," Horace said. "The secret is - don't get a cart. You can only carry so much."

"Good advice," Della answered. Then she paused. "How are you doing? I've not seen you since Addison's closed."

"Actually, quite well," he told her. "I got a better job doing maintenance for the college over in Goshen. It's a little further to drive, but the pay is better."

"That's great news," Della said.

"And how is it at Olson's?" he asked.

"It's just Madelyn and me," she replied. "The guys both got jobs at a big funeral home in Michigan, and last I heard Fred moved there with his family, and Joe was renting an apartment."

"You like it there?"

"It's not the same, of course. We were like a family."

"Especially when Addison wasn't around," Horace said. "He didn't have the best casket-side manner."

Della laughed. Then her face sobered. "We haven't had the funeral of a single person from Town over at Olson's."

"Well, they are pretty pricey," Horace said.

"Somewhat," Della said. "But we scan all the local notices. Nobody has died from here since Addison's closed - and that's almost two months now.

"Really?" Horace looked puzzled. "I didn't know. I've been so busy that I've not paid attention."

"Excuse me," interrupted a woman who was trying to manuever her shopping cart past them.

Horace moved to let her pass. "Well, I'd better go, my hands are freezing."

"Good to see you," Della said, as he hurried off down the aisle.

Horace finished shopping and put his TV dinners in the foam chest he kept on the floor of his pickup, ready to head to his farm east of Town. On a whim, he decided to drive past Olson's, since he'd not been back since the day it closed.

He pulled in front of the building and looked over at the For Sale sign on the tree lawn, now a little dingy from the elements. Then he glanced up at the clock on the overhang of the porch.

"Well, son of a gun," he said to himself. "I never plugged that clock back in." He switched off the ignition and pulled out the keys. "And I never turned in my key. Wonder if it still works?"

He got out of the truck and went up the steps to the door, inserted his key and the door opened. He walked around the room.

Everything was just as it was the day they all left, and it closed down. Even the coffee pot, cups and jar of creamer were on the counter of the little kitchen alcove.

He went down the stairs to the basement and chuckled as he saw the half dozen or so wooden coffins stacked along the walls. Out of curiosity, he pulled off the lid of one. It was empty, of course.

At least there were no skeletons left here, he thought. No ghosts, either. But then, as far as he knew, no one ever died here. They were just brought here, already dead.

He replaced the lid and went back upstairs. Must be going to sell the property lock, stock and barrel, complete with pre-need coffins, he thought. Nobody was probably nuts enough to try running another funeral home here, he figured, and likely the stigma of what the place had been for nearly 100 years was enough to put the damper on anyone thinking of buying it for retail or even as rental apartments.

Oh, well, not his worry. He stopped by the door and tried the light switch. At least they'd kept the electricity on. He went out, locking the door behind him. He moved to the edge of the porch, reached up and plugged the clock back in.

Two days later, Della was entering data into the computer when Madelyn came into her little office, clutching the printout of the latest death notices and schedule for upcoming services.

"There's been a death in the Town," Madelyn said.

"Who?" Della asked. "Was it Mrs. Ellison."

"No," Marilyn replied, "It was Horace Latham. He died of a heart attack."

"Horace?" Della exclaimed. "I saw him just the other day at the grocery store, he looked fine. He told me about his new job and seemed in really good spirits."

"Well, they found his body yesterday," Madelyn went on. "They think he died the day before."

"Where?"

"That's the strangest part," Madelyn said. "He was laying dead on the porch at Addison's."

"Is the service here?" Della asked, not wanting to think about Horace dying there at the place they all knew so well.

"No, some place in Goshen, Mr. Olsen told me," said Madelyn, going back to her office, leaving Della to her thoughts.

That afternoon, Della left at four, telling Madelyn she had finished her work and had a bad headache. Madelyn smiled and told her good-bye.

Della drove back to her small Town nestled in the Fruithills, and made it a point to pass Addison's. She was not surprised when she glanced up at the clock, which had always kept really good time, was now in perfect sync with the time on her watch.

Horace had been a really nice man, she thought. Very conscientious. It would have been like him to make sure the time on the clock was right, even if it wasn't his job anymore. But in a way, maybe it was his job to finalize what could not be changed, and let life and death go on as it should in the Town. Perhaps he was the only man who could.

"God bless you, Horace," Della whispered, and drove away.

THE END

February 29

RoseMary McDaniel a.k.a. Amy Hayle

A mysterious gravestone in a ruined churchyard of a child with the same February 29 birthdate as teenage Abby, made her obsessed with the history of the little girl named Amy Sue, and led Abby and her reluctant friend Ginger to unexpected danger on the evening of Abby's 16th birthday in their small town in the Fruithills, a place that has never lost its ties to a spirit-filled past.

February 29

On one of the rarest days, a time for undoing a wrong...

RoseMary McDaniel

February 29

RoseMary McDaniel a.k.a. Amy Hayle

Maybe it is remembering the cold moonlit night or picturing myself again in that dreary place with the hulking gray granite shapes and rows of low block-like cement stones that brings back that lurking uncertainty - but even though I've tried to forget it, that night is buried deep in my subconscious mind only to emerge every February 29.

Back then, when I was not quite sixteen, once again, my friend Abby Winkler had managed to weasel her way into getting me to promise I'd do what she wanted to do. This time it was her plan for the night of her 16th birthday. She'd been talking about her upcoming birthday for weeks until I literally tried to sing "la, la, la," to myself inside my head, so I wouldn't have to hear her. It never worked very well. She was obsessed with an old cemetery, and she would always correct me when I called it that.

"It's a churchyard, Ginger, not a cemetery. It's a churchyard because there is a church there," she told me.

That didn't make a lot of difference to me. Besides, the church had long since burned down and was just a bunch of rubble piled high with a steeple tower with an old rusty bell sticking out of it. What was left was located on the corner lot of the dead end road that led to Abby's house.

I once tried to make a joke of it - dead at the dead end - but Abby was not amused.

"Show some respect, please," she told me.

She sounded like one of our teachers, and she was always trying to interest me in the history of the place. She told me that the land had been donated by one of the original area settlers who raised apples and peaches and melons in the Fruithills, some distance away.

His wife got her wealthy friends in the east to donate money to help build the church, and many early families were buried in the churchyard. The church itself had been hit by lightening and burned down many years ago. Sometime later, the congregation had built another church in a place less isolated, and the graveyard was more or less abandoned and forgotten except for people like Abby, who had a great bump of historical curiosity.

I'd lived here nearly as long as Abby had, and in fact we'd been best friends since second grade. A case of direct opposites attracting each other. Abby had always been a kind of goofy kid, and from the time we met at the age of seven, we'd been inseparable.

Abby was petite, dark eyed with long brown pigtails and a permanent quizzical look on her pale face. Quick witted Abby questioned everything. On the other hand, I was a too-quiet, a slower moving and thinking moose of a girl, too big for the cute little pastel pinafore style dresses Abby wore in grade school.

"Poor Ginger," my mother would proclaim to our relatives when she didn't know I was listening - and I was always listening.

"She's going to be just naturally big like her Dad's sister, Erma. Got the same frizzy red hair, too."

She'd buy me dark colored over-the-knee skirts and coordinating tailored blouses to try to make my bulky body fade into the background. It didn't work. I kept ripping out the sleeves of the blouses and hems of the skirts when I climbed the trees in our backyard.

Finally, she gave up and let me wear jeans like most everyone else. And when we got to be teens, Abby next to me in her ruffled tops and capris looked like a delicate little china doll next to Godzilla's sister. I could actually pick her up and hoist her into the lower branches of the old walnut tree in my backyard. She was never able to climb up there on her own.

I felt protective of her, more like an older sister, though we were really just a few months apart in age. Her birthday was in February the 29th, which only came every four years. She felt like that made her special, and I guess it did.

My birthday wasn't until April 4th, and I wasn't the typical Aries "have to be first" kind of person. I was content to follow Abby's versatile Pisces leadership, and I wasn't resentful of her good looks and outgoing personality.

So when Abby said she wanted to do something special to celebrate her 16th birthday (actually her fourth by the calendar) - I agreed, thinking she was going to have a party.

Of course she had the perfect place for one in the lower area of the tri-level house where her parents had allowed her to convert the basement into her own private apartment complete with outside entrance/exit.

They were very liberal parents, and Abby did pretty much as she pleased, with very few restrictions.

The house was near the end of a long block with only a couple of other homes nearby. The closest place was actually that old churchyard where Abby loved to go, and drag me with her.

She'd poke around in what remained of the place, surrounded by the scattered gravestones, which had been untended and vandalized for many years. She'd weed around the graves and trim the grass with clippers where she could. But she never tried to move or rearrange the broken stones.

"It's actually against the law to do that," she lectured me with the knowledge she'd learned at a seminar at the old history museum in Town.

But when we were recording the locations, names and dates for a school project the previous semester, and making gravestone rubbings like she'd learned at the museum, she was excited to find an old stone slab crudely engraved with birth and death dates just four years apart, the same as her own birthday, February 29th, but in the early 1900's. The child had apparently died on her fourth birthday.

After that, Abby had taken to tending the little grave, weeding a patch around it and bringing artificial flowers to put in a small metal vase that had been left beside the stone.

When I told her I thought it was a weird thing to do, she only smiled at me and gave me that far away look of hers and replied, "Amy Sue would do the same for me. "

That was the name on the gravestone. Just Amy Sue and no last name and below that birth and death date.

I shrugged. "Honestly, I think it's kind of creepy." I told her.

She gave me her pretty little pout that made boys melt. I ignored it.

Finally she spoke "I did some research at the museum, and I know how she died. An accidental fall, and then she was dead.."

"Didn't a lot of young kids die in those days?" I hesitantly asked.

"She shouldn't have died; it wasn't fair. She had so little time and so little happiness." She turned her attention to pulling the

73

weeds around the stone. I didn't make a reply.

She didn't bring it up again, but every few days when we walked home from school, she would want to stop off there. So we did.

Once winter came, it was rather cold but little snow,that year, so we could continue our trips to her favorite place.

Finally it was her birthday, and even on a school night she insisted that I bring my gear for a sleep-over. So when I got there, I was surprised to see no one else had arrived for the party.

"I didn't ask anyone but you," she said. "And Amy Sue, of course. We're going to celebrate our birthdays together," she continued, directing my attention to a sheet cake on the kitchen counter, that had white icing with "Amy Sue" crudely written in blue gel below the more professionally written "Happy Birthday Abby." The squeezed tube of gel lay next to the cake. I decided to pass on having a piece.

I dumped my sleeping bag on the extra long love seat by the wide screen T.V., and I waited to see what came next. With Abby, you never knew what was coming, and she'd rather you didn't ask, either. You just waited for her to tell you. I started to take off my jacket and hat.

"Just put it on the chair over there," she instructed me. "You'll need it when we go out, to the churchyard later." she added.

Well, at least it was very mild weather for late February, almost springlike, so I guessed it wouldn't be much different than our usual trips there, although we'd never gone after dark before.

Abby headed for the area at the other side of the large basement space. Her parents had spared no expense in making her apartment very up-to-date and complete with her own separate kitchen. So I just sat down and waited while she made some microwave popcorn and brought us each some in a bowl with a soda and then switched on the TV. I wasn't really into some of the movies she seemed to prefer, like ghost stories and the like.

But I sat quietly, diving into my refreshments and letting my mind wander, waiting for her to decide when we should leave. Sometimes I questioned what it was that I liked about Abby, and why I spent so much time with her. We didn't even have a lot in common, if I really thought about it.

But let's face it, the contrast between her lifestyle and mine was very much an attraction. My parents were just blue collar folks, while her parents were both high-salaried professional people, well able to afford to give Abby anything and everything she wanted. For some reason, I guess it must have amused her to have me around, although sometimes I felt more like a pet, than a friend.

The worst times for me were when she'd get caught up in some cause, righting some wrong, like somebody getting the blame for something she was sure they didn't do. Abby didn't give up until it got dealt with, and she was satisfied with the outcome. That was way too obsessive for me.

I often told myself that sometime I was going to go out on my own and get involved with some other people who might do more of the things I thought I would like to do, like sewing or crafts, and social events not based on how much influence you had, but what kind of person you were.

But in the end, even though I had tried a couple of times to pursue spending time with others, Abby always persuaded me to do what she wanted me to, instead. Maybe I was just weak willed or maybe our tie to each other was so strong that I just couldn't get loose all that easily.

I finished my snack and sat the bowl and soda can on the table beside me, and settled back to try to watch the movie, some sort of haunted house thing. Abby didn't like conversation during the movie, so I must have semi-fallen asleep, when I realized that she was talking to me.

"OK, it's time to go," she told me. "Better get your hat and coat on."

I did as I was told, and followed her out the door.

"Here, you carry this. I don't have a pocket," she said and handed me a flashlight that I put it in my own coat pocket.

The air was more chilly now, and the sky was very clear, with bright star points in the darkened sky. There was moonlight, so we really didn't need the flashlight to find our way.

Abby talked as we walked down the street. "Did you know I was adopted?" she asked me.

I must have just stared at her in disbelief.

"It's true," she told me. "I've nearly always known it.

That's why my parents are so generous, I think. Upperclass guilt and over compensation for a poor little orphan."

"I never knew that," I blurted out. "I mean I never knew that you were… "

"Yeah, I didn't think anybody needed to know, not even you. But now it's different."

"Different… ?" I blurted out, her revelation making me less cautious of not asking her for explanations.

"Remember I told you that Amy Sue died in an accident?" she asked.

"Yeah," I answered.

"Well, that's what the obituary said. But when I read further in the old newspaper stories, I found out the truth. Amy Sue's mother had killed her on her birthday. Threw her out of an old barn loft onto a wall, and she died. The mother was crazy of course, and she had been abusing Amy Sue most of her life. They didn't call it that back then, but that was what it was."

"What about the father?" I wondered aloud.

"It just said he was away a lot of the time and never seemed to notice anything wrong, until it was too late." She shook her head as if she couldn't believe it, just as we got to the churchyard, and we went to where a portion of the metal fence had been removed, and headed for the old grave.

"You haven't heard the best part," Abby told me, her voice trailing off.

"Are you going to tell me or not?" I asked, my curiosity raised to a level where I dared question her again.

She went over and sat behind the gravestone, rubbing her fingers gently over the engraved lettering. I stood nearby, waiting for her to continue.

"My adopted mother's great-great grandfather was Amy Sue's father. Amy Sue's mother killed herself, and he married again and had another family."

"So what does that have to do with you?"

She sighed. "My adoptive mother wanted me to feel that I was specially chosen because my mother wasn't able to raise me. So she gave me all the family details on both my real ancestors and her and my adoptive father, when I asked her for information for that genealogy section we did for class." She paused.

"Go on," I urged her.

"The two families are related, intermingled. Amy Sue and I are distant cousins and share the same birthday."

"Lots of people in families have the same birthday," I said.

She was silent a moment, and then stared at me with a look I'll never forget. "But not the same death day," she said with a wry laugh.

Just then, a church bell began to clang and I turned around toward the ruined steeple that had the bell, taking the flashlight out of my pocket and aiming the light in that direction.

The clanging had stopped, and suddenly, a huge piece of the steeple that had hung precariously above us made a tremendous cracking sound and crashed down on top of Abby, barely missing me.

I reached over and tugged and pulled at the metal steeple frame to move it off of Abby, but I knew instinctively that she was dead, laying there so still. More heavy pieces of rubble had broken through the ground, and Abby was actually laying on the shattered wooden coffin that had been buried in the shallow grave: Amy Sue's grave.

I looked away because I didn't want to see what might lay beneath her, and I heard footsteps behind me. I whirled around to see a small child dressed in a white pinafore, much like the ones that Abby had worn years ago, standing there.

"Who are you?" I asked in a fearful voice.

"I'm Amy Sue," she said, smiling at me. "It's my birthday. I'm four years old today."

Then I must have dropped the flashlight and passed out, because I don't remember anything until I heard my mother's voice and opened my eyes. I was laying on a stretcher, but I didn't think I was hurt or anything. I started to look for Abby, but my mother stepped in to block my view.

"Don't look, Ginger. They're taking Abby away now," she told me.

"Is she... ." I couldn't finish my sentence.

"Yes, I'm sorry but she's gone. You're lucky that whatever knocked you out, too, didn't cause serious injuries. Whatever were the two of you doing there? Luckily, Deputy Saunders was on patrol and thought he saw the beam of a flashlight and stopped and found you. He called me as well as the paramedics. They're going to take you to the hospital just to be sure... ."

I sat up, interrupting her and brushing off her attempt to stop me.

"No, Mom, please, I'm Ok, really." I didn't answer her question about why we were there. "Can we please just go home?" I asked her.

Mom and the paramedics exchanged glances and she nodded at me as she said. "All right, if you're sure."

"Really, I am." I looked around in the light streaming from the ambulance and the other vehicles. "Where's the little girl?" I asked.

"There's no one else here," my mother said, giving me a scrutinizing look, and then added hesitantly, "Maybe we should go with the paramedics."

I shook my head. "No, I must have been dreaming or something," I insisted. I stood up. "Let's go."

And without a backward glance, we left.

After the investigation and the funeral, I kept a pretty low profile. My Dad got a new job later that Spring, and I moved with my folks out of town.

My parents never probed me for answers about why it happened, and even offered me counseling, that I refused. I knew no one would believe that I saw Amy Sue that night, and especially not that she came back to life because Abby fell in her grave and died on that same fateful February 29.

I've never gone back to the small Town we grew up in, and I'm glad that February 29 only comes every four years to awaken my unsettled memories. One thing for certain, I'll never know if Abby suspected that death awaited her that particular night. I don't think I really want to know.

THE END

Ghost of a Chance

RoseMary McDaniel a.k.a. Amy Hayle

Uncle Frank and his showroom of vintage cars went missing at midnight years ago. But now it seems that Uncle Frank has come back to haunt his great nephew Howie after disappearing long before Howie was born.

Howie and his friend Luke find the answer to the years' old mystery in the historic cemetery high on the bluff over the river in their small town in the Fruithills - a place that has never lost its ties to a spirit-filled past.

Author's note: Although the stories have been inspired by some actual places and events in history, they are all a product of the author's imagination and not intended to represent any persons, living or dead.

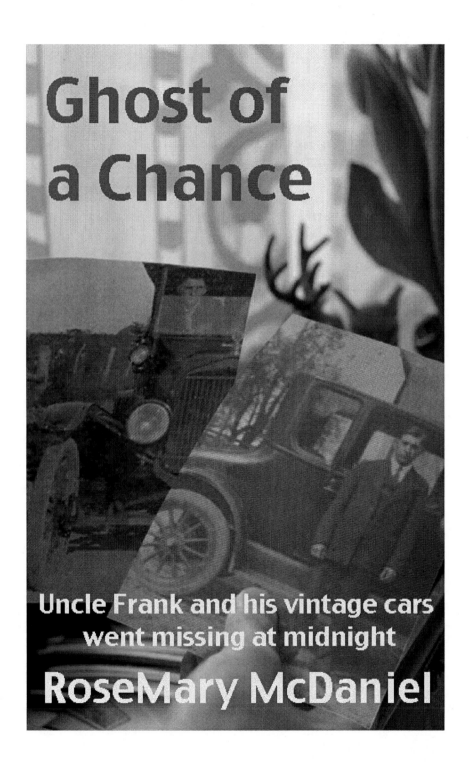

Ghost of a Chance

Uncle Frank and his vintage cars went missing at midnight

RoseMary McDaniel

Ghost of a Chance

RoseMary McDaniel a.k.a. Amy Hayle

"I saw the ghost of my Uncle Frank with his old car in the back yard last night," my friend Howie said, as he sat on his back step, elbows on his knees, with his hands supporting his head. He had a real funny look on his face.

I had wheeled my bike into his yard, looking for him. He was supposed to have met me in the park twenty minutes ago.

"What?" I asked.

Howie looked up and said in a voice that was almost a whisper, "I think I'm being haunted by my Uncle Frank."

I'd never heard of his Uncle Frank before, so I said, "Who the heck is that?" I was annoyed with the delay in our usual Saturday afternoon ride.

Howie looked around, put his finger to his lips, stood up and cracked open the kitchen door. "I'm going riding with Luke," he called out to whomever was in the kitchen.

His mother appeared in the doorway. "Be back for supper by five," she told him.

"O.K.," Howie said, went to his bike and started off, assuming that I would follow. We rode down the short lane that led from Howie's house to the main street.

That's what was great about our little town, nestled in the valley of the Fruithills. In the late 1950s, it was big enough for a gas station, grocery store, post office, library and a few other businesses, but it was small enough for a couple of kids to ride off for the afternoon without worry on their part or their parents that anything bad would happen to them.

Of course, there were farming accidents and kids getting hurt being careless or daring sometimes, but mostly we had nothing to fear in the neighborhoods that were as familiar to us as our own backyards.

Howie and I had just started the seventh grade that fall and were turning thirteen in a few weeks, our birthdays, just a few days apart. Both were in late October, my favorite time of year.

My parents often talked about how great it would be when they could retire to Florida where it was warm all year around, but

I loved the seasons, from the crackling leaves and bonfires of autumn through the snowy winters and into the lazy days of summer. Midwest weather might not have suited them, but it did me.

I knew that I'd have to get Howie to talk about this never-mentioned ghost uncle of his, or our afternoon of freedom and adventure would be ruined. For once, Howie rode quickly, outpacing me, which was unusual. Howie was, to put it kindly, a little too fond of snacks, and tended to be pudgy, which meant he usually dawdled along when we rode together.

He got to the park first and went down by the river to park his bike by a bench. I put mine next to his and went to sit beside him.

"So, give. What's this all about? You probably just had a bad dream. How's come I never knew you had even had an Uncle Frank?"

"Great uncle really," Howie answered. "He isn't usually mentioned outside the family."

"Black sheep, huh?" I asked.

"Not exactly," Howie said. "You know that guy in the Lil' Abner comic strips, Joe something or another, who's always got a black cloud over his head?"

"Yeah," I replied. So what?"

"Well, my Dad would joke about his Uncle Frank saying he had a lot in common with that Joe guy. and because they both were ne'er-do-wells," Howie said.

"You knew him, then?"

"No, he disappeared years before I was born."

"What happened?"

"It's kind of a long story," Howie began hesitantly.

"We've got all afternoon," I replied with a shrug. "Taking our usual ride won't be any fun today, not with you in this mood."

"It's not a mood," Howie insisted. "It was really scary."

"Let's get this straight. You saw what you supposed was the ghost of your Uncle Frank in the back yard with his car. How'd you know it was him, if you never saw him?"

"From photos in the attic," Howie told me. "Aunt Alice, that was his sister, had names written on the back of all of them."

"Getting back to the car," I said. "What kind was it?"

"It was a black 1927 Model T Ford roadster," Howie blurted out.

"How'd you know that?" I asked, then realized how before he could reply. "O.K., more photos, right?"

"Right," Howie said nodding his head. "The last business he ran was a Ford dealership downtown."

"Yeah? Where?"

"You know that one old cement block building on the corner across from the sporting goods store? Well, that was his dealership back in the 1920's. In one of the photos, Uncle Frank was standing out front of his building, with his car. There was even a big glass window like a showroom at one time. Guess they blocked it up afterward when it became a garage"

"When was that?"

"After Uncle Frank went away," Howie said.

"It seems to me there's a lot to this that you're leaving out," I accused him.

"Well, it took me a long time to piece together all the family stories," Howie said. "But after his earlier problems, somehow Uncle Frank had gotten the money together to take over the business from the man who had the dealership to begin with. All it sold were Ford Model T's."

"Money from where?"

"Well, Uncle Jim, my Dad's brother, thought Uncle Frank had gotten lucky on the ponies, and won enough money for a down payment on the place. It was the talk of the town, Uncle Frank and his showroom, with a couple dozen brand new 1927 Model T's. Sales boomed for a while, and Uncle Frank strutted around town with a wallet full of cash. He poured most of it back in the business, and bought more Model T's."

"So what went wrong?"

"Dad said Henry Ford pulled the plug on the Model T in December of 1927, and started making the Model A, so hardly anyone wanted a Model T anymore, and the price went way down. Then in October of 1929, came the stock market crash, and nobody was buying any cars at all."

"So Uncle Frank went broke?"

"Maybe," Howie said. "My Dad and Uncle Jim were just kids, but they remembered Halloween that year wasn't the big deal in town that it usually was. Everyone was depressed, and nobody was in the mood to celebrate the holiday," he paused.

"Go on," I urged.

"Well, Halloween night, was a really dark night, cloudy, chilly with rain falling, and everyone had gone home early. Downtown was deserted. Later, a couple noisy old ladies swore they saw car after car entering the graveyard on the high bluff above the river that night. Cars that went in, but never came out."

"A party in the cemetery?"

"Who knows? But one thing that My Dad and Uncle Jim recall is that Uncle Frank came by their house that night near midnight in his spiffy 1927 Ford Model T roadster and took them for a spin all around town. He honked and they all waved as they drove up and down the streets. People looked out their windows and even opened their doors to see what the racket was.

"Uncle Jim and Dad had the time of their lives riding in that car, and when Uncle Frank finally dropped them off that moonless night, he was smiling as he drove away. No one ever saw him again," Howie finished.

"So, he skipped Town."

"That was what everyone thought the next morning, when it got light and people started to go out. It didn't take long for them to realize that Uncle Frank's dealership with the big glass show window was completely empty. Not a car to be seen."

"Wow," I said. "What do they think happened?"

"Rumor was that Uncle Frank must have hired a bunch of people to come and drive the cars off somewhere, and after he brought my Dad and Uncle Jim home, he took off, too. Then he sold all those cars somewhere for whatever he could get. They figured that he had staged the cars and drivers at the cemetery, and then they all left together after the old ladies had gone to bed."

"And nobody ever heard from him again?"

"Nope," said Howie. "There is something else, though."

"What's that?"

"Months later, because the old ladies kept insisting they saw the cars going to the cemetery that night and not coming out, some thought Uncle Frank must have driven or pushed the cars off the bluff into the ravine that goes clear down to the river so that he could get rid of them and clear out of town," he said

"Nobody ever went down to check?" I asked.

"Nope," Howie said. "Dad said it started snowing in early November and didn't stop till April, and it wouldn't have taken the underbrush long to take over and cover up whatever was down there. Besides, most people figured anybody who liked money as much as Uncle Frank would never do such a thing, and the old ladies were known to have reported all kinds of things that never really happened.

"Seems like somebody would have been curious," I told him.

"Well, Dad had said that after all, it was the depression, and people were too busy worrying about getting food and keeping a roof over their heads to worry about much of anything like that very long."

"Do you suppose your Uncle Frank has come back, then?"

"I think he's dead," Howie said bluntly, "But for some reason, he's haunting me, or maybe the house. The house we live in was originally Dad's grandparents' house, and Uncle Frank did live there at one time."

"How did you know he was out there last night?"

"I woke up when I heard a noise and looked out my bedroom window. He was standing outside in the moonlight, leaning against the driver's door, looking a whole lot like he looked in that photo outside his dealership. Then, I saw him open the car door, reach inside, grab a metal box of some kind, and hold it out for me to see, smiling."

"Didn't you go out to see what he wanted?"

"Of course not! I jumped back in bed and covered my head. I did go back to the window a few minutes later, and he was gone."

"Well, if it wasn't a dream, then he's likely to come back again" I said.

"I sure hope not," he replied.

"I wonder why he picked on you," I pondered.

Howie thought for a moment. "Well, the only thing I can think of is that his sister, Aunt Alice used to make my mother mad by telling her how much I looked like him, and my middle name is Frank."

"That could be it," I agreed. "He feels a connection with you and is trying to communicate. He wants you to do something for him - take care of some unfinished business."

"Like what?"

"I don't know, but I'd say it was a good enough reason for us to ride over to that cemetery and check out whether those old cars are really down there." I told him.

"Are you crazy?" he yelled. "I'm sorry I even told you," he said, and turned away to face the river.

"Don't be a scaredy cat," I said. "I'm sure there's nothing there, anyway."

He turned back with a frown. "If there's nothing there, why go?"

"Come on," I said, "Where's your spirit of adventure? Don't you want to find out what really happened to your Uncle Frank? If we don't put this to rest, next time it may be you who's taken for a ride in the ghost car."

"Don't say that!" he cried. "You don't realize how scary it was."

"All the more reason to settle it once and for all. But if you don't want to go," I paused. "I'll just go without you."

I was pretty fearless in those days, so I climbed back on my bike and headed off down the street. I didn't look back, but I could hear the crunch of leaves on the sidewalk behind me. Howie was following.

I smiled to myself. The pace of the day was picking up. Maybe the whole adventure thing was going to work out after all. Our Saturday exploration usually involved frogs or snakes we'd use to scare some of the neighbor girls, but looking for ghost cars, now that sounded like a real adventure.

It didn't take long to go the couple of blocks to the entrance of the cemetery, and I stopped and waited for Howie to catch up. He didn't seem very enthusiastic.

"Now what?" he asked.

"We explore," I said and took off again, skidding down the gravel road into the cemetery. Once I got to edge of the bluff, where the oldest graves were, I detoured to behind the gravestones, right along the edge of the bluff, and looking down into the tangle of trees and branches, I couldn't see anything but green, with a few touches of autumn red and gold.

I propped my bike up behind an old weathered stone. Next

to it was a big open area that would have been perfect to launch cars down into the ravine. Howie stayed on the gravel road and gave me another frown.

"You shouldn't do that, lean your bike on the stone, it's disrespectful," he said.

I walked around to the front of the stone, and as I turned to answer him, my ankle twisted beneath me, and suddenly the ground under me broke away, and I fell, down, down, down into the ravine.

My only thought as I plunged downward was that if this didn't kill me, my mother would for getting my school clothes dirty. I landed with a big bump mostly on my rear, but I sat up in wonder that I was still alive and looked around me. I'd fallen into some kind of a tunnel or something, and wooden bits of an old coffin and bones had rained down on top of me.

I'd known that the ground beneath really old graves sometimes gave away, as the wooden coffins rotted, but due to my carelessness, now I was in a real pickle.

I could hear Howie up above, screaming my name. I brushed off dirt and assorted debris and stood up. I hurt a little, all over, but nothing was broken.

"I'm O.K., Howie," I called. "Just pipe down, will you?" I heard shuffling far above me, and I saw Howie's face appear in the hole.

"Be careful," I called out to him. "You don't want to fall in, too."

But Howie's extra weight on the already weakened ground was too much, and as I looked up, I saw him tumbling down toward me. I quickly stepped to the side, and was able to break his fall, getting a good rap on my shoulder and arm for my trouble.

Howie shook himself free of debris and looked around.

"You O.K.?", I asked.

He nodded.

To our surprise, it wasn't as dark down here as I'd expected it to be. Light was spilling through the top and sides of the areas on either side of us, and there appeared to be a clear path for some distance straight ahead.

"Where are we?" Howie asked.

"At the bottom of the ravine," I told him, "Along with a

few assorted bones… "

I didn't have a chance to finish before Howie bellowed "Bones from a grave?"

"They won't hurt you," I told him. "Come on, we've got to find our way out, unless you want to spend the rest of the weekend with whatever else is down here."

We started walking along the open area, and I marveled at the how the pathway was lined on either side with some sort of sections of black peeling paint and rust, almost completely covered with leaves, branches and twisty vines.

"Where are we going?" Howie asked.

"Forward," was the only reply I could think of.

Suddenly our path was blocked by a stack of dark colored panels. I reached up to pull some of the foliage away. I laughed as I recognized what it was.

"I think this is one of your Uncle's cars," I said to Howie. "The old ladies were right."

"Are you kidding?" Howie asked, reaching over to pull away a branch. A window and door were plainly visible.

"Looks like a whole showroom full," I said. "So now we know what your uncle did with his inventory."

"But why?" Howie asked.

Suddenly it made sense to me. "He didn't want to be seen as the failure again, not after he had finally shown everyone how well he was doing. So he just dumped them down here, took your Dad and Uncle Jim on a celebratory goodbye spin for the whole town to see, and just disappeared."

"But what really happened to him, and what does he want from me now?" Howie exclaimed.

"We may never know," I admitted, "but right now we have to find a way out of here."

It wasn't easy without any tools or a flashlight, but somehow we struggled out of there, followed along the river and made our way through the woods back to civilization. We ended up with lots of cuts and scrapes and a mean batch of poison ivy, that my Mother said I deserved for ruining my school clothes.

We went back in Howie's Dad's pickup to collect our bikes, since we were now both grounded. The Marshal and the Town Manager met us there with a crew, who armed with ropes and flashlights, descended down into the ravine to check out the situation and confirmed that the cars were down there.

Since they were on town-owned land, the Manager later contracted with a local antique auto dealer who hauled out the more than 20 old cars and sold them with the funds going for the expense of removal and the balance into the town coffers.

Howie and I walked over to spend several afternoons after school watching them bring out the old cars, some of which were in pretty good shape, physically. But the biggest surprise was one car on top of the others, that was less damaged than any of the rest. Howie's whole family had joined us when word of the discovery of this particular car was reported to them.

It appeared to be Uncle Frank's 1927 Ford Model T roadster, in surprisingly good condition. Since the windows were up, the contents of the car had not been disturbed, except by time and decay, but clearly what was left of the remains of Uncle Frank were in the driver's seat, dressed just as Howie's Dad and Uncle Jim remembered him from that last night.

Next to him on the passenger seat was a old metal box, much as Howie had described the one he saw with Uncle Frank in his own backyard. The box was full of cash and other valuables.

There was a bit of a legal tangle over it, but it finally had been decided that it should belong to Howie's Dad and his Uncle Jim. They were able to settle some of Uncle Frank's long-ago debts. That made everyone feel better.

The family got to keep Uncle Frank's car, too, although Howie was a little leery about it, but Uncle Jim agreed to keep it at his home until he could restore it.

Investigators officially determined that due to the position of how this particular car was found, and the likely condition of the bluff that rainy autumn night, it may have not have been Uncle Frank's intention to drive the car and himself over the bluff, but due to the wet and slippery leaves, he may simply have gotten too close to the edge when taking one last look before driving off.

Howie and I like to think that he wasn't planning to skip town that night, and that he was going to use the valuables in the box to pay off his debts and make a new start.

Perhaps that was why he had now appeared to Howie in an effort to set things straight. Whether that was really true or not, it made Howie feel a lot better, and he even agreed to go for rides in the car once his Uncle Jim had restored it to its former glory.

All told, that was probably one of the best adventures Howie and I ever had on our bikes, and it makes me sad that many kids of today will never be able to enjoy the freedom of such an autumn afternoon without worried parents fearing for their safety when they are out on their own.

Howie and I grew up, and we both still live right here in the same little town where we were childhood friends. I became the owner of an Auto Supply Store, and Howie, an local insurance man, and we both ended up with homes and families much like the ones we had as kids.

I just saw Howie yesterday, when he stopped by my store, insisted I take off for the afternoon and join him on an October ride to celebrate our 50th birthdays.

Uncle Jim had left Uncle Frank's car to Howie, who still drove it on special occasions, like today, when two old fogies went to get ice cream sodas at a shop that now occupied the same spot that had once been that old Ford dealership.

I think Uncle Frank would have liked that.

THE END

Haunted Journey

RoseMary McDaniel a.k.a. Amy Hayle

Why was James experiencing visions of a beautiful young girl on a bench at an old railroad station torn down long ago? What tie could he have to a tragic event that had occurred years before he was born?

Would a haunted journey to the past bring him escape from a sad and disappointing present day life in the Fruithills, a place that has never lost its ties to a spirit-filled past.

Copyright 2013, RoseMary McDaniel

Author's note: Although the stories have been inspired by some actual places and events in history, they are all a product of the author's imagination and not intended to represent any persons, living or dead.

Chapter Cover Photo: Courtesy of Elkhart County Historical Museum

Haunted Journey

All aboard for a ride into the Past
RoseMary McDaniel

Haunted Journey

RoseMary McDaniel a.k.a. Amy Hayle

He'd seen her again, sitting on an aged wooden bench in her old fashioned dove-gray dress and a slate-colored hooded cloak, clutching a large quilted bag in her lap.

As he watched, a shaft of golden light glinted off the taffy-hued curls that were piled atop her head, as the last rays of the sun lit up the sky to the west. She was the most beautiful woman he had ever seen.

It was perhaps the fourth time in the last few weeks he'd seen her there, as he took his early evening walk, clicking his stick along the edge of the road to help balance the leg that hadn't been the same since his stint in Nam.

He'd never tried to speak to her, suspecting that the scene in front of the old railroad passenger station, was one that existed only in his pain-fogged mind.

Hallucinations, his doctor would have said, and dangerous for him to be out on his own. Damned pain meds, he supposed. But what did it matter. What did he have left to live for? Parents dead; no siblings to care; and no wife or children to fuss over him.

He only had what was left of him after his medical discharge, years ago now. He'd had nowhere to come back to except the ramshackle home he'd shared with his parents. He'd taken care of them, or they of him until they died.

He was an old man now, alone with the memories of a wasted life. His disability check wasn't much, but enough to exist on here in the little town near the Fruithills where money went a lot farther than anywhere else.

He stood staring across the railroad track at the train station as it had been all those years ago, although it was torn down in the late 1960s, not long after he'd returned home from the war. The trains hadn't stopped there since 1951, and the place had long since disintegrated into a way station for rats and pigeons and a scary hideaway for neighborhood children.

He'd been one of them back in the early 1950s, riding his bike there with Charlie, his best friend, to hide and scare the girls who passed by. They'd gone off together to join the Service when they'd turned eighteen, and a few years later, Charlie was dead, and he was crippled for life.

Some adventure they'd planned; but reality got in the way, and now more than fifty years later, James Elwood felt he was officially no use to anyone, even himself.

As he watched, the young woman put a handkerchief up to her face. James realized that she was weeping silently. He decided to invade his visions even if his dreams had escaped him. He started to cross the track, nearly tripping as the single track had suddenly become double, as it had been all those years ago. He caught himself from falling, and trudged on toward the cement platform where the station stood.

"Are you all right, Miss?" he asked.

She looked up and smiled at him through her tears. "Oh, Sir, do you know when the train heading west will arrive? I've waited and waited, but the station master isn't here."

For a moment he couldn't respond, but finally said, "I don't know that the trains stop here any more," he began.

"Oh, but they must!" she said. "I need to get away as soon as possible."

It was then he noted bruises on her face. "You're hurt. What has happened to you?" he asked, sensing her vulnerability.

She didn't reply, and tried to cover her face with her handkerchief. He stepped up on the platform to sit beside her on the bench. As he did, he thankfully noticed that his leg was no longer stiff, and he slid his stick underneath the bench as he sat down.

"How can I help you?" he asked, and as she lowered the handkerchief from her face, he saw the three initials that were embroidered on it: EDP.

She shook her head. "No one can help here. I must get away."

"What is your name?" he asked.

"Ella," she said shyly, and lowered her head again into the handkerchief.

"Are you running away?" he asked.

She lifted her head once more, the tear stains evident on her damaged face. "Ah, Sir, I cannot take it anymore. I work hard, and still she beats me."

"Who?" he asked.

"I must not say," she told him. "But she is away today, and I must be gone by nightfall or she will find me and I may never have another chance."

"I don't know the schedule," he told her, deciding not to alarm her. "But likely there are only a few a day each way: west and then east."

"Then I must wait for the one west," she said, turning her head to stare off down the tracks and ignoring him.

Suddenly, James felt an overwhelming wave of weariness sweep over him. He'd taken one of his pain pills before he left on his walk, and usually he was back home by now to fall asleep on his bed. Sometimes it hit him hard, especially if he hadn't eaten much that day. He couldn't keep his eyes open, leaning his head back against the high bench, he was instantly asleep.

When he woke, he was chilled, sitting on the ground between two large bushes beside the now single railroad track. Everything else had disappeared: the train station, the bench, and the woman. It was nearly dark. He reached for his stick that lay beside him, and a pain gripped his leg as he tried to stand up.

He was thankful that he was hidden from sight of the road and passersby who would have thought him drunk. Had he been dreaming or had he imagined the conversation with the young lady in distress?

It was as though he had been transported into another time, perhaps one that had been there, years ago. She was dressed in a style that must have dated from the early 1900's, the era of the photos that he had seen of that very station when it was in its height of activity with trains arriving daily, transporting goods and passengers to and from the east and west to Chicago and beyond.

Finally he struggled to his feet painfully, and looked around. Nothing but overgrown bushes and weeds, and certainly no double track, only the single line that carried freight on daily trips through the town. He was glad that no one had seen him, and he made his way slowly back toward home. But once there, after a bowl of soup and a small whiskey, he was wide awake. He went to his makeshift desk where one of his only compromises in accepting modern technology was an ancient laptop hooked to a slow dial-up phone line.

He felt out of place in today's society of social networking and a hurried pace. He wished he'd been born much longer ago when life, though perhaps harder in some ways, was at least blessedly simpler.

He had to find out why he kept seeing her at the train station, a young girl, likely about 20 years old. He knew he didn't dare tell anyone about his visions, for lack of a better word, fearing that he'd be thought more crazy than the town folk who avoided him, already thought he was.

As he searched the Internet for history of the town and the station, he learned that it had indeed employed a station master during the time it was a thriving passenger business, when salesmen would come to town to sell their wares to the local merchants, and buyers of fruit and grain would descend on the station to bid on the bountiful crops that were grown there and shipped as freight to distant cities.

The station master sold the tickets, aided the passengers and did the necessary work about the station. He recalled that his mother telling him that a relative of his had somehow been been connected with the railroad. James never ridden the train himself when it still had passenger service, although he knew that his mother had done so upon occasion when the family's meager resources were able to support that sort of expense.

When he and Charlie had left for the Service, they had been driven to Chicago by Charlie's uncle who had lived there. Once he'd returned, eventually the station had been torn down, He'd had little interest in what went on in the town then, and he never paid attention to exactly when that happened.

At his last appointment, when his doctor suggested he take daily walks to be more active, his route to town and back often led him past where the station had originally stood. Once he had seen the young woman in the backdrop of what was no longer there, he felt compelled to look for her again.

Putting a new search string into Google, he hit a few links to learn about the Lakeshore and Michigan Southern Railroad, or the Old Road, as it had been originally called, before it was taken over by the New York Central line. When he was young, the trains were steam powered. Not long after the steam-powered era ended, the nearly century-old passenger service locally was discontinued. Only freight trains passed through the Town now, and never stopped.

Train travel had been hazardous in the early days, and in his Internet search, he found photos and the account of a passenger train derailment east of town in 1904, after it left the station on its journey west. A young woman was fatally injured, and a member of the crew died trying to rescue her. No one came forward to claim her body, although it was believed she might have been a local resident. Newspaper accounts of the day reported that the only clue to her identity was the handkerchief she had been clutching when she died, with the initials EDP.

James stopped reading and remembered that the initials on the handkerchief of the mysterious girl he'd seen were the same: EDP. She'd told him her name was Ella. A cold chill ran down his spine, and his leg began to ache. He'd been sitting in one position too long, he knew, but his discomfort was more mental than physical.

Why was she appearing to him? What connection could he possibly have to this tragic event? Rubbing his leg to try to relieve the pain, he read more of the account of the accident. There it was, the name of the crew member who had died trying to rescue the young woman, Archibald Witlow. His mother's maiden name. That sparked the memory of his mother telling him that as a young orphan, she had come to this town to stay with the widow of her uncle, who ran a boarding house. An older cousin and fellow boarder had been Archie Witlow, the one who had come west to work on the railroad.

Then James' mother had met and married his father here and seldom went back to her home in the east. James had never known those far-away relatives, since they had died long before he was born, an only child and late-life baby for his mother.

James continued reading the article. As the cleanup and removal of the train wreck was progressing, a reporter at the scene had interviewed another member of the crew who said there had been some unusual events leading up to that accident.

The train crew had seen several times previously in the vicinity of the wreck site, a piercing blue light from a lantern that would appear alongside the train at night, as if waving a warning to them to slow down at the curve. There was a legend that a member of a much earlier crew had died in a minor mishap along the tracks in that area, and although they brought his body back to the Town to be buried, his right arm was missing, and was never found.

The crews believed that it was that missing arm that still held up a blue lantern, at times, appearing to warn the train crew of a dangerous curve of the tracks up ahead. It was at that very curve where the 1904 derailment had occurred taking the life of the unfortunate young lady. Although gravely injured himself, Mr. Witlow had pulled the woman from the wreckage of the car where she had been the only passenger, but they had both died from their injuries.

Archie Witlow's body had been returned to his home town of Grand Rapids, Michigan, to be buried next to his father, and the unidentified young woman had been buried in in an unmarked grave in the old town cemetery, located across the road from the train station.

James' mother had told him about the old pioneer burial grounds, and how the stones were later moved to a newer cemetery, leaving the graves behind, since only a few stones had remained, broken or displaced, and no one really knew who had been buried there or where most of the graves were located.

Was that why he saw the young woman - still waiting for her train west? She had never arrived at her destination and was not at peace? Had his long ago relative established a connection with her that somehow had survived to become part of his own troubled visions? Was the spirit of Archie Witlow also haunting the scene where the wreck had occurred west of the station?

James shut down the laptop, poured a shot of whiskey, and although he knew he shouldn't, took one of his pain meds. What he needed now was sleep.

Once he'd gone to bed, he couldn't escape his nightmares. In them, he was following a path through the woods somewhere outside town that led to a large cabin. In the yard was a old woman who was shaking a frightened young woman, slapping her, and screaming threats at her.

"You stupid girl! You are good for nothing. I am sorry I ever took you in. You can't do anything right." She gave the woman a final shake and pushed her back toward the cabin door. "Get in there and finish the chores. I don't want to hear a word out of you."

As the young woman reached the door, she turned her head toward James, and he saw the face of the girl he had seen on the bench at the station.

James awoke in a cold sweat in the early morning hours. After his dream, he realized what kind of abuse must have made the young woman flee. He knew that girls, often poor relation, were often taken in and made to work as servants in return for room and board, and he'd heard that the lives of many of them were filled with unmitigated terror, until some of them died of beatings and illness due to neglect. No wonder she wanted to escape.

But how could he possibly help? She had been at the mercy of someone who wouldn't hesitate to harm her. Could he rescue her now, as his long dead relative had attempted to do then? Sitting here wasn't going to accomplish anything. He needed to take action, not only for her, but for himself.

Perhaps there was still a way. He got out of bed, clutching the back of a nearby chair, walked painfully to the kitchen and poured himself a breakfast cup of whiskey.

He thought of all the old memorabilia that his mother had kept in the spare room. She hated throwing anything away, and after her death, James had left whatever she'd saved, still intact there. He retrieved his stick and went to the room at the back of the house.

He only had to open a few boxes to find the one he sought. Sitting in a chair, he began looking though the contents of the box. A photo album was on top. His mother, or someone, had been meticulous in carefully printing names below the photos.

Mostly these appeared to be of the Witlow family, and he stopped short as he saw a photo of a young man, identified as Archie Witlow. He was startled by the somewhat familiar features, reminding him of his own as a much younger man. He leafed through the book and saw that the Witlows appeared to be living an upper scale life. His mother had rarely talked about her childhood, but when she did, it was a wistful recall of a lifestyle much different from the austere one she later led.

As he prepared to close the book, he saw some envelopes tucked into a pocket in the back inside of the album, addressed to his mother, dated in the 1920s, with a return address in Grand Rapids, Michigan. Opening one, he found it was a letter to his mother from a relative there. He replaced the letter in the envelope and set them and the album aside.

He moved some other boxes and found an old carpet bag, still quite intact, and put the album and letters in it. But he needed something else. He opened box after box, until he found some old clothes, dating from years ago, still in surprisingly good condition. He and Charlie had worn them for halloween costumes when they were teenagers. He'd not gained much weight since his younger years, and he was pleased to see that the pants, shirt, jacket and shoes still fit him.

Once he'd donned them, he glanced in an old framed mirror that his mother had left hanging on the wall. The clothes might be from Archie Witlow's era, but the face reflected in the mirror was decades older.

He added other clothing items to the bag and then paused over the little jewelry box that had been his mother's. Inside was the jewelry that she'd insisted he promise not to bury with her. She argued that someday he might need money, and at least the wedding ring was pure gold. James had obeyed her wishes. Now the ring might be of value to him.

He added the box to his bag, went into the kitchen and took paper and pen from his desk. He wrote a short letter, which he placed in an envelope and added a stamp. Adding a few more things to his carpet bag, shunning the bottles of medicine on the counter, he picked up the bag and his stick, put the letter in the mail box outside, and raised the red flag for pickup. Then he turned to take one last look at what he was leaving behind and headed for the main road.

His progress was slowed by the weight of the bag, but at last he reached the scene of his visions. The girl wasn't sitting on the bench yet, but it was morning rather than the late afternoon when he usually saw her. The station and tracks were there, as they had been yesterday.

Slowly, he crossed the double track, and stepped up on the platform. The blind was still drawn on the door of the station house, and it appeared no one was around. As he approached it, he stretched out his bad leg, once again felt no pain and discarded his stick. He caught sight of his face in the darkened window of the door. As he had hoped, a younger and more handsome countenance was reflected back at him. He smiled, and sat on the bench to wait.

After a while, he stood up and peered around the building, seeing there a sheltered area not visible from the front containing another bench. He returned to sit in front of the station, and in a little while, he saw the girl crossing the tracks, carrying her satchel, heading for the platform. He picked up his carpet bag, and met her as she arrived.

"Oh, Sir," she said. "I hope I've not missed the train."

"Not all all," he told her. "I've been waiting for you, so we can travel together."

"How kind," she said.

He felt an overwhelming sense of her trusting nature. He felt he must keep her safe.

"The station master isn't here yet," he told her. " There's a shaded bench out back where we can wait, until we hear his carriage."

She followed his lead as he escorted her to the bench in the shade of a giant willow tree, where they sat, side by side. She appeared to recognize him.

"Have we met before?" she asked. "You look very familiar."

"Some time ago," he replied. "I hope that you will trust my judgement in a necessary slight change of our travel plans." He held out his hand, and she shook it, smiling shyly.

"I hope we don't miss the train," she said in a worried tone. "I have yet to purchase my ticket."

"I can do that," he told her.

She reached into her pocket and pulled out a few bills. "Will this be enough?"

He nodded and said, "Wait here," and got up as he heard a carriage drive up in front. Once he had gone around to the front, although he saw that the station master had indeed arrived, it had not been his carriage he'd heard. Instead, an old woman, the image of the one in his frightful dream of the previous night, was arguing with him, demanding to know if a young woman had come trying to leave town on the train.

He heard the woman's claim that after riding off to town

101

that morning, she realized she had forgotten her cash box. Returning back home to get it, and found that the money was missing, and the servant gone. She demanded that the station master detain the girl if she showed up, while she went to get the Town marshal.

The station master merely nodded, but after the woman had left, he turned to James, commenting under his breath. "That old woman can't keep anyone working for her. Don't blame the girl for taking her due and leaving. Are you here for tickets?" he asked, and turned to unlock the door.

James followed him inside. "I need two tickets east, for me and my wife, she's waiting out back for me."

"That train will be here in a few minutes," the station master said as he sold him the tickets.

"Can I send a telegram from here?" James asked. The station master nodded and directed him to a counter, where James quickly wrote a message.

His errand completed, James returned to the girl, who was sitting asleep, leaning against the bench. She looked so peaceful. Sitting beside her, he reached into his carpet bag and pulled out his mother's jewelry box and removed the gold ring. He carefully picked up her hand and slipped the ring on her finger, a perfect fit.

A few minutes later, she awoke, and smiled at him as he held up the tickets.

"The train will be here soon," he told her.

"Thank you," she said, her innocent eyes meeting his. They sat in silence until they heard the approaching train, and he escorted her around the building to board along with half a dozen others, likely salesmen, who had also arrived.

The men let the couple board first. James led Ella through to the second car, while the men rode in the forward car. James put their bags on the upper storage rail, and positioned himself in the window seat, letting her sit on the aisle, out of view.

Shortly after they were seated, the "all aboard" call was made. James looked out of the window as the train pulled away, and saw that the older woman had returned with the Town marshal. She was waving her hands wildly and ranting at the station manager, while he and the marshal stood silently as though they had heard it all before.

Finally, the station manager raised his arms in a gesture of dismissal, shook his head and headed back to the station. Soon the train had left the scene far behind, and James smiled at Ella.

"Here," he said, now that he knew it was safe, "Let's change seats so you can have the window view." They switched, and after a few moments, she had fallen asleep against his shoulder. Glancing down at her, he was pleased to see that her bruises had now disappeared.

Only the clatter of the train wheels interrupted his thoughts, as James envisioned what lay ahead. He was leaving behind nothing of real value; the treasure was the sleeping figure beside him.

The time passed quickly; but the train made a few stops, and James kept a wary eye for the appearance of the law that might have been sent after Ella. Fortunately, none appeared. Once they approached their destination, she was still sleeping, and he gently woke her to follow him off the train to the livery stable in the yard.

He recited the address of the envelope in his pocket, 414 Maple Street, to the driver, and they got into the carriage.

The girl, now wide awake, for the first time looked confused. "Where are we, Sir?" she asked.

"Grand Rapids, Michigan," he replied.

"But I don't know anyone here," she said.

He patted her hand gently as he said. "No, but I do."

"I don't recall your name," she said, as she clutched her small handbag.

"I'm Archie, and you're Ella. You've been ill, perhaps that's why you don't remember."

"We were on another train perhaps?" she said, with a thoughtful look.

"Yes," he replied. "There was an accident, and you were hurt."

She raised her hand to her head. "My head, I think I hurt my head. I was afraid, but I can't remember why I was on the train."

"It doesn't matter; you're better now," James told her. "And I'm here to take care of you. I'm taking you to meet my family. You are my wife. There's my ring, on your finger."

She held up her hand, and as the gold ring glinted in the

sunlight streaming through the window, she smiled. "I think I remember you taking care of me," she said.

"For always and forever," he told her.

They were both silent as their driver joined the other horse and buggies traversing through the tidy streets.

FInally, the driver stopped in front of a huge open field. "Here you are, Sir." he said.

James stared in disbelief. "This can't be 414 Maple Street," he said firmly, trying not to frighten Ella. His heart sank. Gone - what he was seeking couldn't be gone!

The driver shook his head, "No, It's 1414 Maple Street. Isn't that what you said?"

"414 Maple Street," James replied, pulling the letter out of his pocket to be sure. "It must be further on into town, " James insisted.

"Sorry, my mistake," the driver replied, signaling to the horses to move on.

James breathed a sigh of relief a few minutes later, when the carriage stopped in front of a large Italianate style home. He got out, paid the driver with change from the train ticket purchase and then fetched Ella and the bags containing all they had brought from their past lives.

Suddenly the front door of the house flew open and a pretty young girl ran down the steps to greet them.

"You are a wicked brother to give us so little notice. But Mother was so excited to get your wire," cried the young woman as she hurried toward them. As she finished speaking, an older woman appeared in the doorway wearing a huge smile.

"Archie! You're here at last. And this must be Ella, your bride?" the older woman asked, coming down the steps and opening her arms wide to the woman by his side.

Archie was pleased to see that Ella accepted the greeting without question, perhaps as surprised by unaccustomed kindness as a child blinking in unexpected daylight.

"Yes, Mother," he said. "We've come home to stay."

"Welcome, both of you," his mother said, then turned to her daughter. "Trudy, take Ella upstairs so she can freshen up before dinner."

Trudy led Ella into the house, chattering away, as Ella, still slightly dazed, but smiling accompanied her. Mrs. Witlow ushered James into the house, leading him to a small parlor.

"I was so relieved to have the telegram from you this morning," she told him. "I've been so worried. I've had such dreadful dreams about you getting hurt on those trains. I am so glad you came to your senses. But I thought you were determined to work your way to fortune in the west."

"Ella made the difference," James said. "It is because of her that we are here with you now."

"You met on a train?" the older woman asked.

"Yes," James agreed. "Once I met Ella, I realized how much I missed being with the family, so here we are."

"For good?"

"For as long as you'll have me, have us, that is."

"Trudy and I have been rattling around in this big old house alone for too long. Now you are back where you belong." his mother told him. "Your uncle has held open your position at the bank. I told him you were on your way back, and he expects you there on Monday. A shame you don't have time for a proper honeymoon trip, but at least you will have the weekend."

Finally she paused, and let James respond. "We've done all the traveling we care to for a while," he told her. "We want to get back to the everyday."

It was a homecoming such as James had never experienced. In the few hours' notice that she had had, his mother had arranged for an elaborate buffet dinner. Family friends and relatives gathered to welcome home Archie and his new bride. Ella, although shy, seemed happy to be in the center of an adoring family.

After dinner, once the guests had left, Trudy had enticed Ella into a two-handed game of Pinochle. James and Mrs. Witlow sat across from each other in comfortable leather chairs, smiling as the two girls laughed over their game, as Trudy taught it to her.

"Sometimes I wish your father were still alive," Mrs. Witlow said. "But it is wonderful to have you here again. We needed a man in the house."

Just then the clock chimed ten, and James smiled and stood up. "It's time for Ella to rest, now," he said, She's surely tired after the long day."

Trudy put down her hand of cards and looked up as he approached saying to Ella, "Did you ever get Archie to smile in the wedding photo?"

James quickly spoke up. "It was a quick ceremony, and we didn't have time to have any done."

Archie's mother went over to put her arm about Ella's shoulders. "Then we shall have the Parson over for Sunday dinner and repeat the ceremony, and Trudy's friend Neal can take photos. Would you like that, Ella?"

"Are you sure you are up to all that fuss?" James asked, meaning the question for Ella, but Trudy replied.

"Oh, of course we are!" she cried. "Don't you agree, Ella?"

She smiled up at James. "Yes, I would really like to have a wedding photo to remember."

James went over and kissed her on the cheek. "Then that is what we will have."

He turned to Mrs Witlow and Trudy, as he held out his hand for Ella to join him. "Thank you so much for everything. It is good to be home at last," he told them.

James and Ella went up the stairs, and into the room where Trudy had put their things. James knew instinctively that it had been Archie's old room.

"Why don't you turn in, Ella," James told her, spying a box on the night stand opening it and removing the cigar and matches that he had expected to find there. "I'm going outside for a smoke."

"I am tired," she replied, and looked up to meet his eyes. She picked up the nightgown that Trudy had lent her, and James went over to kiss her on the forehead.

"Sleep well, my dear one," he said, and left the room.
He went down the stairs and out the kitchen door into a quiet back yard, tired, but filled with the energy of a younger version of himself.

Tomorrow was Saturday. Sunday would be their wedding day. He would wait until after the ceremony to introduce Ella to the joys of married life. He'd add their wedding photograph to his mother's old album for future generations to find.

Both he and Archie had sought adventure: James joining

the service to see the world, and Archie working on the railroad in his longing to go west. James had suffered a debilitating war injury; while Archie had died trying to rescue Ella.

James gave one last thought to what he had left behind, but knew the letter to his family's lawyer along with the power of attorney he'd already given would guarantee that what was left there would be liquidated and proceeds given to to charity. No one back in his other life would even miss him.

None of the past mattered now, since he had been allowed to step into Archie's interrupted life, so much more fulfilling than his own. Whatever ripples in time might occur in the future, James, now as Archie, was willing to accept the consequences to have an unexpected but much desired second chance at happiness.

THE END

Kindred Spirits

RoseMary McDaniel a.k.a. Amy Hayle

Even as a child, Jane had two passions: horses and the history of the local Indian tribe that had been one of the few who had not left on the "Trail of Tears." Her older sister Sally realized that her younger sibling was unusual and never had a close relationship with her until years later, when as a widow, she rejoined Jane and her older husband Bo on the family farm, then a thriving ranch to raise Jane's beloved Appaloosas.

But still she wondered about Jane's insistence that the spirits of those who came before still lingered in the vast woods that surrounded their childhood farm in the valley of the Fruithills, a place that has never lost its ties to a spirit-filled past.

Author's note: Although the stories have been inspired by some actual places and events in history, they are all a product of the author's imagination and not intended to represent any persons, living or dead.

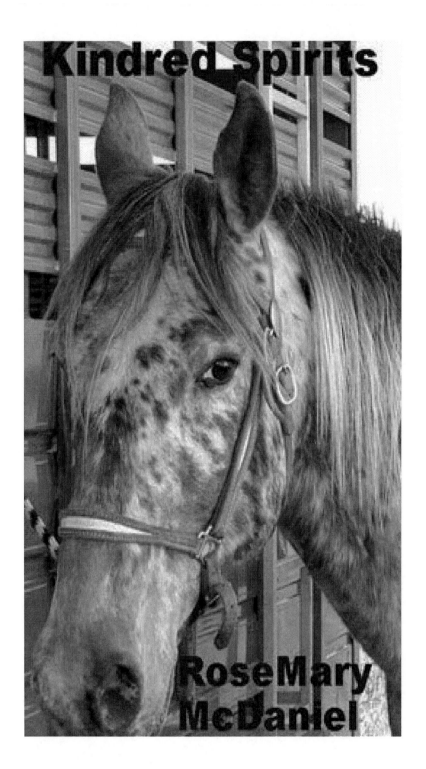

Kindred Spirits

RoseMary McDaniel

Kindred Spirits

RoseMary McDaniel a.k.a. Amy Hayle

"There are more horses than people around here, and the horses are nicer!" declared my sister Jane at an early age.

No producing of any amount of facts would convince her that she was wrong, especially concerning the second part of her argument. She was correct that in our small area of the world, in the valley of the famed Fruithills, we had an abundance of horses, ponies, and the like. I'll admit that I'd never been ill-treated by a horse, but by people, well, maybe Jane was right about that, too.

Being 5 years older, I remember the first time that Dad sat Jane on one of the horses on our farm. She was about 3 years old, and she once she had been on the back of that tired old farm nag, it became her worthy steed. Although she had to be lifted up to ride for some time thereafter, it didn't take her too many years to find a way to mount him herself. Once she did, she was gone for hours on long summer afternoons into the many woods that surrounded our farm, and never missed a chance, once chores were done after school, to ride off into the fields beyond the fence.

I liked riding as well, but my focus was never on the kind of need for freedom and solitude that Jane craved. I was like the boy my Dad never had, and trailed after him and took over chores as soon as he'd let me.

One afternoon, I decided to follow Jane into the woods, curious as to what she actually did during the times she simply disappeared into the thick underbrush and only came home in time for supper. She'd never miss that, of course, delighting in the rich farm table loaded with Mom's home cooking.

I'd let her get ahead of me that afternoon, and after waiting a few minutes, followed her along the trail of downed grasses that marked the path she had taken. I could hear her voice, before I actually saw her, so I slipped off my horse, secured his reins, and quietly approached where I could peer around the trees to see what she was up to.

Her horse quietly grazed beside her, and Jane sat on the ground nearby, earnestly holding a conversation with no one that I could see. She'd ask a question, listen intently, bob her head yes or no, and then speak again. It was like some kind of semi-reality performance, and I slipped closer to catch her words.

Then I froze as I heard her voice clearly, and couldn't understand a single word she was saying. The sounds were clipped, some guttural, and she would laugh in a way that sounded much older than her age then, of about nine years.

As I stepped a bit closer, a branch cracked beneath my foot, and looking up, Jane spotted me.

"What do you want, Sally?" she asked, her tone wary.

I tried to be nonchalant as I replied. "Just out for a ride," I said. "It's a nice day."

"It was," she answered and climbed back on her own mount. She headed for our farm without another word, and I followed without comment.

It wasn't the first time that I'd heard her speak that way. When she was a mere tot, before she really put sentences together, I'd hear her at night sometimes, talking away in her crib in those same sort of utterances. I'd even asked my mother about it, but she merely smiled and said that babies sometimes have their own language, and that it would pass.

Although the night conversations would eventually stop, the fact was that Jane and I were never really very close playmates. Admittedly, she was quite a bit younger, but even when our cousins came to visit and we broke out the board games, she could rarely be coaxed to take part, while cousins her age joined eagerly in the fun.

Nobody seemed to find it strange, except for me. They'd all shrug and say "That's just Jane," should I raise any questions about her actions or non-actions.

At school, she quietly did her lessons, as necessary, but never really developed close relationships with anyone in her classes. By the time she was in the second grade, I was already off to Junior High, and our worlds grew further apart.

Thinking back, with the benefit of knowledge of some of the medical conditions that are attributed to the kind of behavior that Jane sometimes portrayed, I wondered if perhaps she, too, suffered from something more than just a type of personality quite unlike mine. But eventually, I accepted that some people like Jane were just different and left it at that.

Jane had one other main interest, besides horses. She was fascinated by the stories of the Indians who had lived here many years ago. She was always a dedicated reader, and never missed a chance to get new books at the library. Back in our childhood days, the library was our only chance to explore the world of information. Reading materials in our home consisted of newspapers, a few farm magazines and the Bible. There was no Internet, of course back then in the late 1950's, and only the occasional radio show and later a black and white T.V. brought the outside world to our farm.

The cork bulletin board in Jane's room was soon filled with clippings, photos and memorabilia of a local band of the Indian tribe, the Potawatomi. I also learned about the history of tribe called the Pokagon, "Keepers of the Fire". You couldn't help but learn about them being around Jane, it was her passion.

To be sure, the story of how the local band was able to remain on their lands in Michigan and Indiana was intriguing. They did not join a forced march removal of 800 others from their ancestral villages along the St. Joseph, Paw Paw and Kalamazoo Rivers to a reservation in Kansas by the U.S. Government in September of 1838, breaking the promise of several earlier treaties. It was known as the "Trail of Tears," or more accurately the "Trail of Death," due to the many deaths and hardships along the way.

Jane was vocal in her defense of the Indians right to remain on their land, and because of this long-ago event, she formed her unfavorable opinion of government authority in general. My parents viewed it as a phase, something she'd outgrow as she developed interests in other areas, perhaps thankful that at least she was occupied with something that drew her interest.

To be fair, our parents were busy in maintaining the farm in the 1950s and 60's, as my father's business interests and investments grew in the booming recreational vehicle (RV) industry in the area after he started his own business, which expanded and developed beyond the small town where we lived. My mother backed my father 150%, taking over chores as needed, hiring the help to bring in the harvest and providing Jane and me the support of both mother and father, as he spent more and more time at his workplace.

One thing was constant, however, my mother's home cooking. My father had said that she'd made a promise when they married that she'd always have lunch on the table for him everyday, and for many years, she did. Our farm was a few miles out of the little town where his business was located, but he made it home for lunch nearly every day, often bringing co-workers along with him to enjoy the spread my mother provided.

It was nicknamed "The Groaning Table," by those who regularly attended, referring to the groans of "I can't eat another bite," uttered by diners when my mother would set out the wonderful fruit-filled dumplings, puddings and cobblers she made with apples and peaches and strawberries from the local Fruithills, amply covered with real whipped cream. And of course, they would indulge after all in the delicious desserts.

Jane and I partook of these communal meals only during the summertime, since we took our lunch along to school. But Jane usually filled her plate and disappeared outside, while I lingered to enjoy the friendly conversations and the joking back and forth between my parents and those who shared the meal.

Among Jane's treasures were a few arrowheads and other small artifacts that she'd found along the small stream that run behind our home and fed into the river. From what I'd heard from Jane, the Indians who'd roamed the area around the St. Joseph River used the area for hunting and fishing, while their permanent camps tended to be further to the north in Michigan. One day, I noticed that Jane had a little beaded pouch or bag with uniquely woven flower designs. It looked quite old.

"Where did you get that?" I asked.

"From a friend," she replied, but would provide no further information.

Later that week, when I'd gone to her room to look for a sweater she'd borrowed, I saw the bag on her dresser and picked it up to examine it more closely. It seemed familiar, and I glanced up at the photos pinned to her bulletin board. There was a image I'd remembering seeing before of a beaded pouch and a basket, perhaps torn from a magazine.

The pouch I held was similar to the one pictured. Surely, this wasn't something she'd found in the woods, still so well preserved from the past. Yet, I couldn't think of a single person who could be considered a friend who would give Jane such a gift.

I saw my sweater lying on a nearby chair, and feeling a little creepy at spying on Jane's privacy, I lay the bag back where I had found it, and left the room.

As we grew older, Jane changed little in her preference for her own company. She made decent grades, stayed out of trouble, and at least as far as our parents were concerned, was no problem, except for one rainy evening when she rode off on one of the farm horses and didn't return by dark. That was the agreement that our mother had made with Jane. She could go riding as soon as her chores were done, but she must be back home by dark. She was just thirteen and anxious to be independent, even more than she had always been.

On a late summer day, she'd hurried through her chores, filled a saddlebag with snacks and a thermos and she was off, flying across the fields toward the woods. It wasn't long until the clouds turned gray and it was apparent that a storm was headed our way.

Jane wasn't one to let a little rain deter her, so when it began to pour, splashing big raindrops in the barnyard and sizzles of lightening and booms of thunder dotted the sky and air, we figured she'd found shelter somewhere to wait out the storm. But when it became apparent that the rain had stopped and she'd still not shown up, Mother began to worry.

Our father had gone out of town to visit a new customer for his RV components and even when he phoned to check in earlier that night, Mother didn't want to worry him. I'd offered to go looking for her, but mother had decided to wait a little longer. Finally as it neared midnight, she agreed that I could ride after Jane, so I did.

Having ridden with her on the few occasions she allowed me along, I knew the general way she might go, but I didn't find any trace of her. The sky had cleared and the half moon overhead spread a misty light ahead of me. I was just about to turn around and head back, when I heard the whinny of a horse behind me. I saw Jane on her horse, paused at the edge of the woods, and for a split second I thought I saw another mounted figure in the distance behind her and the far off glow of a campfire.

Seeing me, Jane quickly rode toward me, without a word.

"Where on earth have you been?" I scolded her. "Mother is worried silly."

"No need for worry," she announced calmly, "I was quite safe."

"Safe where?" I asked. "There's no shelter in that direction."

Then she edged her horse closer to mine, and smiled that strange faraway Jane smile as she said "I found them, Sally, at their summer camp, just like the pictures in the books I've read."

"What are you talking about?" I said in a harsh voice. "Found who? Some hobos in the forest?"

"Of course not," Jane scoffed. "I found the them, the Keepers of the Fire."

"Are you crazy?" I asked. "There aren't any Indians for miles. They live up in Michigan and don't camp here in the woods."

Jane maneuvered her horse around mine and started back toward our farm. "Don't believe me, then," she said. "But it's true just the same."

She never mentioned it again, and although I tried to bring up the subject later on, she turned a deaf ear to my questions, and eventually, I stopped asking.

After that, I was too busy with my graduation from high school, and then going off to nursing school to pay much attention to Jane. That was basically how the rest of the family dealt with her. Not say too much; not ask questions, and just keep the peace.

When I came back home the following summer, I found Jane with a new horse, taking it through its paces. Although she'd loved all the old farm horses, apparently she had become fascinated with one particular breed of horses, the Appaloosas, originally bred by an Indian tribe in the far northwest.

Father had bargained for the gray dappled colt from a client who'd bought it out East where the breed had become popular, but found it a little too spirited for his young daughter. Jane had no fear and bounded with the colt immediately and had named it "Nikan," which she told me meant "My Friend."

After that, it was as though the two of them were one. With her darkly tanned complexion, deep dark eyes and long dark braided hair, she could have been mistaken for an Indian, herself.

While I, with my paler skin and lighter hair and eyes, avoided direct sun and mostly wore a hat whenever I helped out with chores. Oddly, Jane now filled the tomboy the role that father had originally planned for me, his elder child.

One afternoon before I returned to nursing school early that fall, I sat with mother on the porch sharing a pitcher of iced lemonade and chatting, enjoying the breeze that further cooled that side of the house. I brought up the subject of Jane's future education.

"Does Jane know what college she might like to go to?" I asked.

Mother looked slightly uncomfortable. "I don't think she's thinking about college."

"Not at all or not yet?" I asked.

Mother took a long sip from her glass. "I think she's talked your father into letting her work the farm for him."

"Jane?" I said in amazement. "I've only known her to hurry through her chores and take off on a horse for the woods."

"You'd be surprised how well she and your father have gotten on, lately," Mother replied, and then hurried on, "She's taken over a lot of the managing that I used to have to do," she said.

"At thirteen?" I thought that was beyond belief.

"Nearly fourteen, actually," Mother answered. "She's a whiz at math and very organized. She's extremely efficient at bookwork."

I was silent as I had a pang of jealousy recalling that I'd once thought I'd be the one to work alongside my parents some day on our farm, but I now realized that my earnest desire to have a career in nursing left my spot in the family for Jane to fill.

Sensing that my mother didn't want to discuss it further, I changed the subject. Later, I wondered if my choice of the nursing field was a reaction to my desire to better understand the needs of different types of people, like Jane or perhaps a reflection of the nurturing nature of my mother.

After I returned to school and became more involved in earning my degree, I found nursing-related activities that only allowed time for a short visit to the farm in summer before each new school year began. But in the late summer after my graduation from college, just before I was to take a nursing position at a hospital in Missouri, I returned for a week's stay on the farm.

The first person I saw when I drove into the yard was Jane, looking more than ever like an Indian, talking earnestly to a man I didn't recognize who sat on a tractor.

I got out of my car and walked over to them.

"Hello, Sally," Jane said. "Meet Bo."

The man jumped down from the tractor and took my hand in his enormous paw and shook it heartily.

"A pleasure, m'am," the man said. "Jane's told me a lot about her older sister."

Not sure how to interpret that statement, I merely nodded and said politely "Nice to meet you, too."

"Bo and I were married last week," Jane told me, as he put his arm around her shoulder, towering a good foot taller.

"That's certainly a surprise," I said, and then recovered to add, "Congratulations."

Just then, our father came out of the barn, strolled over and gave me a hug. After that it was a busy time, as cars pulled into the drive, and the usual lunch time crowd still often gathered for a seat at mother's "Groaning Table."

I didn't have a chance to ask anyone about this older stranger who'd suddenly turned up as my barely 18-year-old sister's husband. He was not handsome and not ugly, just big and strong, with a smiling face, dark brown eyes, and a bald head. His high cheekbones made me think that Jane might be carrying her attraction to all things Indian a bit too far.

Later than evening, I joined Dad for a cup of tea on the porch. Jane and Bo had gone to their small cabin, one of several that Dad had built some years ago for guests, and Mom was watching her favorite evening television show. We sat in silence for a few minutes, until I couldn't stand it any longer

"O.K.," I said, "What's up with Jane suddenly married to someone I've never even heard about before?"

Dad sighed and reached across the arm of my chair to pat my hand. "I know it's probably seems odd, but Jane isn't like you. She needs somebody there for her; somebody to depend on. I hadn't wanted to break the news to you until I could do it in person, but your Mom and I won't be around forever, and I doubt you'd want to come back to live here on the farm, so when Bo came along, I knew that it would be the answer to letting Jane take over the farm eventually. Bo would be there for her, even when I can't be. I hoped you'd understand."

Tears came to my eyes as I said, "Of course I do, Dad. You're right, Jane does need somebody, and if you think he's the one, then I know you did the right thing to encourage it. But you and Mom better stick around a long, long time. I want to be able to bring your grandkids back to visit."

I could see Dad's grin even in the gathering darkness. "So, my girl, you've got a likely candidate in mind? When do we get to meet him?"

I laughed. "I'm not ready to bring anyone home to meet the family yet," I said. "But I have met someone, a young doctor, just starting out. With both of us in the healthcare field, we have had a lot to talk about. It might just work out. I just don't know yet. But when I do, you'll be the first one I tell."

"I take it you're not planning to spend the summer with us?" he asked.

"I've taken a position in a hospital in St. Louis," I told him. "But I planned to stay this whole week, if that's all right."

"You know it is," he told me. "And the young doctor?"

"Yes," I said smiling. "It's the same hospital where he's a resident."

"Ah," Dad said. "Then you'll have someone to take care of you," he paused. "Although I know you don't need the same kind of support that Jane does. But it's a good thing for you to have it, just the same."

I nodded my agreement, and just then Mom appeared in the doorway. "How about a piece of my fresh-baked gingerbread with fresh cream on top?" she asked.

"Don't have to ask us twice," Dad replied, and we got up and followed her into the house.

The week went fast, and I enjoyed my time with my family, even letting Jane and Bo talk me into going to the annual Labor Day Weekend Pow Pow in Michigan. He was in his element here, and Jane as his wife was not only accepted but respected. The songs, dancing, food and prayers were a celebration of the Potawatomi way of life. Jane fit in here, and I was pleased to see that she had become a part of Bo's tribal community.

We even visited the Indian casino and although none of us were gamblers, Jane told me it might be my lucky day; and I believed her and actually won $50 at one of the machines for a single quarter.

Before I left, Jane, Bo and Dad shared with me their plans for a new large barn and training facility that they were planning to build on the farm. Having done so well in his RV business, Dad had bought a number of additional acres years ago and there was plenty of room for expansion.

Jane was excited about raising horses, her beloved Appaloosas. I was pleased to see her so happy and animated, and I hugged her when I left. I held out my hand to Bo, who solemnly shook it, and a look passed between us that told me I could trust the care of my odd little sister to this giant of a man.

As the years went by, Dad passed and so did Mother, and I made fewer and fewer trips back to the old farm to see Jane. She and Bo never had any children, but their farm flourished and the horse breeding operation became a big success. I was busy with my own career and marrying that young doctor, who became the most important person in my life, until our children came along. When they were old enough, they enjoyed a few weeks every summer with Aunt Jane and Uncle Bo, while I rarely found the time to accompany them.

But it was my own daughter Lily who provided me with a view into Jane's life on the farm, although Lily corrected me to say that it was now a ranch called Njezhek which meant "just now." I thought it represented well Jane's ability to live in the present, yet honor the past.

She may have not preferred a lot of modern conveniences, but Lily and my son Paul confirmed that that Bo kept up with the modern world, while Jane tended to like simplicity. Lily seemed to have developed a bond with Jane and her love of the woods and accompanied her on her afternoon rides, while Lily's brother Paul preferred working with the horses and in Bo's blacksmith shop.

Paul also liked to assist with lessons, and led the trail rides for the tourists who came to stay at the ranch, and accompany those who came to view the the training facility where groups like the local Marshal's Posse would train and hone their riding skills.

Just before each Labor Day, the local Pokagon tribe still held their Pow-Pow which was a gathering and place for Native people to meet, dance, sing and renew and strengthen their rich culture. Lily and Paul went with Jane a number of times, and they watched as Bo participated in the Men's traditional dances.

Jane and Bo had become acquainted with an orphaned young Native American brother and sister, distant relatives of Bo, who had been on their own since their early teens, when their parents were killed in an auto accident.

Dawn and Ben, (their English names), worked for the ranch, helping with the horses and the events on the farm. Later, they were invited to stay in the small cabin on the farm where Jane and Bo had lived before moving into the big house when my parents died. The two siblings worked full time there and became like part of the family.

Lily and Paul learned much about Native culture from them on their yearly stays at the ranch, and in fact, they were so impressed that they both decided to attend the local South Western Michigan college for a year, where learned more about the history of the local tribe and studied the artifacts and exhibits at the college museum.

Evidently, it affected their future careers as well. Lily went on to major in and earn her degree in Social work with an emphasis on Indian affairs and eventually went to work on an western Indian reservation. Paul pursued a medical education and became a doctor, finally joining Lily on the reservation as a resident doctor.

At first it was a little hard for me to accept that Lily and Paul were so influenced by Jane and Bo, and yet in another way, I was pleased that they were able to connect with her in a way that I never could.

Life went along pretty much as always for a number of years. But my husband Jim died, too young, of a sudden and unexpected heart attack, and I was lonely working in the east, with Jane in the midwest and my children both farther to the west. So, I decided to take a long vacation, perhaps permanently as my 55th birthday dawned and accepted Jane's long-standing invitation to join them on the ranch.

They had added over the years to the guest cabins with a

number of tourist lodges, complete with cooking facilities, and they graciously offered me the use of one for as long as I wanted.

Jane was almost 50 herself, and Bo was, I believed closer to 60, although I never really knew his true age. However, he seemed as vigorous as ever as he worked about the ranch, with Ben's help. Dawn had taken over many of the housekeeping duties from Jane, who devoted her time to working with her beloved horses.

Once I had settled in on the ranch, I noticed that Jane still took those late afternoon rides, heading north westerly into the woods and the beautiful sunsets. One afternoon, I followed her, as I had long ago. I came upon her as she sat on a log, eyes closed as if in meditation, her horse grazing beside her. As I approached, she opened her eyes, not surprised to see me.

"Sit beside me, Sally," she said.

I got off my horse, secured his reins and lowered myself to the log. I looked up to the west, through a clear spot in the trees, and saw the beautiful pinks and oranges of the sunset. "It's very peaceful here," I said.

"It's one of my favorite spots," Jane said, "Always has been. Would you like to take a walk with me?"

"Of course," I answered, not sure where she would lead me.

We walked in silence along the leaf-strewn ground, the dryness crunching beneath our feet to a clearing, several hundred feet from where we had left our horses. Here was the fast moving creek that led toward the river, quite a distance beyond.

"This is where I find them," she said, smiling. "The spirits of those who lived here long ago and still roam this land."

I didn't know what to say.

"No, I'm not delusional," Jane said. "Just sensitive to them. Bo is as well. In fact, your children have felt their presence, too. This where the summer camp was and where those of long ago return in spirit. Do you not feel anything here?"

I stood silent, listening to the rustle of the wind in the trees, the leaves stirring on the branches as they loosened their hold and drifted down to the ground around us.

"I don't know," I said as truthfully as I could. "There is

something here, but what it is, I'm not sure."

"You just need to open your mind to the possibility," Jane told me, putting her arm about me in a rare gesture. "I just wanted to share this with you, as I have with your children. This place brings me peace. I have told Bo that when I die, I want to have my ashes scattered here, not buried in some plot far away."

I didn't know how to reply, but I realized that Jane did not require one. Instead she took my hand and led me back to the place where I'd found her.

She went over to her horse and mounted and rode off toward the farm. I followed her. I wasn't sure how I felt. In one way, I had for a moment entered her world, a place very strange to me, and yet I had shared the peace she felt. Her comment about death was somewhat disconcerting, but frankly, since my husband and our parents were gone, the thought of it had also weighed heavily on my mind.

The autumn weather settled in, and with it, a period of activity began, as late season visitors filled the other lodges and cabins and brought with them a sense of celebration. It had always been my favorite time of year, and Jane's as well, and I felt closer than ever as we worked together with Dawn and the other staff preparing the hearty meals that included seasonal treats like roasted turkey, cream topped pumpkin and apple pies and spiced vegetables. It reminded me of the "Groaning Table," of my parents' era, when there was good eating and joyful times on what was then a farm.

However, the season brought an unprecedented number of storms. Late evening thunder and lightening would awake us, and the rain would pour against the windows only to soften to a patter that would lull me back to sleep.

One afternoon, the storms rolled in early, and the normal activities on the ranch were curtailed as the weather lingered. Bo had gone out to secure the horses, and found that one had broken free and disappeared into the woods. He and Ben set out to find the errant young mare, and each had gone a different route into the back country.

The storm raged for several hours, and although Ben had returned after finding the horse and brought it to the barn, Bo had not come back.

Ben then led a search into the deep woods, and found why Bo was missing. He lay very still under a huge branch from a tree that had been hit by lightening and which had fallen on him as he rode under it. The horse was dead as well, laying beneath him. Ben had been the one to find him, and he had sent Dawn back to find Jane who had been searching in another direction and take her back to the ranch.

But Jane had insisted on going to where they had found Bo. As the others watched, she knelt on the ground next to his body, where only the upper portion was visible. She took his head in her arms, stroking it and speaking softly to him, as the tears flowed down her cheeks.

There wasn't a funeral for Bo, but rather an celebration of his life was held in the forest, and Jane later spread his ashes in the spot she had pointed out to me. My children, Lily and Paul had flown in to attend, and stood beside me, as we watched Jane perform her last act of devotion to her husband.

After Bo's death, Jane seemed more of a shadowy figure than ever. She went about her daily activities as usual, but without the enthusiasm that she had once displayed when working alongside Bo. Ben and Dawn became very protective of her, although they were very careful to include me in any decisions about the ranch business.

Jane was still happiest, it seemed, on her late afternoon rides into the woods. I thought about trying to go along, but decided that what she really sought was solitude and perhaps felt closer to Bo there.

Jane had been unwell for sometime, when Ben and Dawn finally convinced her to visit the family doctor in the next town, and asked me to accompany her. I drove the ranch Jeep, and Jane was her usual quiet self as we went there. She went into the appointment alone, and when she came out, a short time later, she merely nodded to me that it was time to leave, once she had finished her business at the counter.

On the way home, I thought of a thousand questions to ask her, but she responded to the few that I asked with accustomed reticence.

"It's just a skin condition," she told me. "Too much sun."

And that was all she had to say.

I finally had to learn the truth from Dawn.

"She has advanced skin cancer," Dawn told me, after she had taken Jane for several followup sessions at the doctor's office.

"They'll be able cure it, won't they?" I asked. "Chemo or something."

"She's being treated," Dawn said. "But frankly, it's just a matter of time."

I didn't want to believe that. But as I watched silently, day after day, it was as though Jane was fading away before my very eyes. I tried drawing her into conversations about it, but she would only tell me she was tired and go to her room to lie down.

Eventually, she rarely got out of bed, not even taking her daily rides to the woods. It was then that I knew that the end was approaching. I could not believe it. My younger sister, always the energetic one, the healthy one, had a terminal condition. As a nurse, I knew that the form of cancer she had was an aggressive one and often not curable, but still I hoped against hope that she would recover.

As she grew worse, Dawn, Ben and I decided that we would not send her to a hospice, but care for her at home, where she wanted to be. My children Lily and Paul took leaves from their jobs to come back to the ranch to say goodbye to their beloved Aunt Jane, who roused from a mostly medicated state to kiss and thank each of them for coming. It was then a waiting game. On one hand, I didn't want Jane to die, yet I knew that I didn't want her to suffer.

Late one autumn afternoon, My children and I sat on the porch drinking sun tea and watching the colorful sunset, when Dawn and Ben joined us.

"Jane is resting quietly," Dawn said.

"I should go in," I replied.

"No," Ben told me. "Watch the sunset and think of how much Jane has always loved it."

We all sat in silence, watching as the sun sank lower and lower in the western sky. Suddenly, at the very edge of the woods, we saw shadows emerge that had blended into the background. It was the silhouette of a large man, dressed in Indian garb, leading a dappled horse with a similarly dressed rider on its back. Then they stopped, turned toward us, and one last ray of sunlight highlighted their faces.

"It's them," Lily cried. "Uncle Bo and Aunt Jane!"

Then we stood up from our chairs frozen in place as we saw the smiles on their faces. Jane raised her hand in a gesture of goodbye, and as we watched, the light faded, and they blended once more into the darkness and disappeared.

"I must go to Jane," I said, and hurried back into the house, followed by the others.

But as I suspected, Jane was already gone, a peaceful expression on her face. She had joined her husband to follow him to where the spirits of long ago still inhabited the woods beyond our ranch.

Some days later, I went with Lily, Paul, Dawn and Ben and the rest of Bo's tribal family to the woods for a ceremony and later to scatter Jane's ashes where she had lovingly placed his.

Jane and Bo had left the ranch to be shared among Lily, Paul, Dawn and Ben, although it would be Dawn and Ben who would run it. But the lodge where I had been living, and a bit of acreage around it had been left to me for my lifetime. It was home to me now, and here I would remain, until I joined my husband, parents, and Jane and Bo.

Some might say that it was a group hallucination we all shared that autumn afternoon, seeing Bo and Jane as they left us, but I knew that the vision had been a window into the world that they had shared, with a hope for the rest of us that what must die in the flesh is inevitably born into the kindred spirit.

THE END

Last Chance

RoseMary McDaniel a.k.a. Amy Hayle

Chance Givings was devoted to two things: his wife Gena and his career in law enforcement in a small Fruithills Town. When he was given the opportunity to control events, he found himself conflicted. Who should decide life or death in this place that has never lost its ties to a spirit-filled past?

Author's note: Although the stories have been inspired by some actualplaces and events in history, they are all a product of the author's imagination and not intended to represent any persons, living or dead.

Last Chance

RoseMary McDaniel

Last Chance

RoseMary McDaniel a.k.a. Amy Hayle

It was such a loud and horrific crash that Deputy Chance Givings heard it as he sat behind his desk on a Friday afternoon at the Police Station two blocks from the busiest corner in this small Fruithills Town. He tucked his special issue cell phone in his jacket pocket and put steel-toed boots to cement as he hurried off down the street.

Arriving at the scene, it was even worse than he feared. A late model red Jeep SUV had hit a tiny blue Mini-Cooper, crumpling the front end of the smaller car and likely doing much worse to the driver, hardly visible through the window.

Without hesitation, Chance pulled out the phone, entered his passcode and activated the necessary App. He stepped back to scan the area of the accident scene, entered the appropriate request data and hit the activate button. Instantly the scene changed to one of the intersection, devoid of traffic, that had existed ten minutes ago, prior to the deadly crash.

Chance looked around, and then walked over to a crack in the sidewalk, pulled out an errant weed and chucked it in a nearby trashcan. Have to change something always, Chance reminded himself.

He put the phone back in his pocket, and headed for the little coffee shop on the corner, where his superior, Chief Sage Sparrow waved at him from a table in the back. Chance nodded, ordered a diet Coke at the counter and headed for his Chief's table and sat in a chair across from him.

"What's going on?" Chance asked him, checking to see if the older man had registered any of the action that happened right outside the window of the little restaurant.

"Pretty slow day, fortunately," the Chief replied, stirring another packet of artificial sweetener into his brew.

Chance sighed, inaudibly, relieved that the transposition had worked for the second time without an obvious flaw. After a few minutes of conversation, he finished his drink, told the Chief, who'd just ordered lunch, that he'd see him later and headed back to the Department.

As he walked, he recalled the day, nearly a month ago, when he was alone at the Department, and had received a surprise visit from a stranger, dressed in a black suit and dark sunglasses, driving a nondescript tan car.

Chance stood up as the man entered, holding out his hand for a shake. Chance returned the gesture carefully. The man flipped out a photo badge for Chance's examination so quickly he could hardly read it. Then the man looked about carefully.

"Got an office in the back?" he asked.

"Over here," Chance said, directing him to the Chief's small office.

They entered and Chance sat behind the desk; his visitor took the other chair.

"What can I do for you?" Chance asked.

"It's what I can do for you," the man answered.

"I didn't catch your name," Chance said.

"Edwards, you can call me Edwards," the man replied.

When Chance didn't speak, the stranger took a brown paper wrapped package from his pocket and handed it to the younger man.

"Open it," he instructed Chance, when he did not. The man tore off the wrapping himself and handed Chance a cell phone.

Chance looked at Edwards questioningly. "We already have phones here," he said.

"This is a special experimental edition," Edwards told him.

"You'll need to see Chief Sparrow about this," Chance replied, assuming that the man was selling some new communication device for the department.

"I'm not a salesman, Chance," Edwards said, using his first name for emphasis. "This is strictly for you; you've been chosen."

"Chosen?" Chance echoed.

"Turn on the phone," Edwards instructed him.

As if in a trance, Chance turned it on. The screen was pretty ordinary, with an assortment of icons.

"Touch the one labeled 'Official'." Edwards said.

Chance did, and a schematic appeared on the screen. He'd never seen anything quite like it.

"Pay attention," Edwards said, and launched into an explanation of how to use the App that would reverse the previous ten minutes or whatever chosen amount of time and reset the scene to what it had been just prior to that time. He handed Chance a thumb drive.

"This contains the manual on how to use it - complete with cautions. It is confidential and for your eyes only."

"I don't understand," Chance said. "What is this all about? I'll have to tell the Chief."

"You either accept the responsibility yourself and keep it confidential or you don't get this one-time opportunity," Edwards told him.

"Why me?" Chance asked.

"Why not?" Edwards answered. "Believe me, you've been thoroughly vetted for this. You really care about this serving the public good, right?"

Chance reflected for a moment on the times when others had regarded his concern for the welfare of others as a weakness.

"Yes, that's true." he answered.

"Then this is your opportunity to test this new technology, which could be dangerous in the hands of someone less dedicated to serving the greater good. It may have a few quirks, so we need it tested by someone who'll not misuse it. That's you. And if you accept this responsibility, you must not tell anyone about it or what it does. Do you have the fortitude to meet this challenge that could change the world for the better?"

Chance sat for a moment with the phone in his hand. Was this for real? A part of him wanted to believe, and yet his experience in law enforcement had raised his level of skepticism. Before he could reply, Edwards was on his feet with a final few words.

"Read about it and try it out." he said and was out the door.

Chance sat frozen for a moment, and by the time h followed the man to the main office, the strange man who called himself Edwards was gone.

Chance went back into the Chief's office and picked up the paper wrappings from the phone and the thumb drive and returned to the front desk. He threw the plain brown wrapper into the trash, took the phone and thumb drive, tucked them into the personal laptop case that he brought to the office everyday and put it out of sight in a drawer. He'd deal with that later.

A busy day followed, and after Chief Sparrow returned from his lunch, Chance never got around to mentioning anything about the visitor. By then, the civilian clerk was there to man the front desk, and Chance had paperwork in the back to catch up on. When it was time for his shift to end, the Chief had already gone for an appointment, so Chance took his case and left for home.

Over the weekend, he was tempted to open the case, but he was distracted by his concern for his wife, Gena, who wasn't feeling well again. He wished he could help alleviate her suffering, but although they went to a number of doctors and then specialists, none of them were sure exactly what caused her condition. He loved her so much, his bright and cheerful college sweetheart, that he'd wooed and married while they were still finishing their degrees: his in law enforcement, and hers in nursing. It was only after they'd been married for a few years and he was working in the police department in the small town next door to the town where they'd grown up, and where she was now a nurse at the local hospital, that they'd been startled by an odd discovery during a routine test.

They'd both gone to try to find out why they hadn't yet been able to have children, and an unusual result on one of the tests on Gena had raised a concern unrelated to fertility by the doctor.

"It may be nothing," the doctor said, "but we need to do further tests."

And that began their medical nightmare, ending with the diagnosis of an uncommon disease that might be cured by a very risky operation. The doctor advised that they could try to control the symptoms to make Gena more comfortable, while they considered taking the more severe step.

Gena took a medical leave from her job at the hospital. Her medical background helped somewhat, and she rarely complained, but Chance knew that she often suffered in silence, while he was unable to do anything to change the situation.

He had a rough weekend, after his visit from Edwards, as Gena was unable to keep any food down, and spent much of Sunday in bed. By Monday, she was feeling a little better by the time Chance had to leave for his shift. He hated to go, but she insisted she would be fine and had her phone right by her bed.

So, Chance headed off early. Then alone in the office, he

took out the thumb drive and put it in his personal laptop. It didn't take him long to scan through the instruction manual. It was pretty simple, and the proposed ability to reverse time to stop accidents or crime was a very compelling thing.

Chance studied the cautions carefully. Most important was that something at the reversed scene must be changed, no matter how minor, in order that the exact situation not occur again. Other cautions included not being able to change back, once the situation had been altered.

The last caution was a warning that revealed unexpected situations could develop, but Chance felt that was more or less a disclaimer because whomever made the device didn't know what the extent of the capabilities of it were. Chance's intense concentration on the information left echoes of the page text in his mind that he wasn't likely to forget.

A heavy responsibility, Chance thought, and one that he'd not undertake lightly. He'd probably just put the phone back in his case and not use it at all.

So, several weeks went by, and Chance almost forgot the visit and the phone, as he concentrated on his work and concern for his wife and her illness. But one day, when he was in a squad car on patrol on an extra early evening shift, he came across a car on a back country road crashed into a large tree that had just happened.

He stopped and in the gathering dusk, approached the scene. He saw that it was the daughter of a local family who was the driver and sole occupant and who had been partially ejected from the car; obviously dead or nearly so. He hurried back to the squad car to call for assistance, when he saw his case on the seat. His heart ached for the girl and the family, and before he knew it, he had unzipped the case and pulled out the special phone.

Without hesitation, he hurried back to the crash scene and activated the App. His nearly photographic memory allowed him to recall the manual's instructions and he scanned the scene carefully, chose the proper result he wanted and clicked the OK button. The crashed car disappeared. The tree was undamaged as if it had never happened. He stepped over to the tree and broke off a branch. Change something, even if it was minor, was etched into his memory.

He got back into his car and continued his patrol of the

area. Nothing else of significance happened for the rest of his patrol, and he didn't tell anyone about it.

Late that night in bed, as he watched Gena, restless in sleep, he wondered if he had been daydreaming, or imagined the whole thing. But deep down, he knew that it had really happened. He wished that he could go to that young lady who had had the accident and warn her about the consequences of her tendency to speed. which had already earned her several tickets, but he knew that he could not without awkward explanations.

As weeks went by, only a few minor fender benders happened on his shifts, not serious enough to make him consider using the phone. He'd only used it twice, first at the evening accident of the young girl, and second, just last week, at the crash at the busy corner, witnessed by Chief Sparrow who had no memory of it. There'd been no other reason to think about or use the experimental phone.

But in hindsight, he'd wished he could have tracked down the one responsible for that corner accident and also warn him or her about their dangerous driving. That was the problem with playing God without the knowledge or authority to follow through. He could change circumstances to void a particular event, but he knew couldn't affect the fundamental thing that had made it happen or make responsible parties aware of their errors.

At home, Gena's condition was getting worse, and when he took her for her latest doctor visit, there seemed to be no alternative to having the experimental surgery.

"It's OK, darling," Gena told Chance. "I want to do this. I want to get better. Living like this is hard on both of us. I need to do this."

He held her in his arms as tears blurred his eyes. "I'll be with you through it all, sweetheart," he told her.

The operation was scheduled for a Monday morning, and Gena had gone into the hospital on Sunday afternoon. By the next morning, she was groggy as Chance kissed her and told her he loved her, just before they took her into surgery.

It was several hours later, when the doctor came out to talk to Chance in the waiting room.

"It's over," the doctor told him. "It seemed to go well, but the next 24 hours will be crucial. We'll be moving her upstairs in a few minutes, and I'll have the nurse come and take you there when she's settled in.

Half an hour later, a nurse came to take Chance upstairs where Gena lay in a bed hooked up to an array of equipment. Chance sat by her side for several hours, watching as she lay, looking asleep except for the tubes and the monitors. Suddenly an alarm sounded, and Chance stood up as what seemed a crowd o people and a crash cart appeared.

"You'll need to wait outside, sir," an aide told him, and like a robot, Chance complied, standing outside, peering through a gap in the curtains that covered the window of the room, watching them work over Gena.

Eventually, the cart and the crowd withdrew and someone gave Chance the news.

"I'm sorry, but she didn't make it. You can go in now, if you want."

Chance went into the room. He couldn't believe it. His beloved Gena was gone. He reached into his pocket and pulled out the phone Edwards had given him. Some horrible premonition must have made him put it there this morning without conscious thought.

He quietly closed the door and stepped to her bed. With all the equipment removed, she looked like a sleeping angel. He kissed her forehead and said "I love you, Gena."

He activated the special App that scanned her laying in the bed and set the timing for several weeks before the operation and hit "OK."

Then the scene changed, Gena in the bed vanished, and Chance picked up a paper cup from the table, crushed it and and put it in his pocket, realizing that he was now wearing his uniform.

Then he walked out of the hospital unnoticed and went home. To his delight, Gena was there, just back from a doctor's appointment she said, smiling and happy.

"Guess what," she told him. "I've just been to the doctor, and he says it's amazing, truly a miracle. Whatever it was I had, I don't have anymore. And I'm starving. You're home early today, so let's go out for a special dinner."

Chance swept her into his arms and gave her a big hug.

"That's great honey. Just let me change out of my uniform,

and we'll go out and celebrate."

He went upstairs to their room and shut the door. He sat on the bed and took off his boots. He sighed and pulled the special phone out of his pocket and put it on a chair and hit it sharply with one steel-toed boot. The glass splintered, the case split, and the phone was dead.

A device like that was too dangerous, even in his hands, he knew, and he no longer wanted the responsibility for it. Although it could change the world, the potential for misuse was just too tempting.

He'd saved Gena, but likely at a cost somewhere down the road that he was yet unable to comprehend. He had been willing to do almost anything to have her back, but he realized now that even he could be tempted to use the power of the phone for his own needs. If he kept it, he would eventually want other things changed to suit his own circumstances, a dangerous path to follow.

He had to remove that temptation, although he knew this experiment would likely not end with him. Somewhere, someone else would try again to introduce some unsuspecting person to the chance to change the world for the supposed better.

Although he'd never understand why bad things continued to happen in the world, he knew he didn't have the wisdom to play God. He had used his last chance, wisely, he hoped. He felt relieved of the tremendous responsibility, he hadn't asked for. He put the pieces of the broken phone in an old sock and deposited it in his uniform jacket that he hung in the closet. He would dispose of the device chards later.

Then he changed into casual clothes and went downstairs to join his beautiful, restored-to-health, love-of-his life, Gena.

THE END

New Year's Evil

RoseMary McDaniel a.k.a. Amy Hayle

Does evil lurk behind the scenes at a New Year's Eve Mystery Dinner set in the Wild Willow Bed and Breakfast? Before midnight, the scene would be set for a ghostly confrontation of murder victim and murderer. in this small Fruithills Town, a place that has never lost the tie to a spirit-filled past.

Author's note: Although the stories have been inspired by some actual places and events in history, they are all a product of the author's imagination and not intended to represent any persons, living or dead.

new year's evil

RoseMary McDaniel

Midnight Mystery Dinner is Murder

New Year's Evil

RoseMary McDaniel a.k.a. Amy Hayle

The glow of the streetlight outside the bay window spread across the lace table cloth and made the gold edges of the red plates shine, and illuminated the table and chairs, except for the chair on the left, encompassed by a gray-green shadowy mist. The outline of a shapely body was visible inside the blurred edges as the shadow shifted and moved like a person changing position to peer out of the window.

A knock on the door, and the sound of footsteps in the hallway outside the dining room where the decorated tables sat waiting for the evening's event caused the shadow to suddenly disappear just as the snap of a switch turned on the chandelier to light up the room.

Gilda Harrison's hand dropped from the light switch into her apron pocket as she stood silently admiring the scene before her. Then at the second knock, she hurried to open the rear service entrance door that led into the kitchen. It was only Oscar Adams, her husband Guy's friend and helper in renovating this big old Queen Anne home into a Bed and Breakfast.

"Well, come on in," she said, smiling at the man, who held several tools in his hands.

"I found these among mine in my basement, and thought I should return them while I was thinking of it," he said as he lay a hammer and a small saw on the kitchen counter. "Also, I wanted to see how you're doing."

Gilda reached out a hand to touch the hammer, covered with flecks of cranberry-toned paint matching the kitchen woodwork. Guy was never one to be neat; she was constantly picking up after him - that was one of the biggest things she missed.

Oscar cleared his throat quietly; and suddenly remembering he was there, she turned to him, but ignored his probing remark.

"Thanks, Oscar. That was very thoughtful. I'm sure I'll be even more grateful the next time I need to pound one of the old nails around here into place."

"Sure, no problem," he replied. Pushing the baseball cap

138

back on his bald head, he turned to leave.

Then Gilda remembered that he was in somewhat the same situation as she, his wife having died just a short time before Guy. Perhaps he was just lonely and looking for a little friendly conversation. She felt somewhat embarrassed and quickly filled the silence.

"Would you like to see how the room turned out with all the decorations done?"

"Sure," he said and followed her into the dining room.

Four small tables and one larger one were arranged with place settings and holiday decor, ready for the event that evening. Bright colored balloons and crepe paper dangled from the high ceiling and paper hats and party horns were at each place setting.

Gilda turned to him. "I can't thank you enough for all the help that you gave us. If only Guy could have seen this; he would have been so proud how beautiful the dining room is." She sniffed to chase away unbidden tears.

"I just did what Guy needed me to do," Oscar said. "He was the one with the ideas."

"Yes, he was," she agreed, glancing about the room, checking to make sure that everything was just right. So much relied on this particular party going well, she thought. It had to be a success. Again, she remembered her visitor. "You will be coming tonight, won't you? I know Christie is counting on you."

"Well, since she was my wife's favorite cousin, I had to say yes," he admitted. "Fortunately, I'm just part of the backstage crew. She even got me the costume, kinda like the head waiter in a mob joint in the Roaring 20s, but nothing outrageous. I wouldn't have gone for that."

"Guy would have loved it all, the more outrageous the better," Gilda blurted out, and then fell silent, her hand resting on the back of the chair by the bay window.

Again there was an awkward silence, and Oscar lingered a moment before he turned to pat Gilda on the shoulder in a consoling gesture and headed off for the door.

"See you tonight," he said.

"Thanks again," Gilda replied as she followed and shut the door behind him.

She went back into the dining room, and mentally reviewed

what she had done yesterday to prepare the upstairs for guests at her Wild Willow Bed and Breakfast. Tonight's lavish event was a New Year's Eve Murder Mystery Dinner with a meal for eighteen guests, three couples of which would be spending the night in the three guest room suites upstairs.

The event had been arranged by a local author and contributor to many of the charitable organizations in the community. Each of the persons attending was paying a generous sum, not only for the party and lodging, but also to contribute to Christie Warner's favorite charity, an area shelter for abused women.

Christie lived in a large home in one of the fashionable developments in the Fruithills near the town where the Bed and Breakfast was located, and Gilda knew that Christie's influence could help to draw more clients to Wild Willow.

She sighed, as her mind again filled with thoughts of her husband Guy. When they had bought the old home little more than a year previously, she never dreamed that in a few short months, she would be running the place alone and dealing with the myriad of details involved in turning the old Queen Anne residence into a bed and breakfast.

The first months, things had gone well, as Guy retired from his corporate job and pursued the renovation. They'd added in-suite bathrooms to the existing three upstairs bedrooms and completely redecorated with a Art Nouveau theme.

Gilda had loved helping to choose fabric, paint and wallpaper, while Guy did a lot of the restoration work himself with Oscar's help. Guy had met him at the local coffee shop, found out that they both shared common interests and that Oscar was presently employed only part time at an area bowling alley where he was on a team and one of the top bowlers, so he was available to help Guy with the renovation.

By mid-year, the suites were ready, and they tackled the downstairs public area, dining room and professional kitchen makeover, including meeting the many specifications of the local health department. Finished at last with the major work, including the small attached apartment where the couple would live, Guy was ready to build shelves for storage in the basement.

He had begun the project on a sunny autumn afternoon, and

Gilda went to visit a friend having surgery in a hospital in a nearby city. Guy assured her he wouldn't need any help after he'd returned from the Home Depot that morning, his pickup loaded with supplies to build the shelves.

So, Gilda had left, had a good long visit with her friend and stopped for a few groceries on the way back, arriving home late in the afternoon. The house was strangely quiet. She went first to their apartment, expecting to find Guy taking a break to watch the Notre Dame football game. But he wasn't there. She looked out the window to see his truck at the rear entrance still loaded with planks for the shelves and grew concerned.

She opened the basement door and descended the steps, thinking she'd find Guy, smiling as always, working away. But instead, she saw him laying just past the bottom step, not moving.

She bent down and found him unconscious. Alarmed, she pulled her cell phone from her pocket and dialed 911. But it was too late. When the paramedics arrived, they could do nothing for him. He had been dead for several hours. A stroke perhaps, the doctor had declared and noted that Guy had suffered a severe head injury, likely caused when he fell.

The next few days and weeks were a blur as friends and family rallied around her and helped her get through the arrangements and the funeral. But when that was over, she was alone and frightened. So much had gone into their plans for this place, and now with most of the work completed, she would be the one to make the decisions and generate the business needed to support herself.

The first shock was that the portion of Guy's pension and Social Security that she was entitled to was enough to live on, she supposed, but unless the business generated a decent return, she wouldn't be able to afford to keep it going. The second fear was whether she had the skills and the business knowledge to actually make a go of it alone. But she had to try. It had been their dream, and she couldn't just give up.

It was a lonely life now, even with her friends nearby, although her family was in another state. She and Guy couldn't have children, but they were close to nieces and nephews, who though attentive, had their own lives.

So, when Christie Warner brought up the idea of her

charitable event, Gilda couldn't believe her good fortune. She'd opened Wild Willow only a month after Guy died, and already she had received many compliments and promises for return bookings based on the accommodations and especially her flair for unique breakfasts, signature treats and extreme pampering for her guests.

This event could be the very thing to give her the publicity she needed to attract overnight clients, while branching out into hosting teas, parties and dinners for small groups.

She sighed and checked out the freezer to see the containers of delicious desserts that she had prepared ahead. She was already famous for her fabulous cheesecakes and other tasty desserts. Her hand lingered over a container of two-bite cupcakes, but she quickly shut the door. She wanted to fit comfortably into her costume for tonight. She hadn't wanted to play a part in the murder mystery that Christie had written, but Christie had insisted, and Christie was after all the reason for having the event in the first place.

So, Gilda agreed, and had even sown her own costume that was now hanging on the back of the door in the apartment. Gilda was playing the cook for the family in the play, which was quite appropriate, she thought, and shouldn't require much acting ability. Gilda wondered about the rest of the performance, but the identity of the victim and the perpetrator was known only to Christie and the persons she had chosen to play the parts: secret knowledge. The event was based on a whole cast of characters reminiscent of the 1920s gangster life, but strictly scripted by Christie.

Gilda shook her head, time to clear her mind. She had a big list of things that needed to be done before this evening, so she had to get started now, although it was barely 7:30 in the morning. She turned to go upstairs and noticed that the chair at the table in the bay window was slightly askew. She edged it into place with her foot, pausing to brush a bit of gray dust from the padded seat of the old wooden chair and then went upstairs to begin her work.

By mid-afternoon, the air had grown chilly outside, but the heat from the oven where the entrees were being prepared for a quick reheat later and from rushing about had brought Gilda to the refrigerator for a glass of ice water. Her two servers had already arrived and were checking out their costumes: flapper outfits, complete with feathery boas to wind about their neck and scoop neck tops and short shiny skirts beneath little white aprons. Doris, Gilds's friend and a waitress at a local cafe, slipped a feather band on her bottle red hair and glanced in the mirror on the tiger oak buffet in the dining room.

"What'cha think?" she called to Gilda, as she chomped on a wad of gum.

Gilda came through the kitchen doorway into the dining room. She smiled at the sight. "Very classy," she said, deciding to ignore the gum, which was probably actually in character.

Franny, her other server, whom she didn't know as well, seemed uncertain. "I'm not sure about this," she said, clutching the costume that mirrored Doris's, only in bright lemon yellow.

But Doris put her arm about Franny's shoulders to reassure her. "You'll look good and do great. It ain't about us, after all," she said, falling into her role. "We're just background. They won't pay us much attention at all, unless we spill something on them."

At Gilda's horrified look, Doris laughed. "Don't worry, I'm used to dealing with people who've had a bit much of the bubbly."

"Will there be drinking?" Franny, of an Amish background and not used to this kind of an event, asked with a concerned frown.

"Just sparkling grape juice," Gilda replied. "This is a non-alcohol and no-smoking facility."

"Yeah, well, it doesn't take the real thing to get some people tanked up," Doris said. "Besides, those little flasks that the gangster types used to carry means they can bring their own."

"I hope not," Gilda said, and turning to go back to the kitchen, effectively ended the conversation.

Franny turned to Doris. "You think they'll get drunk anyway?" she asked, fretfully.

"Honey, it's New Years's Eve. Anything can happen. Takes a little New Year's Evil to spice things up, if you know what I mean." She removed her feather band and nudged Franny laughingly.

"Need help in here!" Gilda called from the kitchen, and the two flappers-to-be hurried off to comply.

Time passed quickly, and as the five o'clock hour neared, everything was in place; and Gilda was pacing the floor.

"For Heaven's sake, Gilda," Doris said, "You'll wear out the carpet. Everything is cool, so relax."

"I wish I could," Gilda replied. "But I keep thinking there is something, something undone, or that I haven't thought of yet. It's just a kind of ominous feeling."

There was a rap at the rear door, and Doris gave a little pre-flapper shimmy with her ample hips and went to answer it..

"Too late to worry now," she proclaimed to Gilda. "Let the games begin."

She ushered in Christie Warner and her daughter Kendra carrying bags full of their costumes, a couple of suede duffle bags, and several makeup cases. Kendra, tall with dark hair and eyes like her father, was the opposite in looks from her petite blonde mother.

"Your rooms are all ready," Gilda said from the dining room doorway. "I put you in the Pink Petunia room and Kendra in the Red Rose room."

"Wonderful," said Christie. "It will be like a second honeymoon for Kendra and Chuck. Wait until you see him in his costume. He's my handsomest son-in-law."

"We've been married nearly 6 years," Kendra said in a grumpy voice."And he's your only son-in-law at present. Amy prefers to love 'em and leave 'em. I swear you like Chuck more than me."

"Nonsense," Christie replied paying no attention to Kendra's reference to her sister's uncertain love life. "I treat all my dear ones alike."

Arriving at the oak stairway to the suites, she smiled at Gilda and forged up the steps. Gilda smiled back. She'd learned from experience that despite her diminutive size, Christie was undaunted by any challenge and met all difficulties head on, not slowing down for anyone trailing in her wake.

"Would you like me to bring you some tea?" Gilda called after them.

"That would be divine," Christie replied.

Pleased at something useful to do, Gilda headed off to the kitchen. Doris was prepared with a teakettle of boiling water that she poured into the old fashioned tea pot on the tray Gilda was preparing.

"You really go the extra mile to pamper guests," Doris said, shaking her head at Gilda's adding chocolate biscuits and cranberry scones to a lace doily she placed on a saucer.

"I hope so," Gilda replied. "That's what brings them back."

"With guests like that, you can never do enough," Doris muttered under her breath, but only Franny heard and giggled.

Gilda was already halfway up the stairs.

Hearing voices behind the Pink room door at the top of the stairs, Gilda rapped lightly. At Christie's booming "Enter," she went into the room. With costumes and bags spread over the bed, Christie was standing behind Kendra pulling on the lace under chemise worn by her daughter, that cinched her waist and flattened her breasts.

"Ouch," Kendra cried. "That's too tight!"

"Too many slices of pizza, my girl," said Christie.

"No, you're just pulling it too tight," Kendra insisted.

Christie let go of the laces and turned to Gilda. "Thanks, that's just what we needed - well, maybe not the sweets."

"This is what I need, Mother," her daughter said snatching up a scone and taking a big bite.

Gilda, used to the patter between the two, knew they both loved to squabble, but had a close relationship anyway, merely smiled. "Can I get you anything else?"

"No thanks, Darling," Christie answered pouring herself a cup of hot water and selecting a tea bag from the assortment on the tray. "We'll be down at six thirty to make any final necessary adjustments and greet the other guests. I told those husbands of ours to be here no later than that. I instructed them to use the rear entrance since they're bringing a few last minute props."

She reached over and took the half-eaten scone from her daughter's hand and put it back on the plate.

Kendra rolled her eyes. "Give it a rest," she sighed, her way of fending off her mother's tendency to "control freakiness."

"It is extremely important to me and to Gilda that this party is perfect, and that includes how you look in your costume," Christie said, nodding at Gilda who was just opening the door to leave.

"Nothing is perfect," Gilda heard Kendra reply as she shut the door.

Gilda paused at the top of the stairs looking at but not really seeing the greenery and holly decorations that she had spent hours arranging along the oak banister. A shiver passed over her body.

"Goose walking over my grave," she whispered to herself, repeating what her mother always used to say at times like that. She shook her head to rid the feeling of what, she wasn't sure.

Maybe not everything was perfect, she thought to herself, but this event could help build the reputation she needed to prove that the business that was now her sole responsibility would be a success. She went downstairs to finish preparations for tonight.

By six o'clock, Doris had shooed Gilda back to her apartment to put on her costume, promising to take care of things while she was gone. She and Franny had already spent the previous half hour in the downstairs restroom getting into the costumes and the spirit of a gala.

Gilda had merely said "No thanks," when Doris asked how she liked their sparkling peacock blue eyeshadow and offered to share it.

Now alone in the bedroom of the rear apartment, Gilda could sense Guy's presence. What should have been comforting, made her slightly uneasy. It was almost as if Guy was trying to give her some message, but what it was, she had no idea. She shook herself. Listen to me, she said to herself. Someone who won't even watch spooky movies, and I'm imagining things. Get ahold of yourself, girl, she chastened herself.

She reached for the green dress she would wear. It was plain, with a white collar, but the emerald color was a good one for her and brought out some auburn highlights in her hair. Need a touchup soon, she thought, securing the small emerald earrings that Guy had given her on their last anniversary and adding a full white apron and cap to complete the look of a serious cook.

She could heard the tones of the new front doorbell. Oscar had brought it by several weeks ago and hooked it up. A Christmas present, he'd said, that he'd picked up for for a song at a flea market and thought it would be perfect for Wild Willow. It played a tinkling version of "Memories," that Gilda thought seemed quite appropriate.

"I'll get it," she called to Doris and Franny, and made her way to greet the new arrivals. It was a tall man with a rough looking face but a pleasant smile and a thin woman with a serious bobbed hairdo. The woman held out her hand to Gilda.

"I'm Miranda," she said, and this is my husband Jack. You must be Gilda. Christie has told so much about you and your plans for your business."

"Then you're the couple for the third suite," Gilda said. "It's called Calla Lily and has a white and black theme. All the rooms have a flower theme," she explained, finding herself somewhat nervous in their presence.

Suddenly, she realized they were all still standing in the doorway, and stepped aside. "Please come in. Do you need help with your luggage?"

"No," the woman replied, holding a small hanging bag. "I have what we need."

Gilda led them to the stairs. "It's the room farthest down the hallway at the top. Each room has its name and signature flower painted on the ransom. Would you like me to show you?"

"No," that's quite all right. I'm sure we can find it ourselves." Miranda said.

"All right," Gilda agreed. "Shall I bring up some tea?"

"Thanks, we're coffee drinkers, and we've already had enough caffeine for the day. We'll just get ready for the event. Christie wants everyone downstairs by seven."

"Of course," Gilda said, watching as they climbed the steps and went down the hallway to their room. There was something a little odd about them, but she couldn't put her finger on it. She knew most of the people who would be coming this evening, but Christie had said that these two were friends from out of town who had a real interest in drama. Gilda wondered what parts they would play, but she just have to wait and see.

Ted, Christie's husband and Chuck, Kendra's husband soon arrived accompanied by a long-haired young man, whom they introduced as David, Christie's nephew, who looked to be about 18 and wore tiny white earphones stuck in his ears. Gilda thought they were for a music player, which she soon identified sticking out of his shirt pocket.

The men brought in screens, just as Christie came floating down the stairs in her full roaring 20s outfit of lavender lace and what looked like very expensive Austrian Crystal necklace and earrings.

147

"Darling," she said to Gilda. "I'm afraid we must rearrange a few things. We need these screens in place for the performance."

Gilda just nodded, headed for the kitchen, but turned to watch as Christie directed the men to place one of the several white rice paper screens in front of the bay window, and another across the other side of the room angled at a corner. Behind the corner screen, the young man placed a small table and some equipment. She was glad to see that the screens didn't really disturb any of the decor, except to block some of the windows, but since it was winter and dark already, there was nothing to see outside, anyway.

The next half hour was a constant movement of guests arriving in costume, a mix of men and women, young and old. Christie was busy greeting them and providing them with some paperwork and taking a few aside for more in-depth coaching. There wasn't time to introduce them all to Gilda who stood to the side in the kitchen, watching as the guests passed through the hallway past the kitchen into the sitting rooms.

She recognized some of them, like Christie's other daughter, Amy, petite and fair like her mother, who hung on the arm of a good-looking young man dressed like a mobster in a dark suit and jaunty hat. Others she knew were friends and relatives of Christie who supported her causes, whether they wanted to or not. Christie was like the sun, and others were like planets, big or small who orbited about her, called upon as necessary to do her bidding. Most didn't seem to mind, and Christie's fabled generosity made up for any of her overt shortcomings.

Doris and Franny circulated among the guests with glasses of sparkling grape juice, and Oscar in his waiter's mode made trips back and forth to the kitchen to replenish trays of appetizers like oysters wrapped in bacon, garlic and ham in cream cheese spread on cracker triangles and tiny cucumber sandwiches. He caught Gilda's eye as she stood in the doorway and he winked. Embarrassed, she felt herself blushing before hurrying back to the kitchen.

At precisely seven o'clock Christie stood in front of the group who immediately silenced at her "Shhhhh… "

Quickly, she set the scene for the performance, although all of the attendees had received a very thorough email previously, giving them a brief summary of the drama, who they were and

148

what part they played in the overall situation.

Christie and her husband played the owners of a new Speakeasy called "Wild Women," an obvious spin on the name of the Bed and Breakfast. He was a mob boss named Don Leone, and she was his wife Mona.

The rest of the group was divided between various crime mobsters and family members, including the big boss of another family, Don Dimitri and his gun moll Theresa. Don Dimitri's ex-wife Eva was also there, along with a number of supposedly decidedly unsavory characters.

The two newcomers, Miranda and Ralph, portrayed the character of Evan Ewald, an undercover detective and his foreign lady friend Ursula, who wore a silk turban and robe, who stood quietly observing everyone and everything.

Finally, each guest had received a name badge, evidence, personal secrets, information to confront others, and a piece of secret information about another guest. Each was given a task that Christie stressed must be completed by midnight.

She let everything sink in for a moment, and then announced that it was time for dinner to be served. She led the guests into the dining room where there was a specific name card at each setting to show the guests where to sit. Then, she signaled to Gilda to begin serving the meal, and the guests began to play their roles.

Originating behind the corner screen, appropriate period music played softly against the background noise of silverware clanking against china and earnest conversations as the guests followed their individual scripts, using the information they have been given to try to determine who would be the victim and who would be the murderer.

Gilda's meal of house salad with raspberry vinegar dressing, glazed chicken breasts on a bed of rice pilaf, tiny buttered peas, and assorted breads was enjoyed by the guests, as Doris and Franny were kept busy filling the glasses with the bubbly substitute.

On their way back to the kitchen for refills, Doris stopped in the kitchen doorway to watch as one of the mobsters tipped a little flask into his glass and into that of others at his table. She grinned to herself and hurried after Franny, who fortunately did not notice this ad-hoc spiking of the grape juice.

By the time the guests had finished the trays of Gilda's special desserts, it was nearly nine o'clock, and Christie drew their attention by standing up and tapping her fork against her glass,.

"Now we retire to the sitting room to mingle, while this area is rearranged," she said as she led most of the others away.

Doris, Franny and Gilda finished clearing the tables as Christie's husband Ted and son-in-law Chuck shut the sliding doors between the rooms and began rearranging the tables and chairs. Most of the tables were pushed to the side, out of the way, but they left the single table and end chairs in front of the screen covering the bay window.

A short time later, Chuck slid open the doors, and Christie led the group back into the dining room. An area had been cleared for dancing and the chairs were placed in a semi-circle around the edges of the room.Christie motioned for them to be seated if they liked and for the conversations to begin.

The music grew louder, and flasks were multiplying among the guests and shared among more glasses. Doris noticed, but Franny and Gilda were still blissfully unaware as they cleared up in the kitchen. Doris and Oscar kept the grape juice coming, but the flasks were what kept the laughter flowing.

The noise and confusion made it easier for those who were trying to coax information from other guests toward solving the murder to be to focus attention on each other, but when the appropriate Charleston music boomed from behind the corner screen, the younger of the guests got up to show off their dancing skills.

Finally, as the midnight hour neared, Christie once again brought the room to silence.

"Ladies and Gentlemen," she began. "Tonight we have a special treat for you. Madame Ursula, recently arrived from Russia has agreed to conduct a seance for us. She has felt the pull of spirits here looking for release and is asking for our help in encouraging them to speak."

Gilda, in the doorway, flanked by Doris and Franny, kept her emotions from appearing on her face, but underneath her mask of calm, the same uneasy feeling that she had felt earlier in the day returned to put a twinge in her chest. Somehow she felt this wasn't part of the planned playacting.

"Everyone, please find a chair and sit quietly while Madame Ursula prepares herself. Gilda, girls, Oscar, please take a seat here in the front. We need everyone concentrating. Clasp hands with those on each side of you."

The audience responded, reaching on either side for the other hands. The woman Gilda knew as Miranda came forward, and in her imposing outfit walked up to the table in front of the screen and sat in the chair on the right. The chair on the left side was empty. She looked out into the audience and pointed at Oscar.

"You, there," she said in a hollow foreign accent, totally unlike the voice Gilda had heard when she had arrived earlier that evening. "Come and sit in the other chair. I need to anchor the spirits."

Oscar hesitated, but at the urging of the others in the audience, he got up to fulfill her request. He perched on the edge of the chair.

"Sit back and relax," the woman urged. "This won't hurt, unless of course, you have something to hide," she added in a somber tone. Then not waiting for an answer, she raised her hands on either side of her face and closed her eyes.

Her lips were moving without sound, and someone had stepped to the light switch to dim the chandelier until the guests could barely see each other.

Then the woman's voice boomed out over the room. "We are calling the restless spirits to appear before us. Come to us and tell us your pain, your agony. Tell us what we need to hear to set you free from your prison of this unfinished life."

At first it was just a gray shadow that appeared on the white screen behind the table and then the shadow took on the silhouette of a woman. There was a gasp from the audience as another voice floated on the air, softer yet very distinct.

"Why have you awakened me?" was the plaintive cry.

"We have come to help you," replied the woman at the table.

"No-o-o one can help me no-o-o-w," came the answer, stretching out the words.

"Is there not someone here who knows you, who can assist you? Look around you." the other woman asked.

The other voice made a mewling sound, rising and falling, on and on, the tones engulfing the onlookers and sweeping over them. Then the sound reached Oscar seated at the other side of the table. He sat silently staring downward.

"You!" the voice became a piercing wail. "You who pretended to love me and then hurt me and left me like this." The voice seemed to float above Oscar's head, and the shadow shifted and what appeared to be the index finger of a slender hand pointed to him.

Oscar slumped in his chair and then slipped to the floor, seemingly unconscious.

"No!" was a cry from the audience. Amy, Christie's daughter stood up. "He's not the victim; I'm supposed to be the victim!"

Then the woman called Ursula stood up and removed the turban from her head and slipped out of the robe to reveal a business-like suit.

"Sit him back in the chair; he's not hurt," she ordered, and Ted and Chuck lifted Oscar back into a seated position.

He opened his eyes. "What happened?"

Then Christie stood up, ignored him and addressed the audience. "He's not the victim; he's the murderer." She turned to look at Oscar. "Want to tell them how you murdered my cousin, your wife? I guess you thought you got away with it, but you wanted to make sure, and you knew that dead men tell no tales, right?"

"I don't know what you're talking about," Oscar blurted out.

"Then we'll tell you, Mr. Adams," said the woman who'd conducted the seance.

"Your wife's death was suspicious at best, but the authorities had no proof or witnesses that she hadn't just committed suicide as you'd claimed. But later on, you were obviously worried about a witness that you hadn't counted on. You didn't know that your friend Guy Harrison had dropped by that evening and heard you threaten your wife. Mrs. Wilson, your neighbor in the condo next door, saw him come to the door, and when he got no answer, he moved to the window where he must have seen the two of you arguing and just left without letting you know he'd been there. But Mrs. Wilson eventually told you that he'd been by that night. We know because she also told Jack, my partner, that she had, when he interviewed her."

Ursula signaled to the tall man who'd come with her to the party. "I'm Detective Sergeant Miranda Willis and part of the special task force assigned to solve the two suspicious deaths. This is Jack Parsons, our investigator, and he's been following up ever since Guy Harrison was killed."

Gilda stood up with a horrified look and cried out, "Guy? Killed?"

Christie went over and put her arms around Gilda's shoulders. "I'm sorry, Gilda. I didn't want you to find out this way, but confronting Oscar, we'd hoped to get his confession."

"We don't really even need that now," Ursula said and quietly continued. "You see, Oscar, the surveillance camera on the building across the street from this one captured the events of that morning at the Wild Willow perfectly. Few even suspect that there are such cameras in such a small town as this, and neither did you. You saw that Gilda's car was gone, so you parked yours in the bank lot, walked over, supposedly to show him the bowling trophy you'd won the night before, followed him back down the stairs, pushed him and then hit him with that big bowling trophy.

"Oh, you thought you'd wiped clean when you put it back in the display case at the Action Alley. But the fingerprints on the bottom of the trophy and the recovered blood stains on it we found were enough to cinch that it was you. Yeah, Jack had a devil of a time finding that trophy, because even though we figured out what it was viewing it on the surveillance tape, we didn't know where you'd hidden it. But you sure bragged enough about that win, and Jack tracked it down just yesterday at the place you had worked part time."

"But I don't understand, why did you kill them?" Gilda asked.

"She was going to divorce me; said I didn't treat her right, though I had every right to slap her for talking back to me," Oscar exclaimed, no longer able to keep quiet. "She was going to take me for every last penny I had and the house, go to some shelter and tell all. It was just too much.

"So, I spiked her bedtime milk with the powder from

sleeping pills she already had in the medicine cabinet. Once she was asleep, I wore gloves and just left the bottle by the bed and went to bed myself. When I woke up, she was dead, and that was that. They accepted it as suicide, I thought. But later on, a couple of times, Guy looked at me funny and asked some things that didn't add up. After I found out from the old bag next door he'd been there, I knew he'd figured it out and had to be silenced. That was why."

Ursula pulled a pair of plastic cuffs from her suit pocket, showed him her badge and slapped the plastic bands on Oscar's wrists. Then she and Jack steered him toward the door, where Jack recited his rights.

She looked back at the silent audience. "That's all, folks," she said. She turned to Gilda. "Sorry for all the trouble, M'am. Jack already took our stuff from the room upstairs. Real nice place, you've got here." Then the three of them left quietly.

"Is it over now?" Amy asked her mother. "I don't get murdered?"

"No, you don't; and yes, I guess it is over," Christie said. She still had her arm around Gilda who looked shell-shocked.

"Oh, Gilda, I'm so sorry," Christie began, but then Gilda began laughing and Christie looked very concerned, thinking she was hysterical.

"Oh, God, I wish we hadn't done it this way." Christie cried. "But Lydia was my cousin and my childhood companion and I loved her so much."

"I'm all right," Gilda, still smiling. "But look at the screen."

Everyone in the room turned to look at a black and white outline image of a smiling Guy that had appeared on the screen where the gray shadow had disappeared.

"David," Christie's husband Ted called to the young man behind the screen. The young man came out, the earphones still in his ears and the sound turned up so loud that those close could hear and even feel it.

"Oh, sorry, Uncle Ted," the boy said. "I didn't hear you at first."

Eyes on David, Christie pointed toward the screen. "Where did you get that picture?"

"What picture?" he asked blankly.

Everyone turned back to stare at the now blank screen.

"Gee, are you ready now?" David inquired. "I didn't do anything yet, since I didn't get the signal from anyone. I was just listening to my iPod. Are you ready for the voice over and stuff?"

"You mean you didn't broadcast any sound or show anything on the screen?" Christie asked.

"No, I was waiting for your signal to begin the program. Is something wrong?" David asked.

Gilda went over and hugged him. "No, David. Nothing's wrong now."

Just then, the grandfather clock in the corner began to chime.

"It's midnight," Gilda exclaimed. She picked up a glass of sparkling grape juice from a tray on the buffet. "Let's drink to a brand new year."

Doris and Franny passed around the trays again.

Gilda sipped the juice and let a warm feeling come over her. But it wasn't from the grape juice. As the guests counted the seconds down to midnight, she felt Guy's presence roll around her like a soft warm blanket. She knew now that he was with her, and with his support she'd be able to conquer anything.

She turned to cry "Happy New Year," with the rest as the clock stuck its final chime. Then she turned to Christie. "At least it's all settled now, and we'll just have to let the punishment fit the crime."

The other the guests got their coats and quietly began to leave, bidding Gilda and their hostess good night. Ted and Chuck told David they'd take care of packing up the equipment in the morning, and David, still attached to his iPod, left with the others.

Only Christie and her family and Doris and Franny remained.

Franny looked confused. "Then we didn't have a murder tonight?"

Doris removed her feather headband and took off her dangly earrings. "No, we didn't, but we sure got a solid solution. Come on, Franny, I'll take you home."

Gilda's eyes settled on Amy, now sitting quietly with her new boyfriend. "Looks like we've got an extra room tonight,"

Gilda told the couple. "It would be a good way for you two to start off a New Year together, and with your family," she said, knowing how much it would mean to Christie to have both of her daughters in a solid relationship.

"We'd like that," Amy's young man said graciously, hugging Amy who beamed.

Christie murmured "Thank you," but Kendra just rolled her eyes, and snuggled up to Chuck.

Christie's family headed for the upstairs, and she stopped for one last word with Gilda.

"No more apologies," Gilda told her. "In the back of my mind, I alway knew there was something unsettled, unfinished here. I hate it that Guy had to die like that, when someone he trusted as a friend betrayed him, but I'd rather know the truth and that Guy is at peace at last, then wonder why it happened the rest of my life. He'll always be here with me."

"And you'll have me and every person within the sound of my voice supporting you to be sure you turn the Wild Willow into the most popular overnight and dining destination in the County. That's my promise," Christie said.

"That's good enough for me," Gilda replied as they parted at the stairs, Christie heading up, and Gilda returning to the place where she knew that Guy's spirit would always be waiting for her.

THE END

One Bite of the Apple

RoseMary McDaniel a.k.a. Amy Hayle

Jason returns to his hometown after college to try and revive the faded tradition of a family apple orchard and farm. But could his old Uncle Ed be right - has the magic that made the Fruithills famous for abundant fruit been lost?

What would it take to get it back in this place that has never lost its ties to a spirit-filled past??

Author's note: Although the stories have been inspired by some actual places and events in history, they are all a product of the author's imagination and not intended to represent any persons, living or dead.

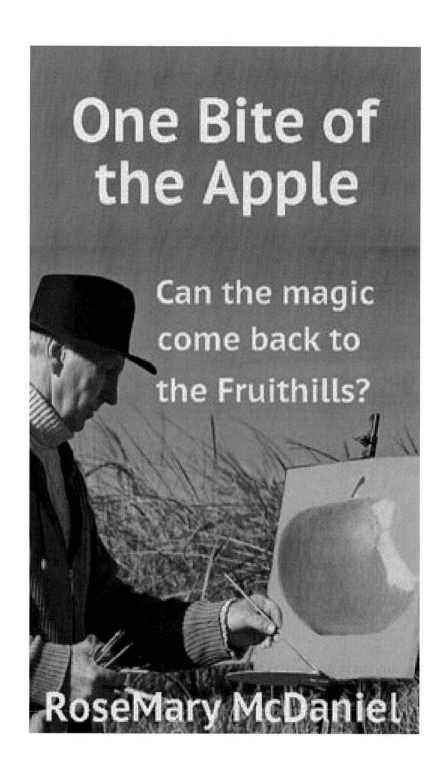

One Bite of the Apple

Can the magic come back to the Fruithills?

RoseMary McDaniel

One Bite of the Apple

RoseMary McDaniel a.k.a. Amy Hayle

"It's like the difference between Good and Evil, my boy," the old man said, when asked about farm life of yesterday and today. He took an ancient pipe out of his mouth and waved it about, then replaced it between his craggy yellow teeth. It was empty, of course, just a habit now. He'd stopped smoking long ago.

His great-great-nephew Jason inched his chair a little closer to his Uncle Ed, wanting to be sure that the older man's 97-year-old ears caught all their conversation.

"Why do you want to know about the history of the Fruithills, anyway?" Uncle Ed continued.

"I bought a little farmette south on State Road 15, sir," Jason began. "There are about a dozen old apple trees left there, and I know that area and the hills above were a prime area for raising fruit in the early days."

The old man's reply was something like a snort. "Bah, ain't no farmettes, only truck farms or commercial operations left around here," he said. "You want to know what made my old Pappy's place such a success, and my time at farming such a failure that I eventually just up and sold the land? Well, I'll tell you. The magic was gone. I didn't have a Clara."

"Clara?"

"Yep, my Pappy's first wife. Came over from Europe she did, and not Ireland or Germany like the most of them who settled here, but from some far-off place, up in them dark mountains. She had the magic."

"How was that?"

"She was a wise-woman, they said, tended herbs and made potions. Hair dark as midnight piled in braids high on her head and eyes like two burning coals. She and several sisters who came here, married some of the old farmers and served up the magic that made those farms spread into acres and acres of bountiful fruits and vegetables, and later the apples, of course, always the apples."

"You mean she cast some kind of spell to make that happen?" Jason asked in surprise.

"She done something, that's for sure. As long as she was alive and doing what she did, his farm thrived like nobody's business. Once she died, and my Pappy married my mother, it was all down hill from there."

"But there were a lot of other fruit growers around," Jason objected. "They did real well for a long time, too, didn't they?"

"Well enough for the first generation that had married Clara's sisters. It even sometimes lasted through the second," Uncle Ed told him. "But eventually only one of them old-time orchards is still doing business today."

"You mean the one with the new winery?" Jason asked.

"That's it," Uncle Ed replied. "Bound to be one still has the magic."

"I heard the old farms disappeared because the descendants didn't want to deal with all the hard work involved," Jason said. "The hand labor got too expensive to compete with the big commercial growers all around the country, and that caused the market for local stuff to dry up. Eventually, the trains didn't stop here anymore to haul the fruit and produce off to market in the bigger cities."

"Some says that," the old man agreed. "But in my Pappy's case, I was willing to pitch in and do my share. Course, he had to run things his own way, and if you think I'm old, he lived till 105, and managed the place till the day he died. Keeled over in the field and suddenly I was left with it. That was the beginning of the end. Never got me a wife like Clara, and I never had the magic."

Jason sat quietly, thinking, and Uncle Ed looked him straight in the eye.

"What about you, boy?" he asked. "Got a wife for that farmette? And what happened to that college education you were were after?

"Haven't found the right one, yet."Jason said. "And I just graduated from the agricultural college last year. I recently took a job with the County Extension Office and then the opportunity came to buy my own place."

"Fancy learning, eh? Well, that might help you grow the beans, corn and lettuce," his uncle countered. "Fruit, now that's a whole different animal."

"But the sandy soil and the weather conditions are ideal for it," Jason said.

"So they say. But you still need the magic," Uncle Ed insisted.

Just then, there was a knock at the door.

"It's time for my evening sponge bath and pills," Uncle Ed told Jason. "This sissy living works out O.K. for an old relic like me. Let her in, will you?"

"Assisted living," Jason corrected and laughed. He got up to open the door to a smiling middle-aged woman in a nurse's uniform who carried a tray and a medical bag.

"Run along now, boy," Uncle Ed said, turning his attention to the woman. "Come back later and let me know how that 'farmette' works out."

Jason bid him goodbye and left the facility. Driving his aging Ford pickup back to his own farm, he thought about what his uncle had told him. Surely hard work, education and genuine effort would still pay off today with the renewed interest in natural and organic foods and the desire of people to know where the products on their tables came from. Apples from Michigan or Oregon were all right, but nothing beat the ones grown right here in the famed Fruithills.

He remembered times from his childhood, when his mother would take him every fall to one of the few remaining apple orchards in the area where you could pick your own right off the tree. It had been a family tradition until he'd gone off to college. When he'd graduated last year and come back to live in the little town at the foot of the Fruithills, his parents had already retired to the Ozark Mountains, near Branson, Missouri, and only one picking orchard was left.

Undeterred, he had searched for his own ideal spot and heard about it, by chance, when chatting with some locals at the downtown breakfast and lunch cafe. The older men were lamenting about the upscale housing development built high in the Fruithills that had replaced the acres and acres of apple orchards and even earlier strawberry fields that had been ripped away, once the last old owner had died and the land sold, with no family left willing to undertake the burden of running such an operation.

A large man in a weather-beaten straw hat mentioned that one of the last few small farms was going up for sale soon, since the owner was finally retiring at the age of 79.

Jason took note of the location, and drove there right after breakfast that day. Mr. Echols, who lived alone, was delighted to have a visitor who'd listen to his stories about the old days and join him in a cup of strong black coffee.

"My daughter says I shouldn't drink the stuff, cause it ain't good for me," he told Jason. "But at my age, I can't see it makes no difference." He added a heaping spoon of sugar, but Jason took his black.

Once Jason had explained that he wanted to buy a small place in his home town, the farmer enthusiastically took him out to tour the gardens and orchard after they finished the coffee. Using a cane for balance, the old man made his way across the field to the rows of gnarled trees.

"Here are my girls," he said, patting a branch on a nearby tree. The leaves were just appearing as it was early spring. "They may not be good-looking, but they still pour beauty every year into their apples."

"I'd imagine you hate to give it up," Jason said, his eyes sweeping down over the dozen or so trees.

"Indeed I do," the old man replied. "But my daughter insists that I come to live with her just outside town and take up some new hobby like oil painting. Her man's dead and kids grown and scattered. She pretends she wants my company, but I know that she just wants to get me under her eye and away from all this." He shook his head, but looked up at Jason.

"You think you can make a go of this, sonny?" he asked.

"I'd sure like to try," Jason told him.

And that was that. The property wasn't even on the market yet, so Jason had no competition, and the old man set a very fair price. Jason was able to cover the downpayment with a small legacy from his grandmother, and get a mortgage from the customer-friendly local bank based on his new job. In a surprisingly short time, he was the new owner of the property.

He helped the old man move what he wanted to take and what his daughter agreed would fit in her home. He left behind quite a bit of furniture, household items and equipment.

"All part of the deal," he told Jason. "No good to me anymore, and don't want the bother of a sale for what little I'd get for it. If you can use the stuff, it's all yours."

Jason was glad to leave the small furnished apartment he'd rented and move into a rural home all ready with most everything he'd need to set up housekeeping..

The barn and outbuildings also had a lifetime's worth of equipment for farming, well-used and not new, but as he climbed on the vintage Farmall tractor and fired it up to hear the welcoming roar, he felt as if he had truly come home.

After that, he'd gone to see his Uncle Ed, not so much for advice, perhaps, but to reassure himself that he was making the right choice in getting back to the land as a farmer, at least part-time. He wasn't sure that what he'd learned from him had been particularly helpful, but at least he now felt he was being realistic about his endeavor. It wasn't going to be easy, he knew.

Jason's first few months on what he now thought of as his home place were filled with ups and downs. By the time he had moved in that spring, it was almost too late to plant a lot of crops, but after work and on weekends, he put in small patches of corn, beans, lettuce, and other vegetables, adding a few strawberry and raspberry plants as well.

Although the year had been reasonably seasonable with moisture in the winter before, the spring got drier and drier. He didn't have any irrigation system so hoses had to suffice for any additional water for the crops. He just about given up on having any yields at all that season, when a change in the weather brought frequent and steady rains to at least save his plants although the yield might be less.

As for the apple trees, they seemed to be doing well. Jason had sprayed the trees, as the old man had suggested, and all he could do was wait for the harvest. But by midsummer, it was apparent that the trees were not developing much fruit.

Jason went late one weekend morning to visit the former owner now living with his daughter. Jason found Mr. Echols out in the back yard sitting at an easel painting a picture of an apple with a big bite out of it."

He looked up and smiled as Jason approached, and waved him closer.

"That looks very real," Jason said, taking a closer look.

"My daughter likes to paint scenery or portraits, but I'd

rather paint what I know." The older man grinned. "Apples are still what I know best."

"That's what I came to ask you about, Jason said, sitting in a nearby lawn chair. "The trees don't seem to be developing much fruit."

"Could just be the weather this year," the other man told him. "Good rains not coming until late. Last year's crop was pretty big, so it may just be lighter this year. That's part of the ups and downs of it."

After they chatted for a few minutes and shared a cup of sun-tea, Jason thanked him for his advice, and said goodbye as his mentor turned back to his easel.

Jason felt a bit down when he left. Perhaps his Uncle Ed was right. Maybe it really did matter that he didn't have the magic. It was discouraging.

Suddenly, he laughed aloud and shook his head in disbelief at what he'd just been thinking. With his education, he should know to concentrate on the scientific evidence of why things occur and how to compensate, and not be influenced by superstition.

Just then the noon siren on the local fire station sounded its daily reminder, and Jason decided that he might just as well stop in town at the local cafe for lunch. The usual retiree table was empty, and Jason remembered that it was the week of the County Fair, so the whole restaurant was deserted.

He sat at the counter and smiled at the pretty new waitress with the bouncy dark pony tail and soft brown eyes, as she gave him a welcoming grin.

"Glad to see you come in," she said. "Kind of slow today with everybody at the County Fair. I'm minding the store for my cousins who never miss going."

"I'd forgotten it started this weekend," Jason agreed, glancing at the menu.

"Would you like today's special?" she asked. "It's a roast beef sandwich with mashed potatoes and gravy."

"Sounds great," he said.

"Would you like a salad or coleslaw with that?"

"No, I don't think so," he replied.

"How about cottage cheese, or maybe the apple sauce. It's good, I made it myself from local apples."

"Apple sauce would be O.K.," Jason agreed.

After he'd been served, he found that his appetite had returned. The meal was really tasty. He saved the applesauce for dessert.

"This tastes terrific," he said to her, as he finished it. "Just the right amount of spices. Thanks for the suggestion. Haven't had anything this good since our last family reunion."

"You live around here?" she asked.

"Got a little farm outside town. I'm trying to raise apples that I hope taste like this. I'm Jason," he said, remembering his manners.

"My family lived here when I was little," she told him. "My grandfather had an orchard, too. I spent every summer there as a child. Grandpa used to call me his lucky charm. My older cousins have taken over the orchard, added a winery and own the cafe in town here as well. Guess I was homesick, so I've come back to help out in the restaurant while I get a degree in herbal medicine."

She reached out to shake his hand. "My name is Claire."

Jason smiled at the touch of her hand in his. "Would you like to go to the Fair with me tonight?" he asked on impulse, the taste of the sweet applesauce lingering in his mouth.

She didn't hesitate. "You bet," she said, meeting his smile with one of her own.

And then he knew. It had taken Adam and Eve only one bite of the Apple to gain forbidden knowledge, but it took him a whole dish full to understand that maybe just bringing Claire into his life might not restore all the magic, but it couldn't hurt to try. He was sure Uncle Ed would approve."

THE END

Rebecca's Journey

RoseMary McDaniel a.k.a. Amy Hayle

Haunted by a persistent presence since childhood, Becky Ann felt compelled to take a journey to her past in the small Fruithills village where she was born nearly 30 years before. Whisked away as an infant by a flower-child mother to California, she felt a renewed pull to that faraway place, when a distant cousin revealed forgotten family history.

What awaited her there was echoed in something that she sought, or that sought her in a place that has never lost its ties to a spirit-filled past.

Author's note: Although the stories have been inspired by some actual places and events in history, they are all a product of the author's imagination and not intended to represent any persons, living or dead.

Rebecca's Journey

RoseMary McDaniel

Rebecca's Journey

RoseMary McDaniel a.k.a. Amy Hayle

Ever since I was a child, in the back of my mind, there was a presence always with me, surfacing when I was least aware, often just as I dropped off to sleep. It generally comforted, rather than frightened me; yet as I grew older, those feelings returned more frequently.

Later as an adult, at work, as I focused on my computer screen, I would glance to my right, feeling someone beside me, just out of view. Instinctively I knew that it was a she, though how I gained that knowledge, I did not know. By gaining my attention, she had insured that I acknowledged her presence.

Sometimes, it was a power struggle between us, but I instinctively knew that her power was greater than my own. For now, she was content to be a silent observer, knowing that sooner or later, I might ease my guard and let her in. I struggled to keep my own identify intact.

Born Becky Ann, in a small Fruithills town, nearly thirty years ago, I had been whisked away to California as an infant by a flower-child mother, wilting in the traditional life of a small, mid-western town. Orphaned early, I had had no contact with my past, until I received an intriguing family tree e-mailed to me by a distant cousin. It outlined five generations of our family nestled together in the quiet countryside It told of a cemetery called Bonneyville, in that small Indiana Fruithills community, where the matriarch, my great-great-grandmother named Rebecca was buried.

At 28, single and bored with my job as a lawyer in San Francisco, I felt an urge to visit the ghosts of my past. It sparked a compelling urge to plan an impromptu trip into history. So I tied an early November vacation to a business trip to Chicago.

I rented a car and drove three hours down the Toll Road Main Street of the Midwest, exiting to follow the directions to the little village where I was born. I cruised down the main street of the town in the late afternoon, and took in the sights. The few stores and restaurants were doing a brisk business, and traffic was steady.

I followed the state highway east where, according to the map. I would go by the Bonneyville Mill Park and then find the cemetery itself. In only a few minutes, I had passed from bustling little town to peaceful back roads. The old Mill glowed a bright red in the late sunshine, and I longed to stop. Later, I promised myself. Now, I had a mission.

I pressed on toward the graveyard, down black-topped roads lined with nearly bare trees that rose and dipped from the many hills. My only observers were cows, black and reddish brown, who lay in the fields, blissfully re-enjoying their morning's meal.

Arriving at my destination, I parked at the edge of the cemetery where a rustic iron fence surrounded it, and only a creaking gate with a high metal arch spanning above it that spelled out "Bonneyville Cemetery," signaled my entrance.

Just inside the gate was the monument of the most famous citizen of this city of the dead, William Tufts, Revolutionary War Veteran, who stood sentinel over the sleeping residents. Only the calls of birds and clicks of crickets could be heard above the crackling of leaves beneath my feet as I walked the narrow pathways between the aged stones.

I consulted the paper in my hand to look for the graves of all of my ancestors, grandparents, great-grand parents, and so on. The first on my list, and supposedly one of the oldest burials in the cemetery was Rebecca Barrett Bacon Sanger, my great-great grandmother.

Dying in 1861, this immigrant from Connecticut was my first link to this place. Her biography, included with the family tree, said that she was a tailor, and the footnote referencing a photo revealed that my cousin still had the huge shears that she had used to ply her trade. Another old photo, digitally transferred to me, had shown Rebecca herself late in life, in shades of gray, wizened and very grim.

But as I stood there, drinking in the crisp early November scent, a breeze stirred like a silent sigh, that familiar feeling came over me. Then I knew that Rebecca was not the grim old woman of the photo, but a strong and robust creature whose essence had survived the long sleep of the grave. Rebecca had been waiting for me. She waited, having learned the patience of more than a century of time.

I knelt in front of her stone, and brushed away the moss that clung to it. An electric surge passed from the stone to my hand. Rebecca was with me. I wandered about the pathways, checking the other inscriptions, identifying those who connected me with the past. But it was Rebecca who remained in my mind.

Random thoughts brought me snippets of her life that I had not learned from my cousin, knowledge that sprang spontaneously into my mind. Rebecca had been the undisputed matriarch of the family in Connecticut. It had been she who had decided, at an advanced age to seek the adventure of the West, and it was she who had commandeered her family to take her there. Indiana had been as far as she was able to go.

In that instant, I realized that she had felt cheated when an illness had ended her life. One by one, her family had followed her here, to the final resting place where they would be together forever. Most had been ready for their last sleep, tired of the struggle. But not she. Rebecca was waiting. For me.

A soft breeze blew over my head, surprisingly warm for the weather, and I stood up, took a few photos and left the cemetery. I headed back to the deserted Mill Park and sat on a bench by the edge of the Mill pond, to grapple with the rush of thoughts that had seized me that day.

Then I walked and walked and thought and thought, and the stillness of the moment was overpowered by the spirits of the past. I was haunted then, I am haunted still.

The interaction with the resting place of Rebecca has shaken me to my soul. Within my veins, though weakened by the many generations that separated us, flowed the blood and strength of a true pioneer.

It was nearly dark when I drove back to town to the bed and breakfast where I had booked a room for the night. Alone in my room, I recorded my impressions and wrote the words that I pledged to myself.

I will carry with me always the beauty of the place that I've never called home. Tomorrow, I will leave this place behind, but I will carry away her spirit. I am compelled to set her free where she can seek the adventure in the West she had only dreamed about.

I make the final decision, look to the right, consciously, and let Rebecca in. The integration is complete. We are one, bringing full-circle to the cycle of life. We begin together at last, Rebecca's journey to the west and to the future.

THE END

Tie a Knot & Hang On

RoseMary McDaniel a.k.a. Amy Hayle

Haunted by a love of reading inspired by her nurturing Aunt Belle, Director Natalie Drew fought to keep her small library relevant and funded to meet technology and maintenance challenges. A simple act of respect triggered help from beyond earthly life.

This story of a small Fruithills Town examines the connections between people and circumstances and the ties that bind them together, in a place that has never lost its ties to a spirit-filled past.

Author's note: Although the stories have been inspired by some actual places and events in history, they are all a product of the author's imagination and not intended to represent any persons, living or dead.

TIE A KNOT
...AND HANG ON

RoseMary McDaniel

Tie a Knot and Hang on

RoseMary McDaniel a.k.a. Amy Hayle

She didn't look very well, and frankly she didn't smell very good either. But Library Director Natalie Drew felt a tug at her heartstrings every time she heard the soft jingle of a chime as the front door opened, and Sadie Hopkins came inside. She would edge sideways into the foyer, usually catching her frayed shopping bag on the door frame as she struggled to hang on to the bag and propel herself inside the main section right by the check out desk.

The desk clerks got very busy in the rear of the book sorting area, until Sadie had passed by the counter on her way to a table at the very back of the library where Natalie kept a special washable cushion on the chair that Sadie always used, and even took it home with her in the evening each time Sadie visited the library. Sadie would spend long hours in that chair, reading book after book.

"Good heavens, Nat," her assistant Jill would say when she saw the Director tuck the cushion into a pre-used plastic grocery bag and set it by her desk so she wouldn't forget to take it with her. "You don't just go the second mile for customer service; you literally take in their washing as well!"

But Natalie only shrugged and smiled. It wouldn't have done any good to respond anyway. The others just didn't understand. When she was a little girl, she had a very old great aunt that lived with her grandmother. Aunt Belle was well taken care of by the family, but they mostly ignored her, except for attending to her physical needs.

Natalie even at seven or eight was an old soul. She'd taught herself to read at four and always had a book under her arm or beneath her nose. Whenever her mother brought her along to grandmother's house, she would quietly go off to see Aunt Belle in her little back bedroom, crawl up on the bed, get a hug that smelled like camphor and then read aloud from her latest book.

If Aunt Belle wasn't a fan of the Adventures of the Boxcar Children, she never let on; and her gentle smile and nod of approval when Natalie was finished, was the best encouragement the little girl ever got.

Her parents, concerned she'd ruin her eyes or something usually tried to pry her away from reading so much, but Aunt Belle, a dedicated reader herself, had been a helper in the Town library years before, so she encouraged Natalie to indulge her love of the printed word. The time spent with her Aunt was one of her best childhood memories.

"There's something noble about reading," Aunt Belle would always say. "It makes a good person, an even better one."

And as she grew older, Natalie found that her peers who loved to read were the ones who could be counted on and who were the most positive influence on others.

Aunt Belle lived a long time and died the year before Natalie went away to college, and was in fact one of the reasons Natalie was able to go to a premier college and get her Master of Library Science degree. Aunt Belle had never married, had no children, and left her bank account, which had grown considerably over the years, to Natalie for her education.

Sometimes she wondered what Aunt Belle would think of all the changes in the way people read today, but Natalie was sure she would have approved and been one of the first to have an electronic reading device.

"You don't get anything accomplished by sticking your head in the sand," Aunt Belle would tell her. "You have to keep up and keep learning."

Natalie still missed her, and she supposed that Sadie reminded her of her own elderly Aunt. The thought that Sadie loved reading so much that she'd struggle her way down the long blocks to the library meant that she needed to be treated with respect and dignity, even if the other staff thought Natalie was crazy to do it.

She knew that the library must be a sort of haven for Sadie who lived alone in a run-down house on a corner bit of ground near the laundromat. From the decaying overstuffed couch on the front porch to the neglected yard and garden in the rear, the property was viewed with disdain by many neighbors and passersby.

Occasionally, some group would take up Sadie's property as a summer service project, but the effort was temporary at best.

Fortunately, a small town was more likely to tolerate its eccentric neighbors than larger communities, as long as the house wasn't considered unsafe for habitation. Sadie wasn't very neighborly, anyway, and most people tended to ignore her, which appeared to be her preference as well.

But Natalie with her soft spot for people like Sadie, provided her with a comfortable chair, situated as far from the busy part of the library as possible, near the rear of the building, not far from Natalie's little library office. Natalie would occasionally leave an unopened bottle of water and a store-wrapped snack on the table when Sadie was gone on one of her perpetual restroom visits.

Upon her return, Sadie would consume them without a word after a quick look and nod in the direction of the window of the office where Natalie did her paperwork.

The situation was static as the year drew to a close, but as the winter weather brought ice and snow, Natalie became preoccupied with a big problem. The aging library roof was leaking badly in several spots as snow on the roof turned to ice and then melted when the weather moderated between freezing and thawing as it seemed to do in the midwestern valley below the Fruithills where the library was located.

She'd had to block off a back section of shelves under some high windows, remove the books and place a few buckets for drips. The library maintenance purse was pretty empty. What was budgeted for repairs had been used to repair the aging parking lot last summer and the few pennies left couldn't be squeezed enough to pay for getting the roof fixed. Not until next spring would they get an infusion into those funds and that was a whole lot of winter away. She only hoped it wouldn't get worse.

Then she received a disturbing call from the Library Board President who had received complaints about the leaks from some of the other board members. If the situation becomes unsafe, he told her; they might have to close the library until something was resolved, perhaps lay off some of the staff to save the money for repairs.

Natalie was horrified. She felt personally responsible, as if she had failed in her mission to keep the library a viable resource for the people of the community.

For the next week or so, she was distracted dealing with the leaks and trying to think of a way to find some funds to fix the problem. She got quotes from several local contractors, but even the lowest, from one who had done work for the library before and was known to be very reasonable, over $3,000.

Natalie had no idea how she could come up with that much money. Even next year's budget didn't have that big a line item for repair. Without a permanent fix, the use of a large section of the library would be curtailed and could lead to much greater damage, she knew.

But laying off staff would also cause hardship for the clerks, one of whom was a widow, and another a single mother. Keeping the library on solid financial footing was a constant struggle anyway, with cuts in funding and the necessity to keep current with technology that changed with the needs of those who used the library.

She closed her eyes and directed a silent plea for a way to fund this much needed work. Her eyes popped open as she realized that anyone passing would assume she was sleeping or at the very least praying on public time. She sighed and put the quotes in her desk drawer. Then a favorite saying from Aunt Belle suddenly flashed across her mind.

"When you've come to the end of your rope, tie a knot and hang on."

She recalled that Aunt Belle had always encouraged her to "Wait on the Lord," and that sometimes you didn't even have to make a decision; someone else would do something that would make it for you. She shut the drawer and went back to work. For now, that was all that she could do.

Then, fortunately the weather turned warm again, and there was a quick thaw. Once the ice had melted and dripped through, and the mess cleaned up, the problem lessened, at least until the next storm.

It was then she realized she hadn't seen Sadie in several weeks, so she asked her assistant, Jill, if perhaps she'd just missed seeing her.

"You sure have been out of it," Jill told her, taking a section from the previous weekend's newspaper off the rack and turning to

177

the back page. To Natalie's dismay, she saw a nearly week-old obituary for Sadie.

"I've even missed the funeral!" Natalie said aloud.

"Look again," said Jill. "There wasn't one. There were no surviving relatives put in a crypt she'd bought some time ago out at the cemetery."

Natalie was devastated; it was like she had failed by not being there at the end, although she knew it likely would have made no difference.

"Don't take it so hard," one of the other clerks told her. "She's better off… "

"Well, I'm not," Natalie said with uncharacteristic anger. "And I hate it when people say that."

The other library employees tip-toed away, and Natalie went into her office and shut the door. She regretted that she had lashed out at the others, but by the time she had cooled down and stopped pouring over paperwork, they had all gone home. She'd apologize tomorrow.

It was late, and time for her to go, too, she thought. Then, she heard the soft chime of the entrance door, and peered out the window toward the front of the building, but saw that no one had come in.

Suddenly, she realized that someone was standing by the chair where Sadie always sat. The person's back was toward her; and in a shabby brown coat and tattered black turban style hat, it looked like an elderly woman: like Sadie. But that was impossible.

Then the figure turned to face the window, and Natalie saw in the dim night mode lights, the face of her old Aunt Belle. Next to her, seated in the familiar chair, was Sadie, holding the seat cushion in her hands. Both woman were nodding their heads and smiling.

Natalie blinked, took off her glasses and then put them back on. She looked out the window again, and both figures were gone. Moving slowly as if in a trance, Natalie got up, went out her door and walked over to the table where Sadie's chair was tucked under the table.

She pulled it out and picked up the cushion. It seemed heavier, thicker. She placed the cushion on the table and unzipped the removable cover.

Several thick packets secured with twine and knotted tightly, fell on the tabletop. She thumbed through the stacks of old $20 and $50 dollar bills, and calculated that there was nearly $5,000 there. A note was carefully tucked under the tie of one of the stacks of bills. In careful script on a torn half piece of stationery, were the words: "For this library to use for whatever needs the library may have." It was signed, simply, Sadie Hopkins and dated 2 weeks previously.

Natalie held the note in her hand and sat down in the chair opposite Sadie's. Who could know that someone who seemed as poor as Sadie could have accumulated so much. Natalie had heard the stories of older people who hoarded their money rather than spend it, but she never would have suspected it of Sadie. She tucked the bundles back inside the cushion cover, chuckling to herself as she looked at Sadie's knots that secured the bundles.

Tie a knot and hang on, indeed; Sadie certainly knew how to hold on to what what little she had; and saving and leaving it to the library had been more important than providing comforts for herself.

Natalie took the cushion back into her office and picked up the phone. She'd need to report her find to the local police, but if things worked out the way that she felt that Sadie and Aunt Belle wanted them to, it would come out all right in the end, and Natalie's hope of fixing the roof and saving the library from further damage and not having to reduce the staff would be possible.

She smiled, picturing Aunt Belle and Sadie together in some great Celestial library sitting and chatting together.

Beginning with their love of reading, she'd bet they had an eternity's worth of things to talk about.

THE END

When Willis Walks

RoseMary McDaniel a.k.a. Amy Hayle

When his westbound train had an unexpected layover in the small midwestern town that had been his boyhood home, a man haunted by memories of his older brother's mysterious disappearance, seeks to uncover the hidden past and find the answer to a mystery buried for over 50 years in this small town in the Fruithills, a place that has never lost its ties to a spirit-filled past.

Author's note: Although the stories have been inspired by some actual places and events in history, they are all a product of the author's imagination and not intended to represent any persons, living or dead.

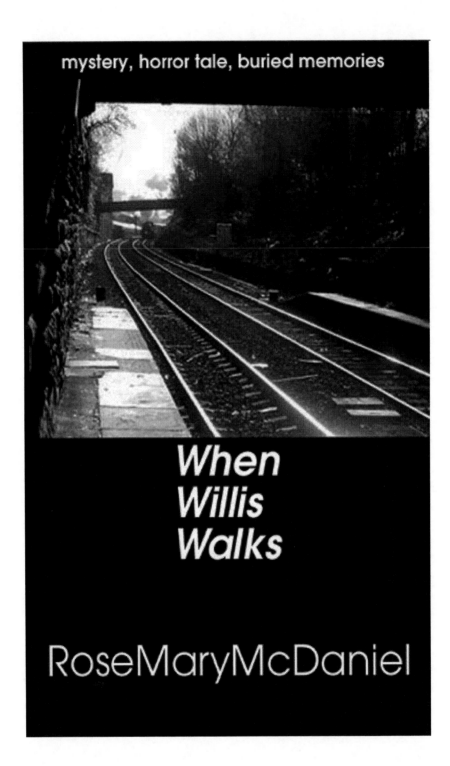

mystery, horror tale, buried memories

When
Willis
Walks

RoseMaryMcDaniel

When Willis Walks

RoseMary McDaniel a.k.a. Amy Hayle

Now that every footstep brings me closer, the madness of it still drives me on, in spite of the chill wind and the biting sleet. Although it is but mid-afternoon, it feels like midnight. Only the crunch of the snow beneath my feet breaks through the silence. Here on this dull winter day of 1970, at last having found the courage to come this far, I cannot turn back until I have satisfied the morbid curiosity that has nagged at me for nearly fifty years.

The unexpected layover of my westbound train in this small Fruithills town that had been my boyhood home was the final impetus that sends me in furious pursuit of God himself knows what. As I leave the boarding house where I had spent the night to walk the lonely streets deserted by more prudent souls who have stayed in the warm refuge of their homes, I am amazed to find how little the town has changed.

My progress is slowed, hampered by a freezing slush, but restrained as well by the weight of the years that have changed me from a callow youth to a man, now nearly sixty years of age. The obsession rooted in the last tragic year that I spent in this small rural community, though dimmed by time and distance, has never left me completely. Now, as I near the edge of town and draw ever closer to that damned and deserted place, the primal scene marking all that came after, I feel the same fear and apprehension that was my near-constant companion when I was but a seven-year-old child.

That fateful year was 1920, and it changed my life. Little did I dream that my twelve-years-older brother Davis, in devising his foolish scheme for us to steal a pumpkin from Neighbor Jackson's field would have set us on a downward path that had no return.

Always the weaker one, always afraid, I had wanted no part of Davis and his daring plan. But once again, Davis won the upper hand, and I followed him, shivering from both fear and the frigid wind that blew with unrelenting fervor across the dark frosty fields.

Our subsequent flight from the field, pumpkins in hand, with Mr. Jackson close on our heels was what had led us into the tangled thicket that lay just outside the cemetery fence. We had crouched in anxious concealment until Mr. Jackson, brandishing his shotgun, had finally given up in disgust. I probably would have waited there all night, fearing Mr. Jackson's imminent return, but Davis, always more impatient, urged our return home. Chilled to the bone, I was easily persuaded to follow.

As I got to my feet, Davis, with glee pointed out the damp piece of stone on which we had been kneeling.. The dull gray surface, cut with crude lettering was now visible in a patch of misty moonlight.

He traced his fingers again and again over the rough-carved single word,"WILLIS." He gave me an evil grin. "You know who this is, don't you, buried here in disgrace, outside the cemetery?" he asked.

I hopped up quickly as if burned. "It's a grave?"

Davis laughed again with the dark lilt that I had noticed in his voice the last year or so. "That's what it is, sissy!"

And I was out of that thicket like a shot! I would probably have completely forgotten the incident, but for Davis and his incessant taunting of me: how scared I'd looked and what a baby I was. I'd certainly wanted to forget it—for I'd never heard of anyone named Willis, and I didn't want to think about him or wonder why his grave was there. I knew, however, that it was not normal for someone to be buried outside the cemetery proper. Mother's relentless shaping our of spiritual lives was always highlighted with weekly Sunday church attendance. The hell and brimstone preaching was lavishly peppered with references to sin and its consequences.

While I was still a faithful adherent to the regimen, Davis found more and more excuses to attend less and less often. Mother's oft-expressed concerns fell on deaf ears as Davis became more interested in his town friends and activities and less willing to participate in our family routines.

It was not until a few weeks later, just before Christmas, that my curiosity had been piqued by a bit of information overheard when Aunt Hattie, Mother's sister, had visited us from out East.

I'd spend most of the cold, snowy evenings by the coal stove in the kitchen, pretending to do my schoolwork, while Aunt Hattie and Mother chatted over their chores. They'd talked mostly about family news and some about Davis spending too much time away from the farm in "dubious" company. I paid little attention to their conversations that mostly rehashed old stories that I'd heard many times.But one night, a casual remark by my mother caused me to listen with renewed interest.

"Ach, Harry," Mother had said, her Germanic roots still poking about the edges of her speech as she spoke intimately to her beloved younger sister, "Old Mrs. Turner is finally gone; God rest her soul!"

Aunt Hattie sniffed with disdain as she replied, "Died of a broken heart, that's for sure."

Mother stopped kneading a loaf of bread and shook her head sadly. "She held out 'till the very end, waiting, it seemed."

"The only one in Leesburg that still believed that boy innocent, no doubt," Aunt Hattie agreed.

"She swore her boy was not a murderer or a thief," Mother confirmed."For over a year, she didn't hear a word from him."

"But when they found him dead last fall, and none of the money was found…" Aunt Hattie's voice trailed off.

Mother had nodded. "She refused to believe he had taken his own life, and she never got over it. Why, she declared until the day she died, that Willis would somehow rise out of his grave, come back to her, and clear his name."

Just then, Mother must have realized how attentively I had been listening, and with a knowing look to Aunt Hattie, changed the subject. But I'd thought about their comments, long after they'd gone on to talk of other things.

The little town of Leesburg wouldn't seem so far away now, but then my whole world encompassed only a few miles and I hadn't ever been there. I'd never heard of Mrs. Turner or her son Willis, but the emotion in my mother's voice and my frightening experience with Davis had made an impression on me that did not soon pass.

That night, after Davis had come home, and we'd gone to bed in our drafty attic room, I'd made the mistake of repeating to

184

him what I'd overheard Mother saying to Aunt Hattie.

He'd laughed and gave me a wicked leer as he shucked off his thick wool pants, the legs stiff with frozen snow. I'd turned my head to avoid his breath that smelled so strongly of spirits, but he'd not denied knowledge of Willis.

After that, it became his favorite subject for ridiculing me. Whenever he was annoyed, which was often, he'd bring up Willis' name. I'd cover my ears, but Davis would beat on me, until I gave up and took my hands away. Then he'd whisper, "When Willis walks... "

The holidays came and went, and Aunt Hattie returned home. We had a brief January thaw, and the afternoon air turned balmy, almost springlike. I was playing in the barn loft with one of the farm cats and her new litter of kittens.

The sun streaming in through the loose fitting wall boards cast beams of warmth on the hay. I lay back in the scratchy softness and lazily watched the dust motes floating in the sunshine, felt the kittens romping up and down on top of me and heard the contented purr of their mother as she snuggled up against my arm. I must have fallen asleep. I woke up to the sound of digging in the ground in one of the stalls beneath me.

Carefully moving a bit of hay on the floor of the loft so that I could see through a wide space in the boards, I saw Davis almost directly below me, shoveling dirt from a corner of the empty stall. After he stopped digging, he hunched over, and his back blocked my view of what he was doing. A few minutes later, I heard the scattering sound of dirt being thrown, the clang of the shovel being set against the wall, and the creak of the closing barn door.

I remained quiet for a few more minutes. Davis hadn't seen me, I was sure, and I'd been avoiding him as much as possible. Finally, my curiosity got the better of me, and gently unburdening myself of the clutch of kittens and their mother, I hurried down the loft ladder.

The soil was soft and loosened now in the spot where he had been digging, and it didn't take me long to brush it away to reveal a small metal box. "Leesburg Bank," was embossed on the front. I rubbed my fingers over the now gritty letters. Cautiously I opened the unsecured lid. Inside was a stack of paper money and many coins.

A pang of fear went through me, and I quickly closed the box and carefully reburied it, replacing the covering of earth. I left the barn in a hurry; I was terrified.

Why was Davis hiding all that money? From where had the box come? From the Leesburg bank was the obvious answer, but the implications of that line of thinking were almost beyond my young comprehension. I only knew that the connection between this box, Davis, and Leesburg caused an aching deep in my stomach that wouldn't go away. I tried to put the thought out of my mind, but it would come, unbidden, whenever I let down my conscious guard.

One morning a few days later before school as I ate my bowl of oatmeal, Davis came in, cold and out of sorts after doing the morning chores. He didn't speak to me at first. He just poured a mugful of the deep, dark-brewed coffee that only he and Father drank. He warmed his hands around the mug and finally looked across the table at me. I was aware of his scrutiny, but I didn't look up to meet his eyes.

"There's the little sissy," he began. "Want to go out and look for Willis this afternoon? Want to go out by the graveyard?"

I didn't reply, and Mother's arrival in the kitchen effectively ended the exchange.

But late in the afternoon, when I had returned from school, Davis surprised me in the barnyard as I struggled to use a saw of Father's to cut a bit of wood for a carving project. Startled, I broke a tooth out of the saw. Davis pounced in triumph.

"Got'cha! Broke it, didn't you? Well, I won't tell Father this time, if you'll come with me to visit Willis," he pronounced in an ominous tone of voice.

For a moment I was frozen with indecision. I couldn't decide if I was more afraid of incurring Father's wrath or going with Davis. Finally, I chose what seemed to be the lesser of two evils, and I reluctantly dogged his heels. But when we got to the edge of the fence row, I refused to enter the underbrush and clung defiantly to a post of the cemetery fence.

"I'll bring him out to you," Davis taunted me and laughed as he pushed back the branches and disappeared inside. Then there was silence. I waited for what seemed a long, long time.

Then I called to him in a harsh whisper, "Davis? Davis, you in there?"

At last I got up enough courage to peer inside the tangled and shadowy thicket. He was gone. A sharp rush of anger and shame swept over me. He must have slipped out the other side, leaving me alone to scare me.

Twilight was streaking purple across the late winter sky as I hurried off for home. Then I went about my own chores, silently fuming inside about the way that Davis had tricked me. I dreaded thinking how he'd laugh when I saw him, only I didn't see him again – ever.

Davis didn't return that afternoon. I didn't tell anyone where we had gone, although I did confess to father that I had broken his cherished tool. But I received only a brief reprimand, because that minor event had been eclipsed by a larger worry. By the time Davis was missed a newly fallen snow had covered all the tracks we had made, and there was no trace of our afternoon expedition.

Father was angry about Davis' absence, supposing that he'd gone into town with some of his friends who were not welcome on our farm. And nobody thought to ask me. But the next day, when Davis still had not returned, Father himself went to town, and learned that no one there had seen him lately. With the help of men from the other farms, Father and the others had searched high and low for Davis, but they never found anything.

I kept my mouth shut about the rest: Davis's taunts, the events of that last afternoon, and the buried cash box in the barn. When I was finally able to slip away to dig it up, I found that it, too, was missing. The soil had refilled the vacated hole, and it was as if the box had never been there.

Life on our farm grew grimmer, as the realization of Davis's unexplained disappearance settled over our family. Father made little comment, and Mother seemed sadly resolved, but thoughts of Davis were never far from my mind.

They said Mother died of the influenza in the epidemic early the next spring, but I was sure it was the worry over Davis that really killed her. I got the same sickness myself, and was so weak, that Aunt Hattie who had come to care for Mother, despaired of my recovery. The doctor had said that I lost consciousness due to my high fever the day I fell ill, the day that Father brought to my room the new hired man who was to take over the work that Davis had done.

"Just call me Willis," the man had said in a strange voice when Father introduced him to me, and I fainted dead away.

Days later, when I was no longer delirious, they told me that Father had collapsed a few days after I had, but that he never recovered. The new hired man had taken care of the chores for a few weeks; but one day he just announced to Aunt Hattie that he was leaving, and nobody ever saw him again. The farm, of course, was sold, and just as quickly as things could be arranged, I went East to live with Aunt Hattie, with never a backward glance.

And all these years, I've just kept waiting and wondering if I'd ever hear from Davis again. But now that nearly fifty years have passed, and I've finally gotten the chance and courage to return, I must find out the answer, although I fear I already know. Yet, I must be certain, however much I dread the truth.

The sleet has softened now, into big fluffy flakes that fall gently to the ground, obscuring the landscape with a chilling whiteness. The silence is deep, and even my footfalls are without sound. I'm just outside the cemetery fence now, and holding my breath, I push aside the snow filled thicket of branches.

I kneel and brush away the covering of snow. The old square stone is beneath my fingers as I trace the rough, carved letters to spell out what I feared, yet always knew it would: D A V I S...

THE END

Widow's Walk

RoseMary McDaniel a.k.a. Amy Hayle

Alexis knew that her friend Jenna was seeking to invent a history of her own, having never known her real parents. The late 1860's house she insisted on buying was one with a haunting history, but Alexis feared that Jenna was taking on more than just a physical renovation. After all, as Jenna herself had said: "The past is still here."

This small Fruithills town is a place that has never lost ties to a spirit-filled past.

Author's note: Although the stories have been inspired by some actual places and events in history, they are all a product of the author's imagination and not intended to represent any persons, living or dead.

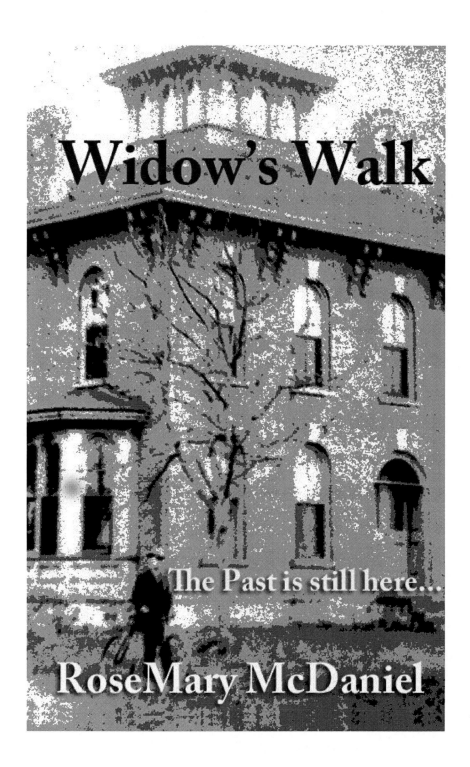

Widow's Walk

The Past is still here...

RoseMary McDaniel

Widow's Walk

RoseMary McDaniel a.k.a. Amy Hayle

The chill January wind swept through the open window and dusted her cheeks with snow that swirled inside, but she didn't move away. Even a harsh voice behind her, failed to stir her from her vigil.

"Drusilla, whatever do you think you're doing? Shut the window," the voice insisted.

When the young woman didn't respond, the owner of the voice surged forward and shut the window herself. The older woman put her arms about the younger, drawing her away from the window. Drusilla didn't speak, her eyes still transfixed on the scene outside. From their perch high above the ground in a structure atop the house that was originally an open platform but which had been enclosed, the view of the land below stretched to the north with a covering of snow that revealed nothing but desolation.

Several hundred feet away, across the deserted road below, lay the ruins of the mill, the sawmill and the furniture factory where her husband and a dozen other men had labored day and night.

"Come, Drusilla," the older woman said, attempting to direct her toward the narrow staircase that led down into the house.

For the first time, the younger woman acknowledged her.

"Minnie, I have to wait for Edward to come home. I always watch for him."

The woman called Minnie drew her into an embrace, as Drusilla buried her head in the ample shoulder of the other woman. Soon Drusilla broke into sobs, and let herself be led slowly to begin her descent down the stairway.

Halfway down, she stopped and stood as if listening. "Do you hear it, Minnie? The music? It must be Edward playing the organ."

She broke away from her escort and quickly ran to the bottom of the stairway, through the door and into the parlor beyond.

Minnie followed quietly, at a slower pace, and arriving in

the parlor, stood in the doorway and watched as Drusilla sat on the edge of the empty bench in front of the organ, and swayed with the sound of the music that only she could hear.

"Oh, Edward, my love" she cried, "You play so beautifully, please don't stop."

There was no one there and the organ was silent.

******

"Open the door, Alexis. I can't wait to see the inside," called the eager voice of the slight blonde woman in the faux fur coat.

"Hold your horses, Jenna," remarked her auburn-haired companion, hands full of paperwork, struggling with the lock box on the front door of the imposing red brick house.

At last she clicked the lock open, and Jenna reached in front of her to turn the knob and was the first inside. "Oh," she said. "I love it already."

"You don't want to buy this house," her companion told her. "It's a dinosaur, needs a boatload of repair, and the owner wants way too much for it."

"But it's historic," Jenna insisted. "It's the place I've always been looking for."

Alexis bit her tongue. She wasn't just Jenna's realtor, helping her find 'the perfect place;' she was her friend. She knew Jenna's own history as an adopted child of a single mother, and who had never known her own parents.

Alexis knew it wasn't just history that Jenna was looking for - she was looking to invent a past for herself. Alexis just shrugged, not anxious to destroy this moment of discovery for her friend.

"What will Jerry say," Alexis finally asked her friend. "He'll have to do a lot of work on the place."

"What do you think I married a guy in construction for, anyway," Jenna said, grinning and rubbing her hands together in glee. "He'll love it."

Alexis wasn't so sure. "It's still overpriced."

"I've got the money that Mom Dinah left me," Jenna said, referring to her adoptive mother who had recently died.

" She intended that for your future," Alexis told her.

"This is my future; the place where I belong," said Jenna.

Alexis knew better than to argue with her friend. All she could do was try to negotiate the best deal possible with the seller, an elderly woman in a nursing home who placed too high a value on the old place. But she also knew that the woman's only living relative, a twenty-something granddaughter, was anxious to sell the property and get the money into the estate, which she managed.

Alexis sighed and followed Jenna as she proceeded through the house, expressing delight in every room.

"Look," she called to Alexis as they entered a small room off the main hallway. "They've left some furniture." She walked over to an old organ and pushed down on the keys. "It even still plays."

Alexis consulted the paperwork she carried. "It says the sale does include all the contents," she told her friend.

"It is so perfect," Jenna extolled. "I can't wait to move in; I've got to make an offer, today."

"It's Saturday," Alexis reminded her. "I'll contact them on Monday. But I'm going to make an offer at a substantial amount below the asking price."

"Don't you dare let me lose this place," Jenna cried. "I'll never forgive you."

"Not everybody is as obsessed as you are to buy a nightmare like this," Alexis replied. "I'm sure you'll be the only one who actually makes an offer, anyway. This house has been vacant for a long time."

"Does that paperwork tell any of the history?" Jenna asked eagerly. "I know it has to have a history."

"It doesn't go into detail," Alexis replied. "But I do know it has had a succession of owners over the years. It was an old folks' home at one time. I've even heard that it's haunted."

"Fascinating," Jenna replied. "There's a history museum here in town. I can research everything locally."

Alexis shook her head. Her friend was an elementary school teacher and dabbled in history and art. Whatever she discovered would be all the more reason for her to keep digging into who lived here and what happened to them. She only hoped that this move wasn't going to be the colossal mistake she was afraid it would be.

******

Alexis was right about one thing; the granddaughter convinced her grandmother to make a counter offer only slightly above the offer Alexis made on Jenna's behalf. When Alexis presented the offer to Jenna, she insisted on accepting it.

So on a mild January day, Alexis accompanied her friend Jenna and her husband Jerry to the home they now owned. Jerry seemed rather subdued, but then Alexis knew that he was never the dominant one in that marriage, generally going along with whatever Jenna wanted.

Alexis was sure it wasn't Jerry who had adopted the big gray parrot from the previous next door neighbors who were moving and couldn't take it along, nor the one who brought a rescued greyhound home to join their menagerie that included a tank of tropical fish. Rescuing was in Jenna's biological DNA, Alexis had decided long ago. So rescuing a rundown old relic of a house wasn't out of line for her. After all, she and Jerry had no children. Perhaps it was a medical issue, or maybe just a choice, but Alexis had never asked, after all, she wasn't even married, herself.

Alexis had arranged for them to use her realty company's box van to move from their small house in the next town to this much larger property. Their furniture wouldn't go far to fill the blanks in the many rooms. Even with what came with the property, she knew that Jenna would spend her upcoming summer break from teaching school to go to auctions and second-hand stores buying just the right items to fill out the decor.

Fortunately, Alexis was able to get the house at a price that left Jenna with at least some of that inheritance, but with what Jenna was planning, she would need to be prudent in her spending on renovation. That was why Alexis was shocked to hear Jenna's plans when she was invited to be their first guest at a meal in their new home.

Jenna had already gone to the museum and discovered a photo of the house as it had been in the 1870's. Jenna pointed out the four tall chimneys on the Italianate roof that had been brick. Over the years, they had been cemented all over, likely due to deteriorating mortar. She would have those chimneys restored, she declared, although Alexis knew that each one would cost several thousand dollars to do. But it was Jenna's most elaborate plan that made Alexis shiver.

"We're going to rebuild the widow's walk on the roof,"Jenna said. "But we're going to do it right - make it a cupola. See, it must have originally been just an open frame, but somebody later added windows, and eventually they must have torn it down when they redid the roof from its original slate. But Jerry has connections to some great Amish carpenters, and they can rebuild it at a fraction of what I got quotes for."

Alexis only smiled and feigned an interest in what she considered complete overkill. She'd been friends with Jenna since childhood, and always felt a protective role when it came to their friendship. She had thought that perhaps Jerry would temper Jenna's ambitious attempts to make the house more than it ever had been, but Jerry's beaming smiles at his wife's suggestions and his silent affirming nods, told Alexis that he was her willing accomplice. She could only hope things worked out well.
******

By mid-summer, Jenna had invited friends, co-workers, and of course Alexis, to a barbecue in the backyard of her new home. Jerry roasted hot dogs and hamburgers on an outside grill, while Jenna took her guests on a guided tour of the progress inside. Alexis had been extremely busy during the previous months, and although she kept in touch with her friend, she'd not seen much of what had gone on.

New wallpaper and paint had helped to remove some of the dreary feeling of the late Victorian era, but Jenna had bigger plans. She was going to have the whole outside of red bricks tuck pointed and the trim scraped and repainted by fall. At the same time, the first chimney was scheduled for repair. Over the winter, she was determined to attack the inside with renewed vigor, including renovating both kitchen and the bathrooms.

Alexis knew that Jenna's savings had been dwindling, and it appeared that Jerry was now engaged full time in repairs on the house, rather than working for wages at his construction job. At that rate, her inheritance would soon all be spent.

But Jenna was overjoyed with her new home as she pointed out to her visitors a log that she was keeping to document in words and photos, the metamorphosis of what she now called "the mansion." She was researching history of the old property as well, and was determined to get it placed on the national historic register.

She had found in old newspaper articles that the original owner was a wealthy man, Edward Dunn who had come here from the East in the early days of the Fruithills, and had joined with a group of local citizens to build an elaborate complex on the south side of the river. It had contained a mill, sawmill, and even a three story furniture factory, powered by a dam on the river. He had brought a shy and refined young woman from the east named Drusilla to be his wife and built her the large red brick Italianate home across the road from his mill complex in the late 1860's.

The home had included a large widow's walk on the roof, which was an open platform. Such structures in those days had a practical purpose, other than the romantic story of the wives of sea captains who would spent hours there, watching for their husbands to return from the sea, although many never returned, drowned in that treacherous trade, Jenna had learned.

The tall chimneys, not always properly maintained, often caught on fire, and the widow's walk offered a quick exit onto the roof, where buckets of sand could be poured down the chimney to quench the fire, preventing a disastrous event.

But the lonely young wife of the wealthy mill owner also used the walk to observe the mill complex across the road where her husband worked day and night, and she was often lulled to sleep by the sound of the machinery in the distance.

Unfortunately, a rival mill owner upstream had complained that the new dam affected his own up stream, and a bitter disagreement arose between the two.

Then, Dun's entire mill complex was the object of a suspected arson, and was burned to the ground by the 1880's. The man, himself, trying to fight the inferno, was severely burned. He was carried back to the home across the road, where he lingered for months. He briefly recovered enough to insist that the widow's walk be enclosed with windows, and it was there he spent his last months, propped up so that he could peer across the road at the ruined complex that he swore he would rebuild.

Eventually, his health deteriorated and he died, with his young wife at his side. She had been pregnant when he was injured, and in the months following his injury, gave birth to a sickly son. A nurse was hired, who tended both the child and the husband, and after the husband's death, was the companion of the widow.

The young child only outlived his father by a few months, and after he was buried beside his father in the old Town burial grounds just a few blocks away, the young widow never left the house again. She had spent most of her time, sitting in the enclosed widow's walk, staring silently across the road, imagining that her husband would soon be coming home, riding his cherished bicycle, that had been one of the few in the Town in those days. The nurse tended to Drusilla's needs, for she would never even have eaten, had it not been for the coaxing of her faithful companion.

One late summer day, a year after the husband died, her companion had come up with a lunch tray, to find the window open, and the room empty. To her horror, she looked out the window to see the young widow Drusilla laying on the ground far below, a suicide. Her parents had come west to bury her and to sell the house, as there were no other relatives.

The next owners, tending to roof repairs years later, had removed the widow's walk.

Jenna loved telling the story over and over to new visitors or even to strangers she met during her extensive research. She related the tales of how the stone bench in the front yard of the home was made of old gravestones, including that of the young widow which had been taken from the abandoned town burial grounds, by some later residence and placed there. So it was no wonder, she thought that the young widow supposedly still haunted the home, looking for her absent husband. Jenna lamented that she had never personally seen the ghost.

******

Several years went by, and Alexis would periodically stop in to see Jenna and hear about the progress on the house. Two more chimneys were redone, and only one remained. The other work, outside tuck pointing work on the house, had been completed, and it was becoming a real showpiece.

Alexis wasn't surprised that Jenna had opened her home for some group events, some charitable, gratis, but also some where groups rented use of the grounds and held tours and tea events that paid Jenna some badly needed revenue. Carefully, she questioned Jenna who admitted that most of the inheritance had now been poured into the work on the home. Even Jerry had had to go back to his contracting work, and Jenna had taken on some tutoring work for extra cash. Jenna's only regret was that she now had less time for her own renovating work and research, but she felt it was worth the effort to keep the project moving forward.

Finally, all four chimneys had been completed, and Alexis received an excited call from Jenna that the work on constructing the cupola had finally begun, with cutting the hole in the attic ceiling to prepare access to the roof and building a staircase. She'd had to cut a few corners in her plans, but at last she would have an observation tower on the world.

"I read that the view was so good from the original walk that you could see nearly to the next town," Jenna told Alexis on the phone.

"Call me when you have the grand reveal," Alexis reminded her. "So, things are working out O.K. for you?" Alexis asked, still concerned about her friend.

"Of course," Jenna replied. "Everything is perfect."
******

Busy with her real estate accounts in the city some miles away, Alexis didn't have time to stop by and view the progress, but in the early fall, Jenna called Alexis called to invite her to the unveiling, as she called it.

"We're going to make it a fall fest," Jenna told her. "Cider, doughnuts, harvest decor all around, next Saturday afternoon at two. Please come."

Alexis promised that she would, and decided to buy the housewarming present that she had delayed for this event. It was a lovely floor model antique tiffany style lamp, which would be perfect for reading at night in the new cupola, she thought.

Alexis wasn't surprised to see a large gathering when she arrived at Jenna's home. Two dozen or more small tables and chairs were set up in the yard and on the small patio outside. Jenna had completely renewed and landscaped the yard, including the small pond on one side and the charming tiled lap pool in the backyard, and added a gazebo.

A tall rustic fence surrounded the entire yard, with a double gate that could be secured. Along the back of the yard, a lower fence edged a dense regrowth forest setting.

"Deer can jump this small fence," Jenna told Alexis, "They come at night to feed or to drink from the pool. I even set out some salt for them."

Alexis was glad to see Jenna so happy, now that one of her most fervent dreams, the new cupola was reality. Jenna offered to take Alexis up to view it, before she opened it to her other guests.

"Wait just a moment," Alexis said, and went out to her car to retrieve the lamp. She carefully removed it from her SUV where it had been wrapped in a quilt and carried it to the house.

"This is for your cupola," she told Jenna, presenting it to her, at the bottom of the attic stairs.

Jenna gave her friend a hug. "It's so beautiful. It will glow like a jewel through the windows. Let's take it there now."

They carried it carefully up the several flights of stairs, finally emerging in the cupola itself. A small sofa filled with pillows, a reading chair and end table were set in place. Jenna sat the lamp by the chair, plugged it in, and turned it on. In the low afternoon light, it shed multi-colored rays about the room. Windows lined all sides, and Alexis stepped closer to gaze out.

"You're right," she said to Jenna. "The view is spectacular."

Jenna smiled. "I told you so," she said.

Then Alexis spied a door to the right of where she stood.

"A door?" she asked.

"Jerry insisted we do it just like the old days, with a quick way to the roof in case the chimney catches on fire."

"Oh, I remember," Alexis said. "Good safety precaution, I guess."

"And a conversation topic, as well," Jenna replied. "So you like my little hideaway?"

"Very much," Alexis answered, noticing the ceiling where her artistic friend had painted a blue sky and fluffy white clouds.

"No ghosts up here?" she asked.

"Not yet," Jenna sounded a bit disappointed. "But I'm hoping whatever spirits might be around will be tempted to enjoy this room as much as I plan to."

"Time will tell," Alexis said, and turned to leave.

"Do you hear that?" Jenna asked her.

"Hear what?"

"A sort of humming sound, rhythmic almost. Like machines running off in the distance," Jenna answered.

"No," Alexis told her. " You know I've always been tone deaf; even got kicked out of choir for singing off key."

"But you could whistle like nobody else could," Jenna said. "Remember how you would stand under my window late at night and whistle, and I'd climb down the trellis and we'd go to your house for popcorn and scary movies Mom Dinah wouldn't let me watch?"

"Indeed I do," said Alexis, forcing a smile, although she also recalled how strict Jenna's adoptive mother had been. She'd been happy to help Jenna escape to a more normal life now and then. So, she couldn't fault Jenna for trying to build the perfect life now, funded by her adoptive mother's money.

They returned to the group and enjoyed a festive time together with a group of congenial friends. Everyone told Jenna how beautiful the house was and admired the view from the new cupola. Alexis was glad to see her friend so happy, and when she left for her own home, she hoped this was the beginning of a time of true contentment for her friend.

******

Once the school year was in full swing, and Jenna was busy with her classes and tutoring, Alexis realized one day that she hadn't heard from her friend for several months. That wasn't like Jenna, who was a frequent text and email correspondent, and usually called Alexis at least once a week, if Alexis didn't call first.

She sent Jenna an email on a Monday, and when she hadn't replied by Saturday, gave her a call. Jenna answered the phone, but appeared to be withdrawn.

"Hey," Alexis said. "You sound down; what's wrong?"

"I've not been sleeping well," Jenna replied.

"Have you been to see the doctor," Alexis asked.

"Not yet," was Jenna's reply. "Can you come over today? Jerry's out of town on a construction job. I could use some company. Bring your PJ's and stay for the weekend."

Her voice seemed more upbeat as she suggested it, and Alexis couldn't refuse.

"Sure, I've just got a little paperwork to finish. How about I come about 5:30?" she told her friend.

"Great," Jenna replied. "We'll make popcorn and watch a scary movie, just like the old days."

"See you then," Alexis said and hung up. After the call, she wondered if things were still going well for her friend. She'd sounded rather depressed, but then she'd perked up when Alexis agreed to come for the weekend. She'd have to get Jenna to tell her what was wrong.

When Jenna opened the door, she pulled Alexis inside and gave her a big hug, followed by what seemed to be a sob. Alexis held her at arms length and took a close look at her face.

"What is it; you've been crying? Is it because Jerry's out of town?"

Jenna sniffed into a tissue she pulled out of her pocket. "No, just a little weepy, lately."

Alexis put down her duffle bag and led Jenna over to the sofa, and they both sat down.

"Then what? What's going on? Money troubles? Jerry troubles?"

"No, we're O.K., financially, and Jerry enjoys the extra work and even the travel. I can't say that I blame him. I guess I've not been very good company lately."

"Are you feeling ill?" Alexis asked. "You probably should see a doctor."

"Maybe, but it's not that. And I'm all right at school, no problem there. It's well, this is going to sound ridiculous, I know. But it's the house. Whenever I'm here alone, I'm sad, and I have strange dreams."

"But you love this house," Alexis exclaimed.

"I do," Jenna replied. "But there's something here."

"I warned you it was haunted," Alexis told her. "What have you seen?"

"I haven't seen anything," Jenna replied. "It's more of a feeling. And I'm compelled to be up there."

"Up where?"

"In the cupola," Jenna answered.

"How do you mean, compelled?" Alexis probed.

"I can't explain it, really. When I'm alone here, I'm totally uneasy sometimes unless I'm up there, staring out the window, across the street. And there's that noise I told you about. It's soothing and it's the only thing that lulls me to sleep. So when Jerry's away, I spend the night on the love seat. It's about the only sleep I get then," Jenna said.

"Come on," Alexis told her. "I want to see for myself."

Jenna just shrugged and followed her as Alexis headed off. When they reached the final stairway to the cupola, Alexis paused.

"You go first," she said.

Jenna moved past her silently and climbed the stairs and went into the room. She immediately moved to the window, where she stood, staring off into the distance.

"Do you hear it now?" Jenna asked.

Alexis concentrated, but she heard nothing but the occasional traffic on the street below.

"What do you hear?" she asked.

"That humming sound, almost like music. It's coming from over there," Jenna said pointing out the window.

"Then let's go down and put on your coat and go and find it," Alexis told her.

They went across the street. On the right was a subdivision, and on the left was the woods that had grown up around the ruined mill complex. Only a few bits of foundation remained. It was deadly silent, except for the occasional passing traffic on the road, as they made their way through the woods to the river some feet below. There was nothing left of the old dam.

"Do you hear anything now?" Alexis asked.

"No, nothing," Jenna replied. "Only when I'm up there."

They both looked back to where they could barely see the house through the trees, but the cupola was visible in the fading daylight.

"Come on," Alexis urged. "It's getting dark. Let's head back."

They didn't speak on their trip back to the house.

"I've got an idea," Alexis said. "Let's go to my place for the weekend."

"No, I've got the bird and the dog to take care of. I can't leave," Jenna insisted.

And no amount of convincing would change her mind. Jenna seemed a little better, now that they were back and downstairs, not in the cupola. They made a supper out of lunch meat sandwiches and soft drinks, and Jenna made microwave popcorn for when they had gotten into their pajamas and settled in a downstairs room where Jerry had a big screen TV.

"He loves sports," Jenna said.

"I remember," Alexis said. "When you two were dating, all he took you to were football and softball games."

"I guess there are worse hobbies," Jenna said, and Alexis agreed.

They settled in to watch a movie channel that featured the type of scary movies they had loved as kids. As the second of a series of creepy thrillers ended, Alexis looked over to see that Jenna had fallen asleep on the sofa. Quietly, she covered her with an afghan that she found on the back of it. She'd let Jenna sleep; she looked like she needed it.

Alexis moved over to a comfy chaise lounge, pulling a coverlet over herself. They'd often fallen asleep in front of the T.V. in the old days, and had to sneak Jenna back to her house in the early hours of the morning. It wouldn't hurt to spent the night sleeping here.

The next morning, Alexis awoke to the smell of brewing coffee and some other delicious aromas. She put on her slippers and headed off in the direction of the kitchen. There, Jenna was smiling and making french toast and heating pre-cooked sausage patties in the microwave. She poured Alexis a cup of coffee, set a plate of food in front of her and pushed a bottle of maple syrup across the table.

"Sit down," Jena told her. "Breakfast is served."

"It smells wonderful," Alexis said. "You look like you're feeling better."

"Slept like a log," Jenna admitted. "Sorry you had to spend the night on the lounge."

"It was like old times," Alexis said. "Remember?"

"How could I forget," Jenna said. "You were my only normal refuge in those days."

"Are you sure you don't want to come home with me, today?" Alexis asked. "We could take the bird and the dog along."

"Both of them in the same car?" Jenna asked, laughing. "They avoid each other at all costs, thank heavens. I don't think they'd like being taken out of their normal environment."

"When is Jerry due back?"

"Monday evening," Jenna replied. "And I've got school all day Monday. Let's just enjoy our girl time. Really, I'll be fine."

Alexis didn't want to break the mood, so she just sat down and began to eat. "This is marvelous," she told Jenna. "I'd forgotten how great breakfast could taste."

Later over lunch, Jenna revealed something to Alexis that she found rather shocking.

"We're thinking of having a baby," Jenna told her.

"Really?" was all Alexis could think to say. She knew that Jenna was her own age, mid-40s, and although Alexis herself had never married or considered having kids, so busy was she with her career, she still thought it was a little late for Jenna to be thinking of motherhood.

"Yes," Jenna said. "I'd like to have someone to leave all this to. After all our hard work, well, I'm looking toward the future. I've been taking the fertility treatments."

"Oh," Alexis said, thinking that perhaps the medication was what was affecting Jenna's moods lately. Perhaps that was the rational explanation.

"Are you sure they're well, safe for you?" Alexis asked.

"Perfectly," Jenna said. "Expensive, of course, but worth it." She paused and went on. "The original owners' had a baby boy who died. Of course he would have been the one to inherit all this. I think she still grieves for him."

Alexis was just about to ask about this strange comment, when her cell phone rang. Excusing herself, she got up from the table to answer it. It was a panicked home buyer having last minute doubts, even on a Sunday. By the time she had calmed her down, Alexis returned to the kitchen to see Jenna clearing up. She was in a happy mood, and again, Alexis wasn't comfortable with continuing the previous discussion, so the conversation moved on to going shopping at a nearby mall, and the two left the house in a jovial mood.

The rest of the day was pleasant, and when Alexis left late that afternoon, she gave Jenna a big hug. "Are you sure you'll be all right until Jerry gets back?"

"Of course," Jenna told her. "Take care, and I'll call you

later in the week."

Alexis got her things together and went out to her car, and stuffed her bag in the back. As she did she glanced up and saw Jenna up in the cupola, looking out the window.

She waved and whistled, the unique one she'd used as a child, but Jenna never looked her way. Alexis drove off, but a concern furrowed her brows as she realized that Jenna would have literally had to bolt up the stairs to get into the cupola and be standing there as Alexis prepared to leave. It was a thought that she didn't want to pursue just then, so she switched on the radio to divert her mind as she headed for home.

******

Midweek, she received an email from Jenna. "Great news," she wrote. "Jerry's back and we went to the doctor today, and he confirmed that I'm pregnant. What do you think of that?"

Alexis considered carefully before she replied. "That's great, Mom. Let's chat tomorrow."

She knew she should be really happy for Jenna, but the ominous feeling that she had had on the weekend returned with a vengeance. She'd be there for her friend, of course, whatever, but something still nagged at her.

Jenna called her the next evening and invited Alexis to lunch on Saturday, telling her that Jerry was leaving for the coast on Friday. Alexis made sure to clear her schedule for the planned meeting.

It was a cloudy gray day when Alexis arrived at the house, and she could see the glowing Tiffany style lamp through the window in the cupola high above. She rang the doorbell, but it seemed to take Jenna a long time to answer. She was out of breath when she opened the door.

"I was in the cupola," Jenna said by way of explanation.

"Are you sure you should be running down the stairs like that in your condition?" Alexis asked in a worried tone.

Jenna patted her middle. "We're fine. A little exercise is good, the doctor said."

They made their way to the kitchen, where Jenna had set two places.

"Hope you don't mind eating out here," Jenna said. "But I've got our meal warming in the oven."

"This is great," Alexis replied, sitting at her place at the table. "Can I do anything to help."

"Got it handled," Jenna replied and donning a oven glove, removed two steaming plates and put them on the table. "It's chicken pot pie. I made it from a new recipe. What would you like to drink?"

"A soda is fine," Alexis said. "Whatever you've got."

They dug into the pies, laughing as they blew to cool them.

"This is really good," Alexis told her. "I didn't realize what a good cook you've become."

"I'm going to be an even better one," Jenna told her. "The baby is due during the summer break, and I've already decided I'm not going back to teaching. I'm going to be a full time Mom."

"Jerry's O.K. with that?" Alexis said, speaking before she thought.

"Oh yes,"Jenna replied. "He's taking longer term assignments and is on the road more, but he's also making a lot more money. Financially, we can make it on one salary."

"That's good news," Alexis said, pausing before she went on. "But what about being alone. Are you still having trouble sleeping when he's away?"

"I won't be alone long," Jenna said. "I'll have the baby. That's all the company I'll need."

Alexis thought it was a odd remark for her to make, as though Jerry wasn't a necessary part of her life anymore, but she let it pass.

"Do you still like spending time in the cupola?" Alexis continued.

"Yes," Jenna replied. "It's my special place, although I think sometimes she's jealous of me."

This time, Alexis couldn't ignore the off-center remark. "Who's jealous?"

"The widow, of course. Her baby died, remember," Jenna told her. "You said yourself that this house has a ghost," Jenna reminded her and then laughed, a sort of strange sound.

Alexis laughed too. Jenna must just be joking, just like they used to do as kids. But even though they had a pleasant visit that afternoon, Alexis still felt a bit uneasy at leaving her alone when she left.

"Are you sure that you don't want me to stay over?" Alexis asked.

"I'm perfectly fine. The house is my refuge, remember." She stopped speaking and then asked, "Do you hear that?"

"Hear what?"

"Music," Jenna replied. "Distant and far off, but beautiful organ music."

"Remember my tin ear," Alexis said, glancing across the room at the silent organ in the corner. "Now stop teasing me. You're going to make me really believe there are ghosts here."

Jenna gave her a hug at the door. "Perhaps there are," she said in a quiet voice. Then she smiled again as she said, "After all, the past is still here."

Alexis drove home in a pensive mood. On one hand, she wanted to believe that Jenna was better and just teasing her. On the other hand, she worried that her remarks were indicative of something more frightening.

Jenna kept in touch with texts over the next few weeks, and Alexis began to hope that things were continuing to going well for her, even though Jerry was gone for longer periods of time. But Jenna seemed happy about the impending birth.

******

Then one night, a strange phone call in wee hours awakened Alexis. Sleepily, she picked up her cell and said "Hello," only to hear distant organ music, and a whispered voice "I think she's going to kill me," and then silence.

There was no caller information, but immediately she thought of Jenna. She looked at the clock on her bedside. Only five a.m. She started to dial Jenna's number and then stopped. Had she really even had such a call? Or was it part of a dream?

She hated to bother anyone at this hour. Surely, if it had been a call from Jenna, her number would have come up. It must have been a prank call or a dream. Alexis decided to go back to sleep and call Jenna in the morning.

When Jenna didn't answer her phone the next morning, Alexis delayed her schedule for the day and drove directly to Jenna's house. As she neared the house, she could see the flashing lights of emergency vehicles in Jenna's driveway. The street was closed off ahead and Alexis had to pull into a nearby street to park, before she ran from her car to the chaotic scene ahead.

She was stopped by officers from going up the driveway. "What's happened?" she cried.

"I'm sorry, Miss. You'll have to stay back."

"Please, the woman who lives here is my best friend. Has something happened to her?"

The officer nodded to a nearby plain clothes officer who came over to Alexis.

"Can you identify her?"

Fear struck Alexis's heart, but she merely nodded and said, "Yes."

The man lead Alexis past the others in the yard and stopped over a silent shape laying in the grass. She had landed on her back, and although a bloody patch stained the grass beneath her head, Jenna looked as though she had fallen asleep there, wearing a long white nightgown.

"Is that your friend?" he asked.

"Yes, it's Jenna Walters," Alexis replied as she realized that Jenna was gone.

"What happened?" she asked in a shaky voice.

"A motorist on the way to work saw her up on the roof, just standing there. The door on the roof was open, just as it is now. The man called 911 right away, but before we could get here, she just walked off the roof and fell where you see her now. She barely missed landing on that stone bench."

Alexis shivered as she now realized that Jenna lay only inches from where Drusilla's gravestone was part of the crude structure in the front yard.

The man led Alexis back down the driveway, away from the body, now attended to by the coroner who had just arrived.

"Do you know any reason for her actions?" the man asked.

Alexis realized that they were already considering Jena's death a suicide. It would do little good to tell them about the call she now knew was surely from Jenna.

"She had been depressed," Alexis answered. "Her husband was out of town much of the time, and she was lonely."

"We found his phone number on her cell phone, and were able to contact him. He's on his way back here, now."

The officer took out his pad and pen and made a note of

Alexis's name and address and handed her his card.

"We may be in touch," he told her. "Please call me, if you think of anything else."

Alexis nodded, put the card in her pocket, and then headed back to her car. She turned, and glanced up at the cupola. It was a gray day, and she could see shining through the window the multi-hued lamp that she had given to Jenna. She looked away, but then suddenly, she heard a sharp whistle and looked up again. There, standing in the window, was Jenna.

Alexis stopped and looked back at the detective, but in her heart she knew that it was a vision that only she could see. Jenna had signaled her now, as she herself had done when they were children. Then she knew that Jenna was still in her beloved house, part of the very history she so desperately sought.

As Jenna had once told her: "The past is still here."

THE END